A few weeks after this, Monnelia's fate was decided. It happened on a warm evening after dinner when a good many gentlemen from the lowlands of South Carolina gathered in formal dress at the Chalmers Street market. It was almost a private occasion, an auction to which only genuine and confidential bidders were admitted. Mr Roberts, the auctioneer, took his place upon a dais in the upper room. Commonly used as a place of public chastisement for errant slave-girls, it made an agreeable venue for the private sale.

Other Books by Blue Moon Authors

Anonymous
The Captive
My Secret Life

Maria Madison
The Reckoning
The Encounter
What Love

Akahige Namban
Woman of the Mountain, Warriors of the Town
Tokyo Story

P.N. Dedeaux
An English Education
Algiers Tomorrow

Elaine Cox
Bombay Bound
Pleasure Beach

Edward Delaunay
Between the Shadows and the Light

Wilma Kauffen
Our Scene
Virtue's Rewards

Martin Pyx
The Tutor's Bride
Summer Frolics

Jack Spender
Rites of Sodom

Don Winslow
Ironwood
Image of Ironwood

The Victorian Era

DEEP SOUTH

Richard Manton

BLUE MOON BOOKS, INC. NEW YORK

Copyright © 1990 by Blue Moon Books, Inc.

All Rights Reserved

No part of this book may be reproduced, stored in a retrieval system, or transmitted in any form, by any means, including mechanical, electronic, photocopying, recording or otherwise, without prior written permission of the publishers.

First Blue Moon Edition 1990
First Printing 1990
Second Printing 1994

ISBN 1-56201-061-1

Manufactured in the United States of America
Published by Blue Moon Books, Inc.
61 Fourth Avenue
New York, New York 10003

Part One

DEEP SOUTH

1
Scenes from the Adventures of Dolly Morton: The Story of a Woman

PREFACE

The most heroic episodes in the history of the American people are bound up with the efforts to destroy the system of slavery which was the worst of many bad legacies bequeathed the Republic of the United States by the British Government. Happily, by Ordinance of Congress in 1787—the same year in which the Constitution was adopted—slavery was abolished or forbidden in the vast northwestern territory out of which so many great states since have been carved. Then, by the Compromise of 1820, a certain line was fixed beyond which current slave empires would not be permitted to extend. However, the odious institution of slaveholding still persisted in the South, and, while most politicians were trying to put off the "irrepressible conflict," as Seward called it, private help was being given by benevolent people all over the northern states to those slaves who were both brave and daring enough to attempt escape. Indeed, some persons, who were so interested in the abolitionist movement that they willingly risked their own freedom to help their unfortunate, dark-skinned fellow-humans gain theirs, organized what since has gone down in history as the "underground railroad."

The "underground railroad" was a network of farms and houses in which escaping slaves were given refuge as they moved northward. At each "station" the fugitive slave would be fed and sheltered, attended to medically when possible, and advised of the route to the next "station." Then he would be sent on his way, the precarious path having been made somewhat less thorny because of the benevolent care of the sympathizer who tended the "station." Professor Wilbur H. Siebert, in a work of great patience,[1] has collected the names of about 3,200 Americans who were engaged in the good work of helping these poor creatures escape, and, in the roll of the world's worthies, there can be few more honoured names.

To help a Negro escape from his master was, it must be remembered, a most perilous undertaking. Many states affixed severe penalties to aiding or abetting a runaway. Men who were caught in the enterprise were beaten, imprisoned, and sometimes even killed. Women, meanwhile, were ruthlessly stripped and whipped; their persons were exposed to the lustful eyes of lascivious men, and, on many of them, other violences of a far more intimate nature were perpetrated. These ardent southern gentlemen who captured them were, after all, men in a sexual sense also, and few men can witness the chastisement and skin-warming of lovely women without feeling promptings of a passionate nature.

In *The Memoirs of Dolly Morton*, the true adventures of

---

[1] Siebert, Wilbur H., Associate Professor of European History, Ohio State University: *The "Underground Railroad" from Slavery to Freedom*. With an Introduction by Albert Bushnell Hart. London: Macmillan.

the brave women of the "underground railway" are related with a candour and a graphic beauty rarely encountered in any literature.

We see beautiful women stripped bare under a Southern sun; we hear their cries and pleadings for mercy as, one by one, their robes and petticoats are torn off or tucked up, their drawers unfastened and rolled down; our eyes are shocked at the sight of the white, well-developed hemispheres laid bare and blushing to our gaze, only to receive the cruel lash—the hemispheres which had never been bared since mother whipped them across her knees, never been rudely handled save in the legitimate caresses of the conjugal bed. Sorry are we, but little can we do: let he that goeth down to war count well the cost thereof. The hairbreadth escapes and the singular adventures are of themselves strange reading, but, when we remember that these adventures were undergone for the highest human ends, interest is merged in admiration for the heroism which could sacrifice so much in the cause of humanity.

The chief of this "underground" system was once Levi Coffin, who was said personally to have helped to freedom over three thousand slaves. The distinguished names of Theodore Parker, Fred Douglass, John Brown, Marshall Giddings, Gerrit Smith, and others all are associated with this most romantic of narratives in the history of the century. And, for adventure, the exploits of the emancipators cannot be equalled. Calvin Fairbanks conducted a whole slave family in a load of straw. James W. Torrence, who exported grain and feathers to Canada, packed runaways inside his crates. Abram Allen had a large three-seated wagon made for the express purpose of carrying fugitives; he called it "Liberator;" it had a mechanism with a bell to record the number of miles travelled. Hannah Marsh took garden produce to the markets of Philadelphia and secured slaves among her carrots and pumpkins. Giddings, a member of Congress, reserved a bedroom in his house in Ohio expressly for runaway slaves. An attic over Garrison's office in Boston was used for the same purpose.

Though heavy penalties were enforced in the cases of those who aided fugitives, and though the work was dangerous and might ruin a man who engaged in it, nothing could stop these dedicated abolitionists who so nobly strove to make poor men free. The reader who peruses *Dolly Morton* will realize more fully what slavery meant, and how much self-denial was needed to press onward the cause of emancipation.

CHARLES CARRINGTON
Paris, France
1899

NARRATOR'S INTRODUCTION

How I made the acquaintance of Dolly Morton, with a faithful account of the circumstances under which she felt impelled to tell me the story of her life.

In the summer of the year 1866, shortly after the conclusion of the civil war between the North and South in America, I was in New York, to which city I had gone for the purpose of taking my passage in a Cunard Steamer to Liverpool on my way back home to one of the midland counties of England after a shooting and fishing trip in the province of Nova Scotia.

My age at that period was thirty years, I stood six feet in my socks, and I was strong and healthy, my disposition was adventurous; I was fond of women and rather reckless in my pursuit of them; so, during my stay in New York, I went about the city very much at night, seeing many queer sights and also various strange phases of life in the tenement houses. However, I do not intend to relate my experiences in the slums of New York City.

One afternoon, about five o'clock, I had strolled into Central Park, where I seated myself on a bench under the shade of a tree to smoke a cigar. It was a beautiful day in

August; the sun, sloping to the west, was shining brightly in a cloudless sky; a light breeze was blowing, tempering the heat and making the leaves of the trees rustle with a soothing sound, and I leant lazily back in my seat, looking at the trim and often pretty nursemaids of various nationalities in charge of the smartly-dressed American children. Then my eyes turned upon a lady who was sitting on the adjoining bench, reading a book.

She apparently was twenty-five years of age, a very pretty little woman with, as far as I could see, a shapely, well-rounded figure. Her hair was a light golden brown and was coiled in a big chignon at the back of her head—it was the day of chignons and crinolines. She was neatly gloved and handsomely but quietly dressed, everything she wore being in good taste, from the little hat on her head to the neat boots on her small, well-shaped feet, which peeped from under the hem of her wide skirt.

I stared at her harder than was polite, thinking that she was quite the type of a pretty American lady of the upper class. After a moment or two she became conscious of my fixed gaze, and, raising her eyes from her book, she looked steadily at me for a short time. Then, apparently satisfied with my appearance, a bright smile came to her face and she shot a saucy glance at me, at the same time making a motion with her hand inviting me to come and sit beside her.

I was rather astonished, as I had not thought from her appearance that she was one of the *demi-monde;* but I was quite willing to have a chat with her—and also to poke her, if her conversation pleased me as much as her looks.

Rising from my seat, I went over to her, and she at once drew aside her voluminous skirts so as to make room for me on the bench beside her. I seated myself and we began to talk.

She spoke grammatically and in an educated manner, and, though she had the American accent, her voice was low and musical—(I do not dislike the American accent when I hear it on the lips of a pretty woman)—and she certainly was a pretty woman. Her eyes were large, clear, and blue, her complexion was extremely good, her teeth were white and regular, her nose was well-shaped and she had a small mouth with red lips.

She had plenty to say for herself, chatting away merrily and using quaint expressions that made me laugh. I took quite a fancy to the lively little woman, so I made up my mind to see her home and spend the night with her.

She had at once noticed by my accent that I was an Englishman, and she informed me that she never before had spoken to a man of my nationality. After we had chatted for some time, I asked her to dine with me. She seemed pleased at my invitation, and at once accepted it so we strolled quietly out of the park to a restaurant where I ordered a good dinner with champagne.

When the meal was over and I had smoked a cigar, I took my companion, who told me that her name was "Dolly," to a theatre. At the end of the performance I engaged a "hack," as the conveyance is called in New York, and drove the woman to her home, which was in the suburbs, about three miles from the theatre. Since it was a bright, moonlit night, I was able to see that the house was a pretty little one-storied building with a creeper-covered veranda standing in a small garden surrounded by iron railings.

The door was opened by a neatly-dressed quadroon woman who ushered us into the drawing room; then, after drawing the curtains and turning up the gas jets in the gaselier, she went away.

The room, which had folding doors at one end, was

prettily furnished; there was nothing in the least suggestive about it, everything being in good style. The floor was covered with a handsome Oriental carpet, the curtains were velvet; there were some good engravings on the walls, and there was a cabinet containing some choice specimens of old china.

My companion told me to sit down and make myself comfortable; then, begging me to excuse her for a moment or two, she passed through the folding doors into the adjoining apartment, which I saw was a bedroom. In a short time she returned, dressed in a white wrapper trimmed with blue ribbons; she had taken off her boots and put on dainty little French slippers, and her hair was flowing loose over her shoulders nearly down to her waist.

She looked so "fetching" that I at once took her on my knees and gave her a kiss on the lips, which she returned, at the same time inserting the tip of her tongue in my mouth. Then I put my hand up her clothes, finding that she had nothing on under the wrapper but a fine, lace-trimmed chemise and her black silk stockings, which were fastened high above the knees with scarlet satin garters, so I was able to feel her whole body with perfect ease.

She was plump as a partridge; there was not a single angle about her figure, and her skin was as smooth as satin. Her bubbies were rather small, but they were as round as apples, quite firm and tipped with tiny, erect, pink nipples. She had a very good bottom with plump firm cheeks, and the hair on the Mons Veneris was silky to the touch.

She gave me a brandy and soda, and we chatted while I smoked a cigar. Then we went into the bedroom, where everything was exquisitely clean and sweet. In a short time we were between the sheets. My breast was on her bosom, my mouth was on her lips, my amatory organ was up to the roots in her den of love, my hands were grasping the cheeks of her bottom and I was riding her vigorously, while she was sighing, squeaking, and bucking up under my powerful digs.

She was a good mount, so I enjoyed the "flutter" very much, especially as I had not "had" a woman for a month. But I had knocked all the breath out of the little woman, and, when all was over, she lay panting in my arms. However, when she had recovered her wind, she said with a little laugh:

"My gracious! You are very big and very strong. I don't think I've ever had such a vigorous embrace in all my life. You seemed to go right through me. But I like it."

I laughed, making no remark, but lying quietly resting, still holding her in my arms and stroking her cool velvety skin till I was ready for action again, making her wince and squeak and wriggle her bottom. We then got between the sheets again, and I made her lie on her side with her back turned towards me while I lay behind her. In this position we fell asleep.

I slept soundly, not waking once till half-past eight o'clock next morning. Sitting up in the bed, I looked at my companion, who was still fast asleep, lying on her back with her long hair streaming over the pillow and her arms stretched above her head. She looked quite young and very pretty and there was a faint pink tint on her round cheeks.

I gently pulled the bed-clothes down to her feet and rolled up her night dress to her chin without waking her. Then I took a good look at her naked charms. And they were worth looking at. Her skin was as white as milk and without a blemish; she really was very well-made, and perfectly proportioned. Her little bubbies stood out from her bosom in high relief; her plump, well-rounded thighs were shapely; she had good legs; her ankles were slender; her belly was without a wrinkle—she evidently had never had a child—and her rose-bed was shaded with fine, curly, golden hair.

I woke her by gently tickling her with my forefinger. She looked smilingly up in my face, her big blue eyes twinkling with fun, saying:

"So you have prepared me for the morning sacrifice. Well, I am ready to receive the stroke."

She then stretched out her legs and in a few seconds the little woman had bucked up more briskly and had wriggled her bottom in the spasm even more lasciviously than on the two other occasions. She really seemed to like the digging I gave her, and I don't think she had pretended to be voluptuously excited merely to please me.

Presently we began to chat on various subjects, her conversation showing that she took an intelligent interest in the affairs of the day. Our talk eventually turned to what was at that period a burning topic, the late civil war, and I asked her which side had had her sympathies.

"I am a Northern woman," she replied, "so I was always for the Union, and am exceedingly glad that the Southerners were beaten and the slaves set free. Slavery was a horrible thing and a disgrace to the country."

"But," I said, "from all the accounts one hears, it seems that the Negroes in the South were better off before the war as slaves than they are now as free people."

"Oh, but they are free now, and that is the great point. No doubt things are bad at present, but they will improve in time."

"I thought that, as a rule, the slaves were well-treated by their owners."

"So they were in many cases," she replied, "but there was no security for them; there was always the chance of their being sold to strange people; and then wives were separated from their husbands, and children from their parents. Besides, there were many owners who treated their slaves badly—working them hard, feeding them scantily and whipping them cruelly for the least offence. Then again, slaves had no rights of any sort. The girls and women, if light coloured and pretty, were not allowed to be virtuous, even if they wished to be. They were obliged to give themselves up to the embraces of their masters, and, if a woman dared to object, she was severely whipped."

"Oh, surely you must be mistaken," I observed.

"No, I am not. I know what I am talking about, for I lived in a slave state before the war, and I had special opportunities for finding out all about slavery and the distressing things connected with it."

"Was it a common thing for women to be whipped?" I asked.

"Yes; I do not suppose that there was a single plantation in the whole of the South where the female slaves were not whipped. Of course, on some plantations there was more whipping than on others. And what made the thing more horrid was the fact that the whippings were always inflicted by men, and very often in the most public way."

"On what part of the body were the slave women whipped; and what instruments of punishment were used?" I inquired.

"Sometimes they were whipped on the back, but most frequently on the bottom; the instruments used were various; there was the hickory switch, the strap, and the paddle."

"What is the paddle?"

"It is a round flat piece of wood fixed to a long handle, and it was always used on the bottom. It does not draw blood, but each stroke raises a blister on the skin and bruises the flesh. The hickory switch, if used with any degree of force, will cut the skin and draw blood. There was another terrible instrument of punishment called 'the cowhide,' but it was very seldom used on women."

"You seem to know all about whipping. Now tell me how it was you came to be living in a slave state," said I.

"I was helping to run a station on the 'underground railroad;' but I suppose you don't know what an 'underground station' is."

"No, I do not, what is it?"

" 'Underground railroad stations' were houses in which the abolitionists used to conceal the runaway slaves. There were a number of these 'stations' in various parts of the South, and the runaway was forwarded secretly by night from one 'station' to another, till he or she finally got to a free state. It was dangerous work because assisting a slave to escape was against the laws of the South, and to do so was considered a very great crime. Any man or woman caught at such work was sure of getting a long term of imprisonment with hard labour in the state's prison. Besides, everyone's hand was against the abolitionist; not only the slave-owners, but also the ordinary white people who did not own a single slave, and it often happened that abolitionists were lynched. They were tarred and feathered, or ridden on a rail or made to suffer in some other way by bands of lawless men."

"Did you ever get into trouble while you were at the 'underground station?' " I asked.

"Yes, I did. I got into bitter trouble, and went through dreadful sufferings. In fact, what happened to me changed the whole course of my life and was the cause of my being what I am now. Oh, how I hate the Southerners! The cruel wretches!" she exclaimed fiercely, her eyes flashing, her bosom heaving, and her cheeks reddening.

I was surprised at her sudden outburst of anger, and it at

once struck me that the little woman had a story. I was curious to hear it, so I said: "I should very much like to hear what happened to you in the South. Will you tell me?"

After a moment's hesitation, she replied: "I have never told my story to a man yet; but I will tell it to you, as you are an Englishman and I think you have a sympathetic nature. The story is a very long one, and there is not time to tell it to you now, but if you will come here tonight at seven o'clock and dine quietly with me, I will give you a full account of my life."

I replied that I should be delighted to dine with her and that it would give me great pleasure to hear her story.

Just then there was a knock at the door and the quadroon woman, neatly dressed and wearing a smart cap on her head, came into the room with tea and buttered toast on a tray, which she placed on a table beside the bed.

My companion sat up, saying to the quadroon: "Mary, give me my wrapper."

The woman handed her mistress the garment, which she threw over her shoulders. Then turning to me, Dolly said with a smile: "Mary was a slave for twenty-five years, and if you'd like to ask her any questions about her life she will answer truthfully. She is not shy. Are you, Mary?"

The quadroon, who was a very buxom, rather good-looking woman, smiled broadly, showing a double row of white teeth between her full, red lips. "No, Miss Dolly," she replied, "I isn't shy."

I was quite ready to ask Mary to give me some information about herself, so to begin with, I said: "Well, Mary, how old are you and what state do you come from?"

"I'se thirty years old, Sah, an' I was raised on ole Major Bascombe's plantation in de state ob Alabama. Dere was one hundred an' fifty field hands on de plantation, an' twelve house servants in de place. I was one ob de parlourmaids, Sah," she added with a sort of pride.

"Was your master a good one?" I next asked the woman.

"Well, Sah, he was a pretty good massa on de whole; he fed us well, an' he didn't work us too hard; but he was very strict, an' dere was plenty ob whipping on de plantation, an' in de house, too."

"Were you ever whipped?"

Mary looked at me with an expression of surprise on her face at being asked such a silly question. "Ob course I was, Sah, many a time," she replied. "I got my fust whippin' when I was 'bout seven years old, an' I got my las' one when I was twenty-five years old; only a week 'fore we was all set free by de President ob de United States."

"How were you whipped?"

"When I was a little girl I used to get spanked; when I grew big, dey whipped me on de bare back or bottom wid de strap or de hick'ry switch; and I'se had de paddle on my bottom several times," said Mary, coolly as possible.

"Who used to whip the women?"

"One ob de overseers gener'ly; but sometimes de massa himself used to whip de house-servants. Dere was a room kep' for de purpose, an' when a gal or a woman was whipped, she was tied face downwards on a long bench, den her close was turned up an' she got her allowance."

"Were the whippings severe?"

"Oh, dey always hurt us dreffully an' made us squeal out loud an' wriggle; an' sometimes we was whipped till the blood come."

Here Dolly broke in, saying: "And when the skin of a woman's back or bottom has been broken by a whipping, the marks never entirely disappear. Mary has plenty of marks upon her body at this moment. Show your bottom to the English gentleman, Mary, and prove the truth of what you have told him."

The woman, without the least hesitation, turned her back towards me. Then she gathered all her clothes up under her arms, exposing the whole lower part of her person. (She was wearing no drawers.)

It was a sight!! Since Mary was rather stout, her bottom was enormous. Her skin was smooth and of a light brown tint, and I noticed at once that both the fat cheeks of her bottom as well as the upper part of her thighs were marked with long, fine, white lines where the skin had been cut by the lash.

She seemed to like showing her opulent charms, for she was in no hurry to drop her petticoats, but stood looking over her shoulder at me with a complacent smile on her face till her mistress said: "That will do, Mary." She then let her clothes fall and left the room smiling.

"There," said Dolly, "you have seen the marks on her bottom, and I can tell you that her back is just as much marked. Moreover, she was seduced, or, to speak more correctly, she had to give herself up to her master's eldest son when she was only fifteen years old. She afterwards passed through the hands of the two younger sons; but the fact of her being the plaything of the three young men did not save her bottom from being blistered by the paddle or striped with the switch whenever she committed an offence of any sort. She has told me that she sometimes had to go to the room of one or another of the young masters while her bottom was bleeding from a whipping. I have another woman about thirty-five years of age in my service as cook; she comes from South Carolina, and her body is even more scarred than Mary's with the marks of the whip."

Dolly paused for a moment or two while she sipped her

tea. Then she said: "Now don't you think it is a good thing that slavery has been abolished in the United States?"

"Yes, indeed I do. I had no idea that female slaves were ever treated in such a way," I replied.

The details given me by Dolly and the quadroon had surprised me very much and had also somewhat moved me. The sight of a woman's bottom always has an exciting effect upon me. So, taking hold of Dolly, I laid her on her back, pulled down the bedclothes, tucked up her drapery and poked her again with great gusto. Then, after refreshing myself with a cup of tea and a piece of toast, I got up and had a cold bath in a small dressing room adjoining the bedchamber.

As soon as I had dressed myself, I bade Dolly goodbye, promising to be back again without fail at seven o'clock. Then, giving her a kiss and a good present, I left the house and made my way back to the hotel where I was staying. After changing my clothes I sat down to breakfast with a good appetite, feeling very well satisfied with my night's amusement.

The day passed rather slowly, and sharply at seven o'clock I was back at Dolly's house, curious to hear her story and fully intending to stay with her all night again.

She seemed glad to see me, and she was looking very nice in a pretty frock of some soft white material. She gave me a simple but well cooked little dinner, with a bottle of excellent Burgundy.

Mary, smartly dressed and beaming with smiles—but perfectly respectful—waited on us, and, when the meal was over and we had gone into the drawing room, she brought some really well-made coffee.

Dolly leant back in an easy chair with her feet, in smart velvet slippers, resting on a stool, and, since her skirts were slightly raised, I was able to see her trim ankles cased in pale blue silk stockings.

I lit a cigar and settled myself in another easy chair opposite her. She then began to tell me her story, which turned out to be a very long one.

The tale was not nearly finished when we went to bed after a little supper at midnight. But, having got interested in the narrative, I wished to hear the end of it, so I paid Dolly three or four more visits and she continued her story each time I saw her until, at last, she had related the whole of her adventures to me. Since I was able to write shorthand, I took down her narrative exactly as she related it, without a break, in her own words.

CHAPTER ONE

A young girl's humiliating experiences; death of my father; how I made Miss Ruth Dean's acquaintance and what came of it; helping to free the slaves.

My name is Dolly Morton, I am just twenty-six years of age and I was born in Philadelphia, where my father was a clerk in a bank. I was his only child and my mother died when I was two years old, so I have no remembrance of her. My father's salary was small, but he gave me as good an education as his means would allow, his intention being that I should gain my living as a school teacher.

He was a silent, stern, reserved man, who perhaps may have been fond of me in his way: but he never showed any outward sign of affection, and he always kept me under strict discipline. Whenever I committed a fault, he would lay me across his knees, turn up my short petticoats, take down my drawers and spank me soundly with a broad piece of leather. I was a plump, soft, thin-skinned girl who felt pain acutely, and I used to shriek and kick up my heels and beg for mercy—which, however, I never received, for he would calmly go on spanking me till my poor little bottom was as red as fire and I was hoarse with screaming.

Then when the punishment was over and my trembling fingers had buttoned up my drawers, I would slink away with smarting bottom and streaming eyes to our old servant who had been my nurse, and she would sympathize with me and comfort me till the smart of the spanking had passed off.

Our life was a rather lonely one; we had no relatives, my father did not care for society of any sort and I had very few girl friends of my own age; but I was strong and healthy, my disposition was cheerful and, fortunately, I was fond of reading, so, though I often felt very dull, I was not absolutely unhappy as a child.

And so the years rolled on, quietly and uneventfully. My childhood passed, I was eighteen years of age and had grown to my full height of five feet, four inches; my figure was well rounded, and I was quite a woman in appearance. I had begun to chafe at the monotony and repression of my life, and was sometimes very wilful and disobedient. But I always suffered on such occasions, for my father still continued to treat me as a child, taking me across his knees and spanking me whenever I offended him. Moreover, he informed me that he would spank me every time I misbehaved until I was twenty years old.

This was very humiliating to a girl of my age, especially since I had become rather romantic and had begun to think of sweethearts. But I never dreamed of resisting my father's authority, so I took my spankings—which, I must confess, were sometimes well deserved—with as much fortitude as I could muster up.

But a change in my life was soon to come. My father was seized with an attack of pneumonia, to which he succumbed after a few days' illness.

I was stunned at first by the suddenness of the blow, but I cannot say that I felt much grief at my loss. My father had never made a companion of me, and, whenever I had tried to interest him in my little affairs, he had invariably shown himself utterly unsympathetic. However I had not much time to think over the past; my position as it was at that moment had to be faced, and a most unfortunate one it was.

My father had died in debt, and the creditors were pressing for payment. I had no money, so the furniture of the house was sold by auction, and, when everything had been settled, I found myself without a cent, homeless, and quite alone in the world.

I lived for a month with my old nurse. She would have kept me with her always, had she been able but she had her own living to make, so she was obliged to go into service again. Then I would have been compelled to seek shelter in the poor house had it not been for the kindness of a lady who, hearing of my friendless and forlorn condition, took me into her house.

Her name was Miss Ruth Dean, and she was at that period thirty years of age. She belonged to the Quaker sect, or, as she called it, "The Society of Friends." She was a virgin, she had no lovers, she was her own mistress and she lived in a large house about two miles from the city. She was well off and she made good use of her money, spending most of it on charity. Her time was chiefly occupied in philanthropic work of all sorts, and she was always ready to give a helping hand to anyone who needed a start in life.

But, before proceeding, I must give you a physical description of Miss Ruth Dean. She was a tall, slender, delicately formed woman with large, earnest-looking brown eyes; her hair also was brown; it was long and soft and she always wore it in plain bands. She had a lovely clear complexion, but there was no colour in her cheeks, though she was in perfect health and was capable of going through a great amount of fatigue. She was a pretty woman, but there was always a rather prim expression on her face, and she rarely laughed, though she was not the least morose.

Miss Dean was as good a woman as ever lived, and she was the best friend I ever had. From the first she treated me as a guest and was most kind to me. I had a prettily furnished bed-sitting room of my own, and the servants, all of whom were devoted to their mistress, always treated me with respect.

Miss Dean had a number of correspondents in all parts of the States, and now my education proved useful to me, for I was able to help my benefactress in answering her letters. She, finding that I was sharp and intelligent, appointed me her secretary, giving me a small salary for pocket money, and also supplying me with clothes. I was very comfortable and never had been so happy in all my life. There were no cross looks, no sharp scoldings, and, above all, no horrid spankings.

As time passed Miss Dean became like an elder sister to me. I likewise grew very fond of her. She admired my face and figure, and always liked to see me nicely dressed, so she gave me lace-trimmed petticoats, drawers and chemises, and also several pretty frocks, though she herself was content with the plainest of underlinen and she always wore the Quaker costume, a plain bodice with a straight-cut skirt of drab, dove-coloured material.

As a matter of course, Miss Dean hated the institution of slavery and was an ardent member of the abolitionist party. She supplied funds to and was in constant communcation with "Friends" in the Southern States who were in charge of "underground stations," and she frequently received into her house escaped slaves of both sexes whom she kept till they got employment. She could harbour the fugitives openly because Pennsylvania was a free state.

I need not enter into the details of my life for two years, as nothing eventful happened. I was contented and happy, I had the society of young people of my own age and I had plenty of innocent amusements. Miss Dean, being a Quakeress, did not patronize places of public amusement of any sort herself, nor would she allow me to go to one; neither did she approve of dancing: but she frequently gave quiet parties, and I often was invited to other houses. I was popular with members of my own sex and had several admirers among the other sex but, since I did not care for any of them, I remained quite heart-whole.

At the time of which I am speaking, the friction between the North and the South was becoming very great, and there were mutterings of the storm which was soon to break—though few people thought that things would end in a long and bloody civil war. Towards the close of the year, the North was startled by the execution, or, as we called it, the murder of the great abolitionist, John Brown, at Harper's Ferry. Miss Dean was particularly shocked and distressed at the news, for she had known John Brown personally and she believed that he had been quite right in getting up the insurrection which cost him his life. Any act, she averred, was justifiable that had for its object the emancipation of the slaves, and she declared that she would not hesitate to do the same thing herself if she thought that it would forward the cause.

As the weeks passed, she became restless. She was not satisfied with merely sending money to the South. She wanted to do something personally to help the slaves, and finally she made up her mind to go South and take charge of an "underground station."

She told me one afternoon what she intended to do, and

she became quite enthusiastic about it. "Oh!" she exclaimed. "I am longing to begin the work of rescue. I am sure that I could manage a 'station' better than any man. Men are suspected and constantly watched by the white loafers, but no one would suspect a woman of running a 'station,' so, if I live quietly and take all the necessary precautions, I am not likely to be found out."

My sympathies had always been with the slaves, and now Miss Dean's enthusiasm moved me greatly. I at once made up my mind to go with her, and I told her of my determination.

At first she would not hear of my doing such a thing; she pointed out the risks of the undertaking and remarked that we might possibly be found out, in which case we should be condemned to a long term of imprisonment. "Not that I am afraid of imprisonment," she added, getting up from her seat and pacing up and down the room, her pale cheeks flushing, her soft eyes sparkling. "But for you, Dolly, it would be dreadful. You are a young, tender girl, and you could not bear—as I could—the hard work and coarse fare. Besides, they would cut off all your pretty hair. I have heard that the hair of female prisoners is cut in Southern gaols. No, my dear, I can't let you go with me. If I did, and anything were to happen to you, I should never forgive myself."

"I am not afraid of the work," I said, "and you have just as pretty hair as I have. If you choose to risk yours, I am ready to risk mine. Do you think, after all you have done for me, that I will let you go alone? I will not be left behind. Where you go, I go, and I will take my chance with you."

I saw that she was much troubled by my fidelity, but still she tried her utmost to dissuade me from going South with her. However, I was firm in my resolve to accompany her, so I met all her arguments and I wound up by saying that "two heads are better than one," and that I could be of great assistance to her.

So, at last, she consented to let me go with her. The point being settled, she kissed me, then sitting down, she wrote to "Friends" in various parts of the South, asking them to let her know a place where a new "underground station" might advantageously be established. We then went to dinner, and, when it was over, we spent the evening talking over our plans and settling to the best of our ability what we should do.

In a few days' time, Miss Dean received answers from all her correspondents. They mentioned several places where an "underground station" might be set up. We discussed the advantages of the various sites, and, after a long deliberation, we determined to go to a place in Virginia, right in the middle of the slave states.

The house which had been recommended to be used as a "station" was situated near the small town of Hampton, on the James River thirty-five miles from Richmond, the capital of the state. Miss Dean at once wrote to a local house-agent, telling him to take the house for her and to have it furnished as soon as possible for the reception of two ladies who wished to spend some time in Virginia.

Presently she received a letter from the agent, saying that he had taken the house for her and that it would be furnished and ready for occupation in a fortnight's time. I need hardly tell you that the agent had not the slightest idea that the house was going to be used as an "underground station."

The following day we began leisurely to make preparations for our departure, and Miss Dean decided to take only one servant, a trustworthy, middle-aged white woman named Martha. She was a Quakeress like her mistress, in whose service she had been for five years. She knew why we were going to Virginia and was quite willing to accompany us.

The other servants were left behind in charge of the house in Philadelphia. Miss Dean thought it would be safer not to let anyone in the city know the exact spot to which we were going, or what we intended to do, so she merely let it be known that we were going for a trip to the South.

A fortnight passed, and one fine morning at the beginning of May we drove quietly to the railway depot and took our tickets for Richmond. On arriving we stayed at a hotel for a couple of days in order to get some stores we wanted. Then, on the third morning at half-past eleven, we left the city in a two-horse buggy driven by a Negro coachman, who deposited the three of us with our trunks at the house after a long but pleasant drive through a pretty country.

The agent to whom Miss Dean had written was waiting to receive us, with a couple of Negro boys to carry in our baggage. He showed us the house, which we found to be in good repair and plainly but comfortably furnished. Everything was in perfect readiness—supplies laid in, wood chopped, and the fire in the kitchen lighted.

The house was very secluded. It was situated at the end of a lane about a quarter of a mile from the main road. It was a wooden structure of one story with a veranda back and front. It contained a parlour, a kitchen, and four bedrooms. In the rear there was a barn, near which grew two hickory trees. The whole place was surrounded by a high, rail fence.

When we had completed the inspection of our new home, the agent bade us goodbye and took his departure, accompanied by the two Negro boys. Martha bustled about the kitchen, while Miss Dean and I unpacked our things in our respective bedrooms. In a short time tea was ready and we sat down in the parlour to a good meal of ham and eggs, fried chicken and hot cakes.

The parlour was a good-sized room with rather a low ceiling crossed by heavy beams. There were two bow windows with latticed panes, and on the sills were pots of sweet-smelling flowers. On one side of the room was a massive sideboard of polished mahogany, and there was an old-fashioned oval mirror with an ebony frame over the mantelpiece. These two bits of old furniture evidently belonged to the house, and they contrasted strangely with the bright coloured carpet and other modern furniture of the room.

When we had finished our meal, Miss Dean wrote to the "Friends" in charge of the "underground stations" north and south of us, with which we were to be in communication. The station south of ours was thirty miles distant, and from it we would receive fugitives, whom we would pass on to the station north of us, which was twenty miles away. Then we had a short chat, but, since we were feeling tired after our long journey, we soon went to bed.

I got up bright and early next morning, feeling in high spirits, and, as soon as I had had my bath and dressed, I peered into Miss Dean's room. Finding that she was fast asleep, I did not disturb her. Instead, going quietly downstairs, I left the house and went for a morning walk along the tree-bordered road, and down lanes flanked with hedges of bright-flowered shrubs of species quite unknown to me.

I rambled about in all directions for an hour without meeting a single white person, though I came across several coloured people of both sexes who stared curiously at me, noticing that I was a stranger. When I got back to the house, I found Miss Dean waiting for me in the parlour, and, in a short time, Martha brought in breakfast, to which

I did full justice, for my walk had given me a good appetite.

We soon were settled down comfortably, and our new and risky life had begun. But neither of us had any forebodings of evil. Miss Dean was always cheerful, and I was quite charmed with the novelty of the whole affair. We stored supplies of bacon, flour, and coffee in the cellar of the house and we hid a couple of mattresses and blankets under the floor of the barn in readiness for the fugitives who might arrive at any moment from the station south of ours.

CHAPTER TWO

My new style of life; redeeming the slave; our first runaways and how we passed them "underground."

The house we lived in was well-adapted for our purpose, owing to its isolated position. Our nearest neighbour lived three miles away and the little town of Hampton, whence we got our supplies, was also three miles distant. The weather was quite warm; however, it agreed with me, and I was in splendid health and condition. Dressed in a plain linen costume with a broad-brimmed straw hat on my head I daily roamed about the country, soon making the acquaintance of a number of plantation slaves, who, seeing that I took an interest in them, were always glad to talk to me; they used to bring me presents of bits of "possum" and "coon," two animals which the Negroes are very fond of, but neither Miss Dean nor I could touch the meat.

I sometimes visited the slaves' quarters on the plantations and always was heartily welcomed. But I was obliged to pay my visits very secretly, for, if the owners of the slaves or the ordinary white folks in the neighbourhood had discovered that I was visiting the quarters, my motives would at once have been suspected. (Though the Negroes whose acquaintance we had made never hinted at the subject, I felt pretty sure that they all guessed why we had taken up our abode in their midst.)

Three months passed, and during the whole of that period the work at our station had gone on smoothly. Sometimes in one week we would have two or three fugitives; on other occasions several days would pass without a single runaway arriving. Whatever the case, they always came after dark to the back of the house and the first thing we did was to give them a good meal, then put them in the barn for the night. Next day we fed them well, and, as soon as it was dark, we supplied them with a packet of provisions and they started off for the next station, walking all night and hiding in the woods during the day. (If, as sometimes happened, the fugitive was a woman who was too tired to go on after one night's rest, we kept her till she felt able to continue her journey.)

The runaways were of all sorts: old men and young men, old women and girls, and sometimes a woman with a baby in her arms. Some of the fugitives were in good condition and decently clothed, others were gaunt and ragged, having come long distances and having been many days on the road. Some had come even from the extreme South of Florida. Many were scarred with the marks of the lash, some bore marks of the branding iron, and others had open or half-healed wounds on their bodies. But all the poor creatures who passed through our hands were intensely grateful to us, and we often heard their stories, which were in many cases most pitiful. I need not enter further into details of our management of the station, but I will give you a short account of one of the cases which came under our notice.

One night Miss Dean and I were sitting as usual in the parlour, chatting and sewing. The lamps had been lit, the curtains had been drawn and everything was quiet and snug. There had been no arrivals for upwards of a week, and Miss Dean had just said: "I wonder if anyone will come tonight." Then, suddenly, we heard a low tapping at one of the windows.

I ran to the door and opened it, and, as I did, a girl staggered up to the threshold, then fell fainting at my feet. I called to Miss Dean, who, with Martha, at once came to my assistance. We carried the girl into the parlour and laid her on the sofa.

She was a very light-coloured quadroon, with a pretty face and long, wavy, dark brown hair, which was flowing in disorder over her shoulders. Her age appeared to be about sixteen, but her figure was fully developed, the rounded contours of her bosom showing plainly under her thin bodice. (Females of her race soon mature.) She was evidently not a field slave, as her hands did not show signs of hard work, and her clothes were of good material, though they were draggled and torn to rags. She was wearing a neat pair of shoes, but they, as well as her stockings, were covered with mud. We soon brought her round, and she opened her great brown eyes which had a hunted look in them, while her face wore an expression of pain and weariness. We gave her a bowl of soup, and some bread and meat, which she ate ravenously, telling us that she had had nothing for twenty-four hours.

Because the girl was so weak and ill, we did not send her to the barn. Instead, as soon as she had finished her supper, I took her upstairs to the spare room, telling her to undress and go to bed. She looked bashfully at me, but after a moment's hesitation took off her frock and petticoats. She wore no drawers, and I noticed immediately that the back of her chemise was plentifully stained with spots of dried blood. I knew what that meant! Going up to the girl, I raised her chemise and looked at her bottom. The whole surface was covered with livid weals, and the skin was cut in a great many places.

I soon got her to tell me why she had been so severely whipped. It was the old story. She belonged to a planter, a married man with young children, who lived about twenty-five miles away. She was one of his wife's maids. Her master had taken a fancy to her and had ordered her to be in his dressing room at a certain hour one evening. She was a virgin, and she disobeyed the order. Next day she was sent with a note to one of the overseers who took her to the shed used as a place of punishment. He then informed her that her master had sent her to be whipped for disobedience.

She was stretched over the whipping block. Her wrists and ankles were held by two male slaves. Then the overseer laid bare her bottom and whipped her with a hickory switch till the blood trickled down her thighs. She then was allowed to go, being told that if she did not obey her master she would find herself on the whipping block again.

But she was a plucky girl, and she determined not to surrender her maidenhead. So she ran away that night, sore and bleeding as she was, and made her way for twenty-five miles through the woods and byways until she reached our house. She had heard that we were kind to slaves, and she thought that we would hide her from her master.

We did hide her, keeping her for a week. Then we sent her on to the next station along with a man who happened to arrive just at the right time.

Now I will return to my own story, and that of Miss Dean, for our fates at this period became linked together even more closely than they had been.

Time passed and everything continued to go on quietly.

Miss Dean was still full of enthusiasm for the work, but I had got rather sick of it. The stories of cruelty I constantly was hearing and the sights which I sometimes saw made my heart ache. Moreover, I was tired of the loneliness of my life. I wanted some companions with whom I could laugh and chatter freely and frivolously. Though Miss Dean was always sweet and amiable, her conversation was not of a light sort.

Occasionally, too, a feeling of fear would come over me: we might be found out. I did not feel so brave as formerly. I dreaded being put in gaol and having my hair cut. And I did not like the idea of the hard labour and the scanty fare.

However, so far, I had had no cause for alarm. We had come to be well known by the people in the neighbourhood, but no one suspected that the two quiet women living by themselves in the lonely house were engaged in unlawful practices. There had never been an instance known of an "underground station" being run by women.

The ordinary white people—and by that expression I mean the white folks who did not own slaves—were always civil to us whenever we had anything to do with them. Many of them were very rough-looking fellows, and there were some lazy loafers. But there were also a number of respectable, hard-working men with wives and families. Strange to say, all these whites, though not one of them owned a Negro, were staunch upholders of slavery. They sold us venison, wild turkeys, and fish, all of which were welcome additions to our usual homely fare.

CHAPTER THREE

I am chased by a bull in the country and saved by an unknown gentleman who, in the sequel, proves a far more savage bull, differing only in outward shape.

I still continued to amuse myself by wandering about the country. But it was dull work alone, and I often wished for someone to talk to and to keep me company during my walks. At last my wishes were gratified. One afternoon I was strolling along a road, when, on turning a corner, I came suddenly upon a small herd of cows, headed by a savage looking bull which, on seeing me, stopped and began to paw the ground, its head lowered in a threatening way and its eyes gleaming angrily. If I had stood still, the animal might have passed on. But, since I was frightened, I foolishly turned around and ran away as fast as I could.

The bull, bellowing hoarsely, at once pursued me. I heard its breathing close behind me as I ran, shrieking loudly. I expected at any moment to be transfixed by the creature's horns. Just in the nick of time, however, a gentleman on horseback leaped the hedge and, charging the bull, belaboured it with a heavy whip till the beast turned tail and dashed up the road. The gentleman then dismounted and came to me. I was trembling all over and nearly fainting, and would have fallen to the ground had he not put his arm round my waist and held me up.

He gave me a draught of wine from a flask which he took out of his pocket. Then he made me sit on the grass at the side of the road while he stood in front of me with the bridle of his horse over his arm, looking down at my face.

"Don't be frightened. The danger is past," he said. "It was lucky, though, that I happened to hear your cries and was able to get to you in time."

I soon recovered myself, then I thanked him warmly, at the same time taking a good look at him. He was a tall, handsome man, about thirty-five years of age, with very dark hair and eyes. His face was clean shaven except for a long, drooping mustache, which hid his mouth, and he was dressed in a well-fitting riding suit. Fastening his horse's bridle to a tree, he sat beside me on the grass and began to talk in a lively and amusing way, putting me quite at ease. Soon I found myself chatting and laughing with him as freely as if I had known him for a long time.

It was delightful to have a merry companion of the male sex to talk to. My spirits rose and I felt quite gay. I think we must have talked for an hour. He told me that his name was Randolph. I had often heard of him. He was a bachelor, and was the owner of one of the largest plantations in the neighbourhood. His place, called "Woodlands," was about three miles from our house, and I knew some of his slaves. But I did not tell him that.

He asked me my name, and, when I told him, he smiled. "I have heard of you and also of Miss Dean," he said. "In fact, I am your landlord; the house you are living in belongs to me."

I was rather startled at hearing that. "Oh, are you?" I said.

"Yes," he replied, laughing. "And somehow I had got it into my head that my tenants were two ugly old Quaker ladies."

I could not help smiling at the way he had spoken. "Miss Dean is a Quakeress," I said, "but she is not ugly, nor is she old. She is only thirty-two years of age. I am her companion, but I am not a Quakeress."

"You are a very charming young lady, and I am glad to have made your acquaintance," he said, looking hard in my face.

I blushed, feeling rather confused by his bold glances; but nevertheless I was pleased with his compliment. I was not accustomed to having compliments paid to me. The few young men I had known in Philadelphia were Quakers and were not given to paying compliments.

He went on: "You two ladies must find it very dull living all alone, especially in the evenings. What do you do with yourselves?"

This was an awkward question. "We read and sew," I replied.

"Well, I must give myself the pleasure of calling on you some night. I suppose you are always at home," he observed.

My heart gave a little jump, and I felt hot and uncomfortable. It would never do to have him calling at the house, so I racked my brains to find something to say that would prevent him from paying us a visit. "I must beg you not to call. Miss Dean would not like it. She is peculiar in her ways, and I have to humour her," I said, rising to my feet and thinking that I had better get home as soon as possible so as to avoid being further questioned by him.

He also stood up. "If that is the case I will not intrude on Miss Dean, but I hope to have the pleasure of seeing you again. Will you meet me here tomorrow at three o'clock?"

I thought there would be no harm in meeting him. Besides, if I did not, he probably would call at the house, and that was a thing to be prevented if possible. So I promised to meet him the following afternoon at the hour he had named. Then, shaking hands with him, I bade him goodbye.

He held my hand longer than necessary and he also pressed it, at the same time fixing his gleaming black eyes upon mine with a look which made me feel rather uncomfortable again. "Goodbye then, Miss Morton, till three o'clock tomorrow," he said. Then mounting his horse, he touched it with his spurs and cantered off, turning round in the saddle to wave his hat to me.

My eyes followed him with admiration, for he was a graceful rider and his horse was a magnificent animal. Moreover, I felt grateful to the man, for he had undoubtedly saved me from serious injuries, if not death.

I walked slowly home, thinking over the whole affair, and feeling very light-hearted. A bit of romance had come into my hitherto quiet life, and I was pleased. In the future I should have someone to talk to and to walk with. I had an idea that Mr. Randolph and I would often meet, but I had not the least thought of harm.

On reaching the house, I found Miss Dean looking, as usual, sweet and placid, making shirts for ragged fugitives. Kissing me affectionately, she said: "You are looking very blooming, Dorothy. What has made your cheeks so rosy this evening?"

I laughed, telling her that I had been frightened by a

bull. But I did not inform her of the danger I had been in, nor did I mention Mr. Randolph. I thought it best to keep silent about him, for Miss Dean was very strict in her ideas, and she never would have allowed me to meet him.

I took off my hat, and we went in to dinner. It was a plentiful meal, consisting of fried trout, grilled wild turkey, corn bread, buckwheat cakes and honey. The evening was spent in the usual way. We read and sewed till it was time to go to bed.

Next day at the appointed hour and place I met Mr. Randolph. He evidently was glad to see me, and, taking both my hands, held them, gazing with a look of admiration in my face. (A woman always knows when she is admired.) After exchanging greetings, he politely offered his arm, which I took, and we strolled along the road till we came to a secluded dell with mossy banks shaded by trees. In this nook we sat side by side on the grass. Then he questioned me about myself.

I told him that I was an orphan and that I had no relations of any sort. I told him also how I had come to be a companion to Miss Dean. But, of course, I did not hint at our reasons for coming to live in Virginia.

His manner to me was perfectly respectful, and I remained chatting with him for upwards of an hour. Then I went home, promising to meet him again in three days' time. I did meet him, and, from that time, we became very friendly, meeting each other two or three times a week. I did not love him in the least, but I liked being in his company. He was so utterly different from any man I had ever known. He amused me with stories of adventures—he had travelled all over the world—and he interested me with his descriptions of European countries, which I was always longing to visit.

I soon found out that he was cynical and that he had a very low opinion of women, and, from the way he sometimes talked, I had an idea that his disposition was cruel. However, he seemed to exercise a sort of fascination over me, so invariably I met him whenever he chose to ask me.

Up to this point he had treated me politely, but in a condescending sort of way, and I was quick-witted enough to perceive that he considered me very much his inferior. He was a rich planter, one of the aristocracy of the South, and a member of one of the "FFV's," as they called themselves, meaning "First Families of Virginia," while I was only the daughter of a poor clerk of no particular family, earning my living as companion to a Quaker lady.

As time passed I got to like him a little better and consequently was more familiar with him, while he became warmer in his manner towards me. But as yet he had not attempted to take the least liberty with me. (Little did I suspect that he was only waiting for a favourable opportunity.) He lent me books of poetry which were a great source of delight to me, and he often used to read aloud to me passages from Byron, Shelley, or Keats.

One afternoon we were sitting side by side in our favourite nook, and he was reading poetry to me. I do not know who was the author, but I remember that the poem was about love. Randolph had a musical voice, and he read with passionate feeling, every now and then looking into my eyes. I became deeply moved by the sweet but rather warm verse, my cheeks flushed, my heart began to beat rapidly, and my bosom heaved. A sensuous feeling such as I had never experienced took possession of me. I closed my eyes and sat in a soft waking-dream.

Soon Randolph ceased reading and everything was perfectly still except for the far-off song of a mockingbird. Presently I felt his arm steal around my waist, then he drew me onto his lap and pressed his lips to mine in a long kiss.

It was the first time that I had ever been kissed by a man, and I felt a thrill pass through me from head to foot. But I did not attempt to get away. The kiss seemed to have me mesmerized.

Pressing me to his breast, Randolph now covered my face with kisses, calling me all sorts of endearing names and telling me that he loved me. I lay quietly in his arms, feeling unable to move, and my quietness emboldened him. After a moment or two, he put his hand up under my petticoats and felt my bottom through the slit of my drawers.

Now my senses returned. The touch of the man's hand on such a part of my body acted like a galvanic shock. My sensuous feeling was instantly changed to a feeling of outraged modesty. I realized my danger and began to struggle violently in his arms, at the same time calling out to him to let me go. But he paid no attention to what I said, and I was unable to free myself from his powerful grasp.

Laying me down upon my back, he pulled up my clothes, and, tearing open my drawers, tried to separate my thighs, which I instinctively kept pressed together. I resisted with all my power, shrieking and buffeting him in the face with both my hands, but he soon prevented my doing that by seizing my wrists and holding my arms down at my sides. Then, pressing his chest upon my bosom, he crushed me under his weight. Thrusting his knees between my legs, he forced my thighs apart, in spite of all my efforts to prevent him.

I was strong, healthy, and in good condition, so I fought hard in defence of my virginity, at the same time uttering a succession of loud shrieks. It was a terrible fight! All my muscles were aching from the strain. Every nerve in my body was strung to the utmost tension. His weight was squeezing the breath out of me. My bosom heaved as though it would have burst, my eyes were starting out of my head, and I was filled with a horrible feeling of loathing. But I continued to resist stubbornly, until, at last, fearing, I suppose, that my screams would be heard, he ceased his efforts to rape me, and, uttering a bitter curse, let me go. Then, rising to his feet, he buttoned up his trousers.

I sprang to my feet, panting for breath and trembling all over. The tears were streaming down my cheeks. I was hoarse from screaming. My clothes were torn. My hair had come down and was flowing in disorder, partly hiding my scarlet face. Overwhelmed with shame, I was about to run away when he seized me by the arm, and, glaring at me with a cruel look in his eyes, hissed out in a savage tone: "You little fool! Why did you resist me?"

"Let me go, you horrid wretch!" I exclaimed fiercely. "How dare you look me in the face after what you have done to me? Oh! You beast! But I will have you prosecuted. I will go to the police and have you put in gaol."

He smiled an evil smile and darted a baleful glance at me. "Oh no, my little girl; you won't go to the police when you have heard what I am going to tell you," he said, pinching my arm. "Now you needn't struggle. I'm done with you for the present, and I'll let you go in a moment. But you must first listen to what I have to say. I know what Miss Dean and you are doing. You are keeping an 'underground station.' I suspected you both from the first, so I watched the house at night on several occasions, and I soon found out the game which was being carried on. For certain reasons, which I daresay you can guess, I did not give the information to the police. But you and Miss Dean are in my power, and if I choose now to let the authorities know what you have been doing, you will find yourselves in a very short time at hard labour in the state's prison."

I was startled and frightened, for I saw at once that we were entirely at the man's mercy. But I was so thoroughly upset by the outrage which I had suffered that I could not find a word to say. I could only weep.

Changing his tone, he went on: "But I don't want to inform against you. I wish to be your friend. I am fond of you, and, when you let me kiss you so quietly just now, I thought that you were willing to let me go further. I am sorry I treated you so roughly and I apologize. But I want you. Leave Miss Dean and come live with me. You shall have everything a woman can desire, and I will settle a thousand dollars a year on you for life. And I will promise not to lay information against Miss Dean or to interfere with her in any way."

As things turned out, it would have been far better for me had I then accepted his offer. But at that moment I was full of rage and shame. Moreover, being a perfectly pure girl, I was utterly revolted at the cool way in which he had offered to buy my virtue. Though I dreaded the prison, I said to myself that I would rather go there than surrender to the man.

"No! No!" I exclaimed. "I will not leave Miss Dean. You may tell the police, if you are such a brute. I will go to gaol, but I will not live with you. I hate the very sight of you! Oh! Go away and leave me, you wretch!"

Again the cruel look came to his face and he pushed me roughly, saying in a tone of suppressed anger: "Very well, Miss Dorothy Morton, I will go away now. But we shall meet again some day, and I think that you will be sorry for having refused my offer."

Then, bowing to me with mock politeness, he turned on his heel and walked rapidly away, leaving me weeping and dishevelled.

CHAPTER FOUR

The results of my resistance; the inutility of goodness; an unwelcome visit, which leads to the humiliation of our persons and the ravishment of my virgin state.

As soon as he was out of sight, I twisted up my hair and arranged the disorder of my attire as much as was possible; then I hurried home, and fortunately got up to my room without being seen by either Miss Dean or Martha.

Locking the door, I undressed, for my clothes were in a dreadful state; my frock, a white one, was torn at the gathers nearly all the way round, and the back was stained green; the strings of my petticoats were broken, my chemise was torn, and my drawers were hanging in ribbons about my legs; my thighs were covered with black marks made by the pressure of the man's fingers, and I was sore and bruised all over.

After I had put on clean things I threw myself on the bed, buried my face in the pillow and cried. But my tears now were angry ones, for the keenness of my shame had somewhat worn off.

I was enraged at my foolishness in having trusted myself alone with Randolph, for whom I had a feeling of distrust ever since he had expressed to me his low opinion of the virtue of women. I also felt degraded in my own estimation that he should have taken for granted that I was the sort of girl who would give herself up to a man for the asking. I am sure that I had never given him the least encouragement.

Then I remembered that he had said that I would be sorry for not accepting his offer. I had made an enemy of him, so most probably he would give information about us to the police.

It was not pleasant to think of. I felt that I ought to let Miss Dean know that we had been found out, but, had I done so, I should have been obliged to enter into all the details of my affair with Randolph. And I could not bear to tell her of the outrage which I had been subjected to. Altogether, through my imprudence, we were in a dreadful fix, and there was nothing to be done but wait miserably for the end, which would be in the gaol. (Already in my mind I pictured Miss Dean and myself clad in coarse prison garments, and with our hair cropped short, toiling at some hard labour.)

Presently Martha knocked at the door to tell me that tea was ready; so I had to pull myself together and go down to the parlour. I could not eat much, and Miss Dean noticed at once my want of appetite; she also saw that my face was pale and my eyes red, and she asked me what was the matter.

I told her that I had a bad headache, which was the truth. On hearing that, the kind-hearted woman made me lie on the sofa while she bathed my forehead with *eau de Cologne*. Then she recommended that I go to bed, so that I might have a long night's rest and sleep off the headache.

But I did not sleep well. My rest was broken by a succession of horrid dreams in which I fancied that I was struggling in the arms of a man with an enormous member, who always succeeded in overcoming my resistance and taking my maidenhead. In the morning, while dressing, I wondered where we should be in twenty-four hours' time, for I fully expected that Miss Dean and I would be arrested before the night came.

The day wore slowly away. I was uneasy and restless, I could not settle down to my usual routine of work. I was constantly peeping out of the window watching for the arrival of the police.

They did not come. But, at nine o'clock, a runaway made his appearance in a starving condition; and, in attending to the poor creature's wants, I forgot, for the time, my own precarious position.

Several days went by quietly and I began to think that Randolph after all was not going to be so mean as to inform on us. But all the same I was very anxious to get out of the state of Virginia, so I said to Miss Dean that I thought we had now done our share of the work and that we ought to go back to Philadelphia. Miss Dean however would not hear of such a thing. She said we were doing good work and that we must go on with it, for some time longer at any rate.

Another fortnight passed, during which period three fugitives arrived, two men and a woman, all of whom we had sent on to the next station without, as far as I knew, exciting any suspicion, and, since nothing had occurred to alarm me, my spirits rose and I became quite myself again.

I had not seen Randolph since the day he had assaulted me, but I often had thought of the shameful affair, the recollection of it always sending the blood in a hot flood to my cheeks. I had a hatred for the man and hoped that I should never again set eyes on him.

But, alas! I was fated to see him before long, under the most painful circumstances. One afternoon, about five o'clock, we were sitting in the veranda at the front of the house. Miss Dean, looking very sweet and pretty in a dove-coloured dress, was as usual usefully employed in making shirts for the runaways, while I was engaged in trimming a hat for myself. Martha was in the kitchen washing up plates and dishes, for we had just finished tea.

I was in good spirits, and as I worked I sang to myself in a low voice a plantation song I had learned from the Negroes, called "Carry Me Back To Ole Virginny." It was strange that I should have been singing that particular song, for I was very anxious to get away from "Ole Virginny" and had I been out of that state I certainly would not have asked anyone to carry me back to it.

Presently the stillness of the evening was broken by the clatter of horses' hoofs mingled with the sound of loud voices in the distance, and, on looking down the lane, I saw a number of men, some of them mounted, some on foot, coming towards the house. Miss Dean and I gazed at them as they came along, and we wondered where they were all going; people very rarely entered our secluded lane.

To our surprise, the party stopped at the house, the men on horseback dismounting and hitching their horses to the fence. Then the whole crowd came into the veranda and gathered round us as we sat, in silent astonishment, on our chairs. I noticed, however, that there was a hard stern look on the face of every man, while some of them scowled at us with angry glances.

There were fifteen men, all of whom were quite unknown to me, even by sight. Most of them were bearded, rough looking fellows, dressed in coarse cotton shirts of various colours, with their trousers tucked into boots reaching to the knees, and wearing slouch hats on their heads. But there were some men better dressed, and evidently of a higher class.

My heart began to flutter, and a vague foreboding of evil came over me, for, though I had not the least suspicion of what the men's intentions were, I guessed from their looks that they had not come to pay us a friendly visit.

One of the intruders, a man about forty years of age, who was addressed by the others as Jake Stevens and who appeared to be the leader of the band, stepped forward, and laying his hand on Miss Dean's shoulder, at the same time looking at me, said sternly: "Stand up you two, I've got sumthin' to say to you."

We both rose to our feet, and Miss Dean asked in a quiet tone: "Why have you and your companions invaded my house in this rough manner?"

The man laughed scornfully, saying, "Well, I should say you orter pretty well guess what's brought us here. You ain't so innocent as you look, by a long chalk." Then, with an oath, he went on: "It has come to the knowledge of the white folks in these parts that you are keeping an 'underground station.' Since you have been here you have got away a great many slaves. Now I jest tell you that we Southerners don't allow no derned Northern abolitionists to run off our slaves. When we ketches abolitionists we makes it hot for them, and now that we've ketched you and your assistant, we are going to bring you before Judge Lynch's court. The boys who have come here with me are the gentlemen of the jury. Isn't that the right talk, boys?" he said to the men round him.

"Yes, yes, Jake. That's the talk. You've put it the right way," shouted several voices.

I sank down on my chair, horribly frightened. I had

heard dreadful stories of the cruelties perpetrated under the name of "Lynch."

Miss Dean again spoke calmly: "If you have found out that we have broken the law of the state, why have you not informed the police? You have no right to take the law into your own hands."

There was an angry movement among the men, and a hubbub of voices rose. "We've got the right to do as we please." "Lynch Law is good enough for the likes of you." "Shut your mouth." "Don't waste any more time talking to her, Jake. Let's get to business," was shouted.

"All right boys," said Stevens, "we'll go into the garden right away and settle what shall be done with the prisoners. We know they're guilty, so we've only got to sentence them, and then we'll proceed to carry out the sentence of the court."

Miss Dean and I were left on the veranda while the men, all trooping out into the garden, gathered in a cluster and began to talk; but they were too far off for us to hear what was being said.

I sat huddled up in my chair, with a dreadful sinking at my heart. "Oh Miss Dean," I wailed, "what will they do to us?"

"I do not know, dear," she replied, coming over to me and taking my hand. "I am not very much concerned about myself, but, oh, my poor girl, I am so sorry for you. I never should have allowed you to come here."

Too miserable to say another word, I sat pale and silent. The men continued talking together, and there seemed to be differences of opinion among them, but I could not catch a word that was said. The suspense to me was dreadful, my mouth was parched and I turned alternately hot and cold. But Miss Dean, who still held my hand, occasionally pressing it, was quite calm.

At last the men seemed to have agreed, and they all returned to the veranda. Then Stevens, assuming a sort of judicial manner, addressed us, saying: "The sentence of the court upon you two is that you are each to receive a whipping with a hickory switch on the bare bottom, then you are both to be made to ride a rail for two hours, and, further, you are warned to leave the state of Virginny within forty-eight hours. If at the end of that time you are found in the state, Judge Lynch will have something more to say to you."

When I heard the shameful and cruel sentence which the lynchers had passed upon us, my blood ran cold and I trembled all over. There was a singing in my ears, and a mist came before my eyes. I rose from my seat, my legs shaking under me so much that I had to hold the back of my chair to support myself.

"Oh, you surely don't mean to whip us!" I exclaimed in piteous accents, stretching out my arms appealingly to the men. "Oh, don't put us to such awful shame and pain. Have pity on us. Oh, do have pity on us."

But there was not the least sign of pity on any of the faces surrounding us. All were stern, or frowning, or stolid. And one man called out: "Serves you right, you darned little abolitionist. You both ought to be stripped naked and tarred and feathered after the whipping and then perched on the rail. You would look like a queer brace of birds."

At this coarse joke, there was a burst of laughter from the other men and I again sank down on my chair wringing my hands in despair while the tears streamed down my white cheeks. Miss Dean, however, faced the men boldly. She turned very pale, but her eyes were bright and she showed no signs of fear. Addressing the leader, she said without a tremor in her voice: "I have often been told that the Southerners were chivalrous in their treatment of women, but I find that I have been misinformed. Chivalrous men do not whip women."

"I don't know nothing about chivalrous," said Stevens gruffly, "but when women acts like men and sets to running an 'underground station' they must take the consequences."

The men in various terms, garnished with oaths, expressed their approval of what their leader had said.

Miss Dean calmly continued: "I wish you all to know that I am the only person in this house responsible for what has been done. The young lady is not to blame in any way. She is my paid companion and has acted entirely under my orders. You must let her go free."

"Oh no we won't," exclaimed several voices at once. "She must have her share of the switch."

"Let me do the talking," said Stevens. "We know very well, Miss Dean, that you are the boss of this yere show, but the girl has been helpin' you to run it, so she's got to be whipped. But she won't git such a smart touchin' up as you will. Isn't that right, boys?" he asked.

"Yes." "Yes." "That's all right," some of them answered. "Let the gal off a bit easier than the woman."

Just then one of the men called out: "Whar's the hired woman? She ought to have her bottom switched, and get a ride on the rail as well as the others."

"Certainly she ought," said Stevens. "A couple of you go and bring her here. I guess she's hiding somewhere in the house."

Two of the men went into the house and while they were away the others talked and laughed with each other, making ribald remarks that caused me to blush and shiver. But Miss Dean did not appear to hear what was being said.

She stood quite still, her hands loosely clasped in front of her and a far-off look in her great, soft, brown eyes.

In about five minutes' time, the two men returned and one of them said with an oath: "We can't find the bitch anywhere in the house, though we have looked well. She must have run off into the woods."

"It's a pity she's got away," said Stevens, "but anyhow we've got the two leading ladies of the show, and I guess we'll make them both feel sorry that they ever took a hand in the game."

"You bet we will, Jake," shouted the men. "We'll make them sorry they ever came to Virginny. Let's get to work at once."

"Very well," said Stevens. "Bill, you run to the barn and fetch the ladder you'll find there. Pete and Sam, you go and cut a couple of good, long, springy hick'ry switches and trim them ready for use." Then he added with a laugh: "I daresay these yere northern ladies have often eaten hick'ry nuts, but I reckon they never thought they would feel a hick'ry switch on their bare bottoms." The men all joined in the laugh, while I shuddered and my heart swelled with bitterness at our utter helplessness.

The ladder and the switches were brought, then all the men went into the garden. The ladder then was fixed in a sloping position against the rail of the veranda on the outside, and Stevens took up his position near it, holding one of the switches in his hand, while the other men stood round in a ring so that they might all have a good look at what was going to be done.

"Bring out the prisoners," said Stevens.

Some of the men took hold of us by the arms and led us out of the veranda to receive the cruel and indecent punishment. I was trembling and crying; but Miss Dean was calm and silent.

Stevens said to her: "Since you're the boss, you shall be whipped first. Tie her up, boys."

She immediately was seized by two men and laid upon the ladder. Her arms were stretched out to their full extent above her head and her wrists were tied with thick cords to the rungs of the ladder. Her ankles were securely fastened the same way. She had not shown the least resistance nor had she uttered a word while being tied up, but now she turned her head and looking over her shoulder at Stevens said: "Can you not whip me without removing my clothes?"

"No, certainly not," he replied. "You were sentenced to be whipped on the bare bottom. Turn up her clothes, boys."

Her skirt, petticoats, and chemise were rolled high above her waist and tucked under her body so that they could not fall down. She had not on the ordinary drawers with a slit behind, such as are usually worn by women, but was wearing long pantalettes which were buttoned up all round, fitting rather closely to her legs and reaching down to her ankles, around which the little frills at the end of the garment were drawn in with narrow ribbons.

"Why darn me, if she ain't got on white trousers!" ejaculated Stevens in a tone of astonishment. "I never seen such things on a woman before."

The other men also seemed surprised and very much amused at the sight of the trousers, and various remarks were made by some of the spectators. I suppose that women of their class in that part of the country never wore drawers of any sort.

"Take down her trousers," said Stevens.

Again Miss Dean looked around. "Please leave me my pantalettes. They won't protect me much. Do not expose my nakedness to all these men," she pleaded earnestly.

But no attention was paid to her entreaty. One of the

men roughly put his hands in front of her belly and after some fumbling unbuttoned the pantalettes and pulled them down to her ankles, leaving her person naked from the waist to the tops of her black silk stockings.

When her last garment had been removed, her pale cheeks blushed scarlet. Even the nape of her neck and her ears became red. A shudder shook her body from head to foot, she bent her head down and she closed her eyes. I was being held by two men close to the ladder, so I could not help seeing everything.

The men pressed closer to the ladder, and I could see their eyes glisten as they fixed them with lecherous looks on Miss Dean's half-naked body. Stevens, after gazing for a moment or two at her straight figure, exclaimed with a laugh: "Je-ru-sa-lem! What a little bottom she's got. It ain't no bigger than a man's. By gosh, boys! Perhaps she is a man!"

This was meant as a joke. It amused the men and they all laughed, one of them calling out: "Well, Jake, you can easily find out whether she's a woman or not."

"Why, so I can, now that you have put it in my head," drawled Stevens, grinning and pretending to be surprised at the suggestion.

Miss Dean flinched convulsively, uttering a startled cry. Then, looking round at the man with an expression of intense horror on her face and with her eyes flashing, she exclaimed: "How dare you touch me like that?! Take your hand away! Oh, whip me and let me go!"

She writhed and twisted, the man saying with a coarse laugh: "She's a woman sure enough, boys."

Then he said to her: "My hand won't hurt you. But if I and these other gentlemen were not decent sort of chaps who only intend to carry out the sentence of Judge Lynch, you would soon find something different to a hand between your legs. Now I'll whip you right away, and I guess you'll soon be begging me to stop whipping you."

He withdrew his hand, and Miss Dean ceased struggling. Her head drooped forward. She again closed her eyes and lay silently awaiting the shameful punishment.

Stevens raised the switch and flicked it about so as to make it hiss in the air. Then he brought it down with considerable force across the upper part of her bottom, the tough hickory spray making a sharp crack as it struck the firm flesh which quivered involuntarily under the stinging stroke.

Miss Dean winced, drawing her breath through her teeth with a hissing sound. A long red weal instantly rose on her delicate skin.

Stevens continued to whip her ruthlessly and slowly, pausing between each stroke. The weals increased in number and her skin grew redder until at last there was not a trace of white to be seen on the whole surface of her bottom. Her flesh twitched, she winced more sharply, she writhed more and she jerked her loins from side to side as the hissing strokes fell. Then, raising her head and looking over her shoulder, she fixed her eyes, which had become dialated and wild looking, on the switch every time it rose in the air.

But the brave woman never once screamed, nor did she make an appeal for mercy. Her fortitude amazed me.

At last Stevens stopped whipping and threw down the switch which had become quite frayed at the end. Then, bending down, he closely examined the marks of his handiwork on the sufferer's bottom.

"There, boys," said Stevens, looking round at the spectators, "I guess that will do for her. I touched her up pretty smartly, as you can see by the state of her bottom. She won't be able to sit down comfortable for two or three days, and I don't think the marks of the whipping will ever be quite rubbed off her skin." He then pulled down her clothes and unfastened her wrists and ankles.

She seemed oblivious of everything except her pain. But, after a few moments, she recovered herself a little and, taking her handkerchief from her pocket, wiped the tears from her eyes. Then she pulled up her pantalettes and with some difficulty—for she was trembling very much—buttoned them around her waist, her cheeks again reddening when she noticed the grinning faces and leering looks of the men standing round her.

Two of the men took her by the arms and led her into the veranda, where they left her. She laid herself down at full length upon a couch and hid her face in the cushion, weeping.

CHAPTER FIVE

I am stripped naked and receive a most terrible whipping; the coarse observations of the men; my shame and terror, showing from experience that chastisement by the opposite sex awakens sensations sometimes far from pleasurable.

I have told you all these things precisely as they happened, and I have used the exact words and phrases which were spoken by the band of lynchers who tortured us that day. I daresay you wonder at my remembering all the little details. But such an experience can never be forgotten: all the incidents which occurred during that dreadful period were indelibly printed on my memory so that I have still a vivid recollection of them.

But to resume. You can imagine my feelings as I listened to the coarse language of the men, language such as I had never before heard, and as I watched the proceedings at once so cruel and so utterly revolting the feminine delicacy. I was torn with various emotions. I was horrified at what I had heard and seen; I was filled with pity for Miss Dean; I was consumed with impotent rage against the men in whose power we were; I dreaded the coming exposure of my person, and I was awfully afraid of the whipping before me. I never could bear pain with any fortitude. In fact, I must confess that I am morally and physically a great coward.

Stevens picked up the unused switch and straightened it by drawing it through the fingers of his left hand. "Now, boys," he said, "put the gal on the ladder and tie her up, but let me do the stripping."

The awful moment had come, and I became quite frantic at the thought of the shame and pain which I was about to undergo. An insane idea that I might escape came into my head. The men were holding me loosely, so I easily slipped from their grasp and made a dash for the garden gate. Several of the men gave chase, and, though I exerted myself to the utmost, I soon was caught and dragged to the ladder, shrieking, struggling, and begging them not to whip me. But my entreaties evoked only laughter. I was lifted up, was placed in position with outstretched arms and was securely bound at the wrists and the ankles.

Stevens now began to strip me and seemed to take as long a time over the work as possible, slowly rolling my garments up one by one. A sensation of unutterable shame overwhelmed me. To be exposed in such a way before fifteen men!

And such men! Oh! It was horrible! I knew that they were all gloating over my nakedness, and I seemed actually to feel their lascivious glances on my flesh. I was hot with shame, yet I shivered as with cold.

But worse was yet to come. Stevens put his hand on my bottom, stroking it all over and squeezing the flesh with his fingers, making me thrill and quiver with disgust. In fact, my feelings of shame and horror at the moment were far greater than they had been when Randolph assaulted me.

"Ah!" said Stevens, chuckling and continuing to feel me with his rough hand, "this gal has got something like a bottom. Now, as to the punishment of the gal. I propose to give her a dozen strokes, but not to draw blood. Remember, she's only an assistant in the business."

The men were divided in opinion. Some said that I ought to be whipped just the same as the "missis;" but the majority was in favour of my receiving only twelve strokes. And so it was settled. Even in my fear and shame, I felt a wave of relief at hearing that I was not going to be whipped so severely as Miss Dean had been.

One of the men called out: "Mind you, lay on the dozen right smart, Jake. Make the young bitch wriggle her bottom."

"You bet I'll lay them on smart, and you'll see how she'll move. I know how to handle a hick'ry switch, and I'll rule a dozen lines across her bottom that'll make it look like the American flag, striped red and white. And when I've done with her I guess she'll be pretty sore behind, but you'll see that I won't draw a drop of blood. Yes, gentlemen, I tell you again that I know how to whip. I was an overseer in Georgia for five years."

It fell with a loud swishing noise. Oh! It was awful! The pain was even worse than I had anticipated. It took my breath away for a moment and made me gasp. Then I uttered a loud shriek, writhing and twisting my loins in agony.

I had forgotten all about my nakedness now. The only sensation I had at the moment was one of intense pain. When the twelve strokes had been inflicted, I was in a half-fainting state.

Pulling down my clothes, he now loosened me from the ladder and led me, crying, sore, and miserable, back to the veranda where Miss Dean was still lying on her side upon the couch with her hands over her face. He then went off to the other men, a few of whom I saw were engaged in work of some sort near the fence.

But I was so thankful at having got out of their hands and sight that I did not particularly notice what they were doing. I thought they would soon go away and that all our troubles were over. I had quite forgotten that Stevens had said we would have to ride a rail for two hours after being whipped.

Miss Dean looked mournfully at me. Her sweet face was very pale and her soft eyes were full of tears but the tears were not for herself, they were for me. She beckoned to me, and, when I went to her, she folded me in her arms, pressing me to her bosom.

"Oh! My poor, poor girl," she murmured in tones full of compassion. "How I have felt for you! Your shrieks pierced my heart. Oh! The cruel, cruel man, to whip you so severely!" (She seemed to have quite forgotten the shame and pain of her own whipping in her pity for me.)

"He did not whip me nearly so severely as he did you," I said. "He gave me only a dozen strokes and no blood has come. But I could not help screaming. I am not so brave as you are." Then we kissed and cried and sympathized with each other, comparing notes as to our feelings while we had been on the ladder exposed to the eyes of the men.

After a moment or two I put my hand under my petticoats and touched my smarting bottom, feeling the weals which had been raised on the flesh by the switch. They were exquisitely tender and I could hardly bear to touch them.

"Oh! Dear me!" I wailed. "How dreadfully sore I am. But you must be much sorer."

"I certainly am very sore," said Miss Dean, wiping her eyes. "I can neither sit down nor lie on my back. My bottom is still bleeding, I think, and my pantalettes are sticking to my flesh. But, oh, oh! The awful exposure, and the shameful touch of the man's hands was worse than the whipping!" she exclaimed, wringing her hands while the tears again began to trickle down her cheeks.

I pressed her hand in sympathy, and she went on: "Our sufferings are not over yet, Dorothy. Don't you remember that the man said we would have to ride a rail for two hours?"

I now did call to mind what Stevens had said about our riding a rail, but I was not much frightened at having to do so. Of course, I knew that it would be very uncomfortable —if not downright painful—to have to sit with a sore and smarting bottom on a rail for two hours. But that was all I thought about the matter at the moment. Ah! I little knew what a terrible torture riding a rail would prove to be! I don't know whether Miss Dean had any notion of what it actually was, but anyway she did not say a word more on the subject, and we stood, both of us being too sore to sit down in comfort, with our arms round each other, weeping silently and waiting miserably for the men to come for us.

We had not long to wait. In a couple of minutes, four of the band came and, taking us by the arms, led us out of the veranda to the fence beside which the other men were standing, some of them holding pieces of rope in their hands. The fence was about five feet high and of the ordinary pattern, made of split rails, the upper edge of each rail being wedge-shaped and sharp.

Stevens, with a cruel smile on his face, said: "Now you

are going to receive the rest of your punishment, a two-hour ride on the rail. I guess your bottoms must be very hot jest now, but they'll have plenty of time to cool while you are having your ride. And to prevent you from falling off your horses, we'll tie you on them. Get them ready, boys."

I thought that we merely would be tied in a sitting posture on the fence with our clothes down. But I was soon undeceived! We were each seized by two men who held our arms while a third man raised our petticoats and pulled our drawers entirely off our legs. Then our skirts were held high above our waists so that the whole lower parts of our persons, both behind and before, were exposed to the lustful eyes of the horrid men.

After looking at our naked bodies for fully five minutes, the men went on with their work. A long piece of rope was passed several times round our bodies so that our arms and wrists were lashed closely to our sides. We then were lifted bodily up and, to my intense horror, seated astride one of the topmost rails of the fence, facing each other and about six feet apart.

The rail passed between our naked thighs, and our bare bottoms rested on the sharp edge of it. On each side of the fence and close to it the men had driven stakes into the ground, and to these stakes our ankles were securely tied. When the men had fixed us in this painful position, they allowed our clothes to fall about our legs. Our nakedness was covered, but our torture had begun.

Stevens looked at us with a grin on his face, saying: "There now; you are properly mounted on your horses. We're done with you and we're all going away. But at the end of two hours one of us will come back and loosen you. And I reckon you'll both be mighty stiff after your ride."

Then the band of lynchers took their departure, laughing and shouting coarse jokes which made us, even in our pain, grow hot with shame. The clatter of the horses' hoofs and the loud laughter of the men gradually died away in the distance. Then all was perfectly still.

CHAPTER SIX

On the rack; moral torture is allied to physical; I make the great decision of my life and consent to become Randolph's mistress; his revolting cynicism.

It was a beautiful, calm, bright evening. The sun was just setting and the house, the garden, and our two unfortunate selves were bathed in a flood of amber light. At first I had entertained a faint hope that Martha would come back once the men had gone and would release us. However, she never came, and there did not seem to be the slightest chance of anyone else's coming to the house at that hour. Thus, escape being seen as impossible, I resigned myself to the thought that Miss Dean and I would be forced to undergo the whole of our dreadful punishment.

From the first moment of our being placed astride the rail we had been suffering pain. Now it was increasing every minute. We did not speak to one another—our sufferings were too great!—so we just sat in silence with the tears, which we could not wipe off, trickling down our pale cheeks, while every now and then a shuddering sob or a groan of anguish would break from our parched lips.

As the minutes slowly passed, the pain grew more and

more excruciating. In addition, my bottom was still smarting and the weals on it still were throbbing. I felt as if the wedge-shaped rail were slowly splitting me.

Sharp, lancinating pains darted through my loins and up my back. Since my ankles were tightly fastened to the stake, I could not alter my position in the slightest degree. If my arms had not been bound to my sides, I might have gained a little temporary ease by resting my hands on the rail and thus taking some of the weight off my bottom. But the men, in their devilish ingenuity, had taken care that we should not have even a moment's respite from our tortures. Even if we had fainted, we would not have dropped either forward or backward, but our legs, tied to the stakes, would have remained straddled over the rail, and the sharp edge still would have remained between the cheeks of our bottoms.

Before long, every nerve in my body was throbbing with agony. A cold dew of perspiration had broken out on my forehead. I groaned and writhed and twisted about, but the more I did so, the more firmly the sharp rail was embedded in my tender cleft.

I began to scream, and, but for the grace of God, might even have cursed. Miss Dean, meanwhile, was crying, and her face showed the anguish which she felt. However, she made no outcry.

A few minutes more of agony slowly passed. Then I saw a man enter the lane and come towards the house. He was not one of the lynchers, so my heart bounded with joy. We should be released in a few moments!

I redoubled my cries, begging him to come quickly to our assistance. However, he did not hurry himself in the least. He walked deliberately and slowly up the path, and, alas, when he got a little nearer, I saw that he was none other than Randolph.

A few days previously I had hoped never to set eyes on him again. But now I was intensely delighted to see him. "Oh, Mr. Randolph!" I gasped out in a choking voice, with tears streaming down my cheeks. "Take me down! Oh! Take me down quickly!"

He came close to the fence and stood looking down at Miss Dean and me. He had a smile on his face.

"Oh dear, Mr. Randolph!" I again wailed. "Take me down! Do be quick and take me down!"

But, to my horror, he did not move. "Well," he said mockingly, "if it isn't Miss Ruth Dean and Miss Dorothy Morton. This is what slave-running has brought you. And it is to me that you owe your present position. I let the 'white' people know of your doings, and you have been rightly and smartly punished. I told you, Dolly, that we should meet again, and we have met. I knew that the men were coming to pay you a visit this evening, so I came with them, and, though you did not see me, I saw both of you getting your bottoms whipped. I must say, Dolly, you squealed just like a pig being killed."

He paused to laugh, and a sickening feeling of despair came over me. The cruel man, not content with having set the lynchers on us, had come to mock us in our agony.

He continued: "I am afraid that your bottoms—especially yours, Miss Dean—must be very tender after the smart switching, and I am afraid that you both must be extremely uncomfortable on your present seats."

Miss Dean's face was working with pain and her eyes were full of tears. But, when she heard Randolph's coarse and indecent words, she put aside her suffering and was consumed with indignation. Her pale cheeks grew red. Looking at me, she said in a quavering voice: "Dorothy, do you know this boor?"

Randolph answered for me: "Oh yes she does! Miss

Morton and I once were great friends. But we had a little tiff one day and she told me to go away. Is that not the case, Dolly?"

I hated the man, but at that moment the dreadful pain which I was suffering overpowered every other feeling. "Yes! Yes! That is the case!" I exclaimed fretfully. "But don't stand there talking! Take us down at once!"

Randolph smiled, but did not make a move to release us.

"Oh! Oh!" I shrieked with pain, enraged at his utter callousness. "How can you stand there and watch two poor women suffering agony? Oh! Why don't you release us? Have you no mercy or pity?"

"I am not a merciful man," he replied coolly. "I am a Southerner. As a rule I have no pity for abolitionists when they get into trouble for interfering with our slaves." Then, grinning lasciviously, he added: "But I don't mind making an exception in your case, Dolly. I will take you down if you will promise to come and live with me."

Upon hearing what he said, Miss Dean again fixed her eyes on me. She said earnestly: "Oh, Dorothy! Don't listen to the man! He is a cruel scoundrel to try to take advantage of your sufferings. But be brave, dear. Don't give way. I am suffering as much as—if not more than—you are, but I would not accept release on such disgraceful terms."

Randolph laughed scornfully. "I have not the least intention of offering the terms to you, Miss Dean," he said. "As far as I am concerned, you may sit on the rail till the two hours are over. The view I had of your naked charms did not tempt me in the slightest."

"Oh! You hateful man!" exclaimed Miss Dean angrily—for, after all, she was a woman, and no woman likes to hear her charms, whatever they may be, spoken of in disparaging terms.

But Randolph ignored her. "Now then, Dolly," he chuckled. "You have heard what I said. Do you intend to come home with me tonight?"

The coarse way he put the question shocked me, so I tried to pluck up a little spirit. I partly succeeded. "No, no, I won't go home with you," I said. But, I fear, my tone of voice was far from determined.

"Very well then," replied he. "Stay where you are. You have an hour and a half more to sit on your perch. By that time you'll be in a terrible state between the legs. And you'll be half-dead with pain. Rather a dreadful prospect, isn't it?"

Alas, it was! I moaned and shuddered at the thought of the long period of agony before me. Again I piteously entreated him to take me down.

He made no answer, but coolly lit a cigar and began to smoke. Then, leaning against the middle of the rail, he looked first to his right at Miss Dean, then to his left at me. His physiognomy was a study in perfect unconcern as we writhed, wept and groaned in anguish—and as the sharp edge of the rail pressed harder and harder against the tender flesh between the cheeks of our bottoms.

For a few minutes more, I bore the pain, which was growing more and more intense. Then I gave way utterly. I could no longer endure the anguish. I said to myself: "What does anything matter, so long as I can escape from this terrible torture?! I can't bear it for another hour and a half! I'll go raving mad, or die!"

No doubt it was weak of me, but I was in a half-fainting state, and, as I have told you before, I am physically and morally a coward. "Oh!" I cried. "Oh! Take me down! Take me down at once, and I promise to go home with you!"

When Miss Dean heard me promise to go with Randolph, she said: "Don't! Oh, don't go with him, Dorothy! Don't wreck your life! Try to bear your sufferings! They soon will be over! If I were you I would rather die than yield my body to the man."

"You are not she, Miss Dean," Randolph said curtly. Then, turning to me, he asked: "Have you quite made up your mind, Dolly?" And, so saying, he touched his hand to the knot of the rope binding my arms.

"Yes! Yes!" I cried impatiently. "Oh! Do be quick and release me!"

"Oh, Dorothy!" sighed Miss Dean in a sorrowful tone. "Oh, you poor girl! I pity you! You do not know the horror and shame which lie before you!"

Randolph soon untied the ropes which fastened my arms and ankles. Then, putting his arms around my waist, he lifted me off the rail, carried me into the veranda and laid me, limp and faint, on the couch. I was stiff and sore and aching from head to foot, but I was not suffering much pain. And, oh, the intense relief to find myself no longer astride the sharp rail!

When I was situated comfortably, Randolph fetched me a glass of water, which I drank thirstily, for my mouth was parched and I was quite feverish from the torture which I had undergone. Then, when I had recovered a little, I thought of Miss Dean and I asked Randolph to release her. However, he was very bitterly set against her, and would hear nothing of my pleas. It was not until after I had begged for her with all the pathos at my command that he finally consented to release her before we went away.

"Now, Dolly," he said, "I'll go for the buggy. I left it just around the corner of the lane. I shan't be gone long, so you lie here quietly until I come back." Then he added meaningfully: "You had better not attempt to escape, for the men still are somewhere in the neighbourhood and if they see you they'll put you back on the rail." So saying, he took his leave.

The thought of escape never entered my head. At that moment I was so weak and frightened that all my senses were in a half-torpid state. I did not fully realize the horrors which lay ahead of me, and I lay languidly on the couch, thinking only that it was so delightful to be free at last from pain.

Presently Randolph drove up with the buggy and, after hitching the horse to the garden gate, came to the couch, "Now then, Dolly," he said to me, "come along. Never mind your things. My women can supply you with everything necessary for the night, and I will send for your trunks tomorrow morning. Can you walk to the buggy, or shall I carry you?"

I replied that I could walk. But, on attempting to do so, I found myself so shaky and stiff that I could barely put one foot before the other. Noticing how feeble I was, Randolph lifted me up in his arms and carried me to the buggy. Then he placed me inside and wrapped a rug around my knees. I reminded him of his promise to free Miss Dean before we left, and he dutifully went to the fence and untied her bonds. However, he did not take the trouble to help her off her painful perch; the poor creature was forced to climb from the rail without assistance of any sort.

Miss Dean was weak, pale and suffering. Her feebleness was such that she had to lean against the fence for support. But her thoughts still were for me. "Don't go with that man, Dorothy," she said again, her tone urgent and earnest. "Never mind your promise. It was extracted from you by torture, so you are not morally obliged to keep it. Stay with me."

I did not want to go with Randolph, and I would have

been only too glad to stay with her. But my cowardice ruled the day. Afraid of being placed once more astride the rail, I could only cry out feebly: "Oh, I must go with him, my dear friend. I am in his power."

"Yes, indeed you are," Randolph observed. "And if you were to attempt to break your promise you would very soon find yourself back 'in the saddle.' " Then, addressing Miss Dean, he went on: "Remember, Ruth, what the men told you. If you are not out of the state before forty-eight hours have expired, you will receive another visit from 'Judge Lynch.' " He then got into the buggy beside me, and, as he did so, I shrank as far away from him as possible, hating him and despising myself even more.

Randolph touched the horse with his whip and we drove off, leaving Miss Dean standing with drooping head by the fence. After we had gone a short distance, I looked back and saw her lonely figure still in the same position. She did not move, and I kept my eyes fixed upon her until the buggy turned the corner of the lane. Then I sank back on the seat and, covering my face with my hands, wept bitterly. I had parted with the only friend I had in the world.

CHAPTER SEVEN

A Rabelaisian banquet of nude demoiselles; a shocking orgy; ten naked waitresses and their bashfulness; hot viands and bottom-spanking escapades, and the inevitable sequel!

Three months passed, during which period I went through some varied experiences and saw some curious sights. If I were to relate everything that occurred, my story would be too long. However, I will describe one or two of the incidents just to give you an idea of what sort of man Randolph was.

I have already mentioned the dinner parties he frequently gave for his male friends, and I have told you that these gatherings were always of a very free and easy sort. At one of these dinners the proceedings were of a more licentious character than usual. Randolph had invited ten guests, which was the usual number.

He was very particular on these occasions that all the girls should be nicely dressed, so Dinah used to parade them for my inspection just before the guests arrived. I merely had to see that the girls should be nicely attired outwardly, but Dinah, before bringing them to me, had to see that each girl was clean in person and that she had on clean underlinen.

On the day of which I am speaking, after my own toilet had been made, I went down to the hall and inspected the girls, finding them all looking clean and smart.

Then I went into the drawing-room where Randolph was lounging on a chair turning over the leaves of a large illustrated book of Rabelais, which he was very fond of reading.

I told him I had seen the girls, and that they were all looking very nice in their black frocks. To my astonishment, he burst out laughing, and said:

"Oh, they won't wear frocks this evening. I have got such a splendid idea from a picture in this old book. I wonder it never struck me before."

"What is it?" I asked.

"I have just been reading the chapter which tells how Pantagruel and his companions were entertained at a banquet by the Papimanes, and were waited on by a bevy of nude damsels. The dinner tonight shall be a reproduction of the scene described. There are ten men coming, and each man shall be waited on by a naked girl. It will be great fun, and also quite a novel entertainment for my guests."

Although I was accustomed to his vagaries this new freak horrified me. I should have to sit at the table with ten men, while the same number of women displayed their naked bodies.

The idea was most repugnant to me and I blushed, a thing I had not done for many a day.

"Oh George!" I exclaimed, "don't do such a thing. It is too shameful."

"Yes, I will," he said, laughing heartily. "Why Dolly, you are actually blushing! I thought you had got over all your squeamishness by this time."

"Oh, but this is a particularly horrid idea," I observed.

"And if you are determined to carry it out, don't make me come to table. Just fancy what a dreadful position it would be for me to have to sit among a lot of men, surrounded by naked women. I should not know which way to turn my eyes!"

He again laughed, but there was in his pupils a stern gleam which I had got to know, meaning that he had determined to have his way.

"It does not matter which way you look," he said. "You are looking very pretty and that's sufficient. You will have to take your place at table as usual, and you must appear to be quite unconscious that the women are naked. None of my guests will insult you by word or glance."

I still remonstrated, but he sternly told me to shut up, or it would be the worse for me. I held my tongue, for I was afraid of him, knowing him to be a man who would stick at nothing, and it struck me that if I made any more objections he might take it into his head to whip *me*.

Sending for Dinah, he told her what he intended to do, and gave her orders to have ten of the young women stripped naked in readiness. He named the ones he wanted, selecting those who had the best figures. Seven of them were quadroons, the other three were octoroons, one of them being Rosa. Dinah received the order, and also some further instructions he gave her, with a perfectly unmoved countenance.

"All right, sah," she said. "De gals shall be ready."

She then left the room.

It was nearly seven o'clock, and the guests began to arrive. Some came on horseback, others in buggies, and in a short time the whole party had assembled. All the gentlemen were more or less known to me, and everyone on entering the room shook hands with me in a most polite manner. They were of all ages: the youngest being about twenty-five years of age, while the oldest was upwards of fifty. Most of them were bachelors, but I knew that some of them were married men.

Presently Dinah, looking very smart in her black frock and white cap, made her appearance with a tray of cocktails, and while the guests were imbibing them, Randolph said with a smile on his face:

"I suppose, gentlemen, that most of you have read Rabelais. Those who have perused the book will remember the description of the banquet given to Pantagruel in the island of Papimany. I intend our dinner tonight to be, as nearly as possible, a counterpart of that celebrated banquet. I think I can give you as good fare and as good wine as Homenas gave Pantagruel and his companions. I also think that the 'she-butlers' will please you. They may not be so fair-skinned as were the damsels of Papimany, but in all other respects you will find that the 'waitresses' will answer the description of the ones mentioned in the book. They are 'tight lasses,' good-conditioned; comely, waggish, and fit for business."

The men who had perused Rabelais and knew what was coming, laughed and clapped their hands, but the men who had not read the book looked puzzled. However, knowing Randolph's little ways, they guessed that something funny was going to happen. In a short time, dinner was announced, and then the oldest of the guests, a gentleman named Harrington, who I knew had grown-up daughters, offered me his arm and led me into the brilliantly lighted diningroom. The other men followed, and we took our places at the table, which was beautifully decorated with flowers, and glittering with plate and glass.

Randolph took his place at one end of the table; I faced him at the other end, and five of the guests sat on each side.

When everyone was comfortably settled, Randolph touched a small handbell beside him, and then the door at the far end of the room was opened. Dinah came in, followed by the ten naked young women with their long black, or dark brown hair flowing loose on their shoulders; each girl, without hesitation, taking up her position behind one of the guests. Dinah had told each waitress where she was to go. They all, without exception, showed signs of bashfulness, for although every one of them had passed through the hands of gentlemen on various occasions, singly in a bedroom, they had never been exposed stark naked before the eyes of a number of people. Some of the girls blushed, the colour showing plainly on their olive cheeks; others cast down their eyes and fidgeted as they stood, while all of them placed their hands over the "spot" between their legs.

I felt horribly uncomfortable, hot thrills passed over me, and my cheeks grew scarlet. The men smiled, casting amused glances at one another, then they looked with gleaming eyes at the naked girls. Some were slim, and some plump; some tall; some of medium size, and some short; but all of them were pretty and had shapely figures, with firm, round titties and good bottoms, while the brilliant light, shining on their naked bodies, made their smooth, olive-tinted, and in some cases, nearly white skins, glisten. The hair covering the "spots" was, in all cases, black or dark brown, and one of the quadroons, a plump little girl, nineteen years of age, named Fanny, who had been whipped a couple of days before, still bore on her bottom the pink stripes left by the switch. Rosa was the prettiest of all the girls; she had also the best figure, and she was the lightest in colour; consequently she attracted the most admiration. The dinner was soon in full progress; the girls, directed by Dinah, bustled about bringing in the dishes, changing the plates, and filling the glasses with champagne. Some of them, not being accustomed to waiting at table, were rather awkward, but whenever a girl made a mistake she received from Randolph the next time she came within reach of his arm, a sounding slap on the bottom which made her jump and squeal, and clap her hand to the place.

But no one took the least notice of these little occurrences, the gentlemen continuing to talk and laugh as unconcernedly as if they were quite accustomed to being waited on by naked women, and also to seeing them smacked whenever they made a mistake. But it was a most trying time for me. I sat with my eyes fixed on my plate, and with a very red face, making a pretense of eating, and hardly listening to the conversation of Mr. Harrington, the old gentleman who had taken me into dinner, and who was sitting on my right. He chattered away to me, but I noticed that he kept leering lecherously at Rosa's full bosom and broad bottom, as she tripped gracefully here and there. She had evidently taken his fancy more than any of the other girls, and I felt sure that later on, my pretty maid would be poked by the old satyr. The dinner was a long one, but at last it was over, and the gentlemen settled down to smoke their cigars and sip their coffee, while the conversation turned upon slaves, and the price of cotton.

No improper remarks of any sort were made by the men, but their eyes were frequently turned with lustful looks on the naked girls standing in various attitudes about the room.

When the cigars had been smoked, we all went into the drawing-room, the girls being told to follow. I tried to slip away, but Randolph ordered me to remain. He told his guests to sit down on a row of chairs at the end of the room, and when they had done so, he posed the naked girls in groups in various positions with their arms round each other, some standing, some kneeling, and some lying on their sides at full length, so that their figures could be seen both back and front. These *poses plastiques* greatly pleased the spectators, and they gloated over each lascivious tableau, applauding vigorously; while the girls, utterly astonished at what they were being made to do, gazed timidly at the men with their big, ox-like eyes. At last, Randolph exhausted his ingenuity in inventing fresh tableaux, and I thought he would at least let the girls put on their clothes. But he did not. He had not yet done with their naked bodies.

"Now, gentlemen," he said, "if you will go into the corridor I will let you see young mares' races. Some of them are rather fat, but I daresay I shall be able to make them show their best paces."

The men, laughing boisterously, trooped out of the room and stationed themselves at intervals on each side of the long broad corridor. The races were to be run in heats, the course being from one end of the corridor to the other and back, twice over. Before starting the girls, Randolph got a long heavy whip, and cracking it in the air, warned them that they had better run as fast as they could. Then as soon as the first lot was off, he took up his position at one side of the corridor half-way down, and as the runners dashed past him in the several heats, he flicked the bottom of any girl who appeared not to be exerting herself, the touch of the whip extracting a shrill cry from the victim, and making her increase her speed, while a red mark instantly showed on her skin where the end of the lash had fallen.

The men grew excited, they laughed, cheered, and bet on the girls as they raced up and down the corridor, their long hair flowing loose behind them, their titties undulating and their bottoms swaying.

The final heat was won by a tall, slender octoroon girl, twenty-one years of age, named Jenny.

After the runners had a rest, there was what Randolph called a "Jockey race." The five strongest girls had to take on their backs the other five girls, who held on by putting their arms round the necks and their legs round the loins of their respective "mounts."

This time the course was once up and down the corridor, and heavy bets were laid by the men on the women they fancied.

The signal to start was given, and the race began, the gentlemen whooping and shouting as they watched the extraordinary sight. Five naked women staggering along the corridor as fast as they could, each woman carrying on her back another naked female!

The muscles of the thighs and bottoms of the carriers quivered under the strain, while the legs of the riders, being stretched apart by the position in which they clung to their steeds, the cheeks of their bottoms were slightly separated, so that the spectators could see the hair in the cleft of the thighs. And nearly every one of the bottoms was marked either with the prints of Randolph's fingers, or with the red dot made by the flick of the whip. Two of the girls had both finger-marks and whip-marks, and when all was over only three girls out of the ten had spotless posteriors.

The men's eyes gleamed, their faces were flushed, and I could see that they were all in a state of great sensual excitement. After a close struggle, the race was won by a sturdy young quadroon woman, twenty-five years of age, named Eliza, who had carried the youngest of all the girls, a slightly-built, shapely octoroon named Helen, who was only eighteen years old.

Then we went back to the drawing-room, the girls being

allowed to sit down, and Randolph told Dinah to give each of them a glass of wine and water. They were all very thirsty, some of them had tears in their eyes, and one or two were rubbing their bottoms, while the girls who had been carriers were panting for breath; their bosoms heaving tumultuously, and their naked bodies moist with perspiration. As soon as they had recovered their breath, the ten were made to stand in a row with their hands by their sides. Then Randolph said:

"Now, gentlemen, will you each choose a girl, either for a short time, or for the whole night? You can please yourselves."

The men laughing and joking, began to make their selections, and in cases where two or three wanted the same girl, the matter was settled by tossing up a coin.

Rosa was the favourite, five of the men, including Mr. Harrington, wanting to have her, but finally the old gentleman, as the senior member of the party, was allowed to take her. The selections being made, each man, followed submissively by the naked girl he had chosen, left the apartment and went upstairs to a bedroom.

Randolph and I were left alone.

He had been very much pleased with his evening's amusement.

"Oh, Dolly," he said laughing, "what fun it has been! I've never had such a game before. I'll do it again some day or other and when I do, every woman in the house shall strip for the races."

I did not feel at all mirthfully inclined. I had been wretched and uncomfortable throughout the whole proceedings, moreover the sight of so many bare bottoms, naked bosoms, and uncovered "spots," had given me a feeling of disgust. A woman is not excited by seeing the nakedness of other women. At any rate I never am.

"I think it was all very horrid and shameful," I observed.

"I don't care what you think," he replied. "It pleased me, and amused my guests, and that's all I care about. But it has been very exciting work, I am feeling very randy, and my tool is aching from its prolonged erection, so I must take the stiffness out of it at once. I will 'have' you sitting down, so as not to crumple your pretty frock."

So saying, he seated himself on a chair and let loose his member, which stood straight up with its red tip uncovered.

"Come along now, Dolly, you know what to do," he said impatiently.

I did know what to do. Turning my back to him, I raised my petticoats above my waist, and pulled open the slit of my drawers as widely as possible, exposing the whole of my bottom; then straddling over his thighs, with a leg on each side of him, I lowered myself down upon his standing member, which he guided between my thighs into its place, and the weight of my body forced the weapon up to the hilt in the sheath.

He clasped me round the waist under my clothes, while I, raising myself up and down on my toes, did all the work until the spasm seized me, and I felt the hot torrent inundating my inside. Then I lay back panting against his breast. As soon as I had received all he had to give me at the moment, I got off his lap, pulled my drawers into their place, and shook my petticoats straight, as some of the men might be coming back at any moment. As it was, we got done only just in time, for we had hardly sat down before one of the gentlemen made his appearance, and he was followed at intervals by others, until at last all had re-assembled except three, who had elected to stay all night with their girls. The other lasses, after being poked, had been allowed to go away to their own part of the house. Dinah brought in a tray of liquors and the men refreshed themselves. Then they all sat down to play cards, and I slipped out of the room and went to bed, glad to get away from the men, although not one of them had said an improper word to me during the evening.

It was very late, or to speak more correctly, it was early in the morning when Randolph came to bed. I was fast asleep, but he soon woke me up by pinching my bottom, and then in a moment or two he was working away at me. As I was very tired and sleepy, I did not respond to his movements in the least, so when he had finished, he said crossly:

"Damn it, Dolly, you lay just like a log of wood. You did not even move your bottom at the finish. What's the matter with you?"

I said there was nothing the matter with me only that I was sleepy. He growled out something uncomplimentary, then turning his back to me, went to sleep, and I speedily did the same.

2
The Last of Fort Sumter

Colonel Randolph stood in the piazza window of his summer mansion that looked out across the bougainvillea and magnolia of his garden to the East Battery and the Charleston waterfront. The ornate plaster swags and cornucopia of the inner arch framed the scene. No sign of light appeared in the deep bay of Charleston harbour, nothing but the phosphorescence of the breaking waves that came gently ashore. Silence and darkness were supreme. He let the velvet curtain fall and looked out upon the scene.

"Alea jacta est," he said to anyone who might hear him. "The words of Caesar upon crossing the Rubicon. The die is cast."

It was midnight and the sickle moon had scarcely risen. From the flat land enclosing the bay came a distant rumble of gun-carriages. The artillery of Charleston limbered up and moved forward until it commanded the best field of fire across the water to the walls of the Union garrison on the little island. Along the other piazzas of the East Battery mansions, in a perfume of oleanders, ladies in the finest evening gowns of London and Paris crowded with their menfolk to watch the great event. The length of the Battery and its raised waterfront promenade, from the dark trees of White Point Gardens to the beginning of the East Dock, the warm night air stirred with a buzz of conversation. It was now known that Colonel Chesnut had given the Union battery on Fort Sumter an ultimatum which expired at four in the morning.

Like his neighbours in the classic beauty of the waterfront houses, the colonel enjoyed a fine and private view as the old world passed into history. It was almost like a box at the theatre. He sat there, visible so far as the head and shoulders but hidden below that by the balustrade. He was even able to continue a conversation with his neighbour in the intervals of shell-fire, describing in diplomatic French the fate of an insolent young woman in whom he had had an interest. The pretentious young wanton had passed into the keeping of a tyrannical master in Cheluna, where the most interesting things had been done to her.

While he related this scandal and while history was made across the bay at Fort Sumter, Colonel Randolph was waited upon by a most charming adolescent girl. She was a nymph of Scandanavian beauty in whose elfin figure the fuller shapes of womanhood had not yet developed. "Nina" Katrina Frederiksen was a demure little blonde with slim and lightly sunbronzed limbs. Though the face of this pretty little creature had a rather straight and solemn look, the widely-spaced blue eyes, the firm lines of nose and chin gave her a delicious appeal. The little blonde had her hair casually curled on her forehead and drawn back into a silky-soft pony-tail that swung and brushed her collar as she walked.

In the heat of the night, Nina, as she was called by her

pet name, had been only too glad to change into a white sleeveless blouse and a pair of white cotton shorts whose hem came down no lower than the very tops of her silkily tanned thighs. She had slim straight legs suited to a girl on the threshold of adolescence. The trim rondeur of her elfin hips and buttocks had a primness that seemed proper to beauty in bud but not yet in blossom.

While two armies gathered in the night, Katrina Frederiksen brought him a tall glass on a silver tray. Colonel Randolph sipped it and described in murmured asides to his neighbour the ordeals inflicted upon the proud young woman of twenty-six whom he had consigned to white slavery. She was, he recalled, a firm-hipped young beauty with a self-assured swell of bottom-cheeks as she walked. Her light brown hair was worn a little tousled to her collar and her face had a certain prim disdain.

"Nous aimions la mettre nue. Miss Susan Webb était placée à plat ventre, à travers un sofa de cuir. On attacha la jeune esclave étroitement par des liens de cuir aux mains, aux poids et autour de la ceinture nue. Le monstre aimable, caressait longtemps les fesses blanches de Sue Webb. Doucement il nommait Miss Webb une jeune putain, une garce provoquante. Et il avait raison!"

Nina rested her dainty elbows on the rail with her back to him and leant forward a little. Colonel Randolph continued to describe Sue Webb's fate to his smiling neighbour in diplomatic French, in order not to rouse the unease of his little Scandanavian blonde. But his eyes dwelt on the youngster as he spoke. In the intimate white shorts, little Miss Frederiksen's slim thighs were bare and silkily sheened with gold from the sun. The tightening of the thin white cotton as she leant forward on the rail suggestively shadowed the cute little cheeks of Nina-Katrina's bottom. From time to time she reached back and plucked down the hem of the shorts with finger and thumb as if nervous that she might be showing rather too much to the man behind her.

Colonel Randolph stared at the view she offered and returned to his account of the prim young bitch, Susan Webb, who was vigorously impaled by her bottom way while held over the sofa.

"Le bombe de sperme éclata dans la croupe de la jeune femme. Il a fait sentir Susan Webb beaucoup de la vase chaude dans les entrailles. La putain hardie cria sa detestation de son sperme dans sa derrière. Elle avoua que ça la donna une envie à vomir. Il donna Susan plus pire, un peu après."

His eyes caressed the sight that Katrina Frederiksen offered him. The thighs lacked mature womanhood but not femininity. His neighbour was impatient to hear more of the pretentious young woman of twenty-six whom they had left strapped over the leather sofa. Colonel Randolph obliged him.

"On veux faire souffrir Susan Webb, cette jeune garce avec le visage impudent. J'ai choisi pour elle une punition très forte. Sue Webb était liée étroitement à plat ventre. Elle étatit nue et blanche, les fesses bien levées par des coussins de caoutchouc placés sous les hanches. Les valets écartaient les fesses nue de cette putain. L'anus de Sue Webb était barbouillé avec du savon mouillié. Le bourreau enfonça dans le trou postérieure de Miss Webb le nez d'un soufflet de forge. J'ordonnai au bourreau que les entrailles de la jeune putain doient gonflées sans pitié par la route de sa derrière. Pendant une demi-heure il pompait, jusqu' elle a evanoui deux fois! Susan Webb passait une nuit très, très dure!"

Colonel Randolph's crony replied, amused at the fate that had overtaken Sue Webb and inquiring if something of the sort might be arranged for young Nina. Since the youngster could not understand the conversation, Colonel Randolph saw no need for pretense.

"Je veux écouter Katrina Frederiksen—cette petite Nina—hurler à haute voix," said Colonel Randolph laughing. "Je pense à Nina avec le trou mignon élargi par le soufflet de forge, les fesses bien punies d'un fouet de cuir et la derrière caressée d'un cigare chauffé au rouge . . ."

What other indiscretions might have followed, it was impossible to say. Just then, a shooting star appeared to rip through the sky above Charleston harbour. A tail of fire streamed behind it and there was a dull explosion. But the projectile expired in a harmless puff of magnesium brilliance high above the wide anchorage. It hung in the sky a moment before falling slowly to extinction in the dark water. Its effect was to illuminate briefly the entire harbour and the forts upon their islands.

The colonel drew back within the doors of the upper floor, so that he might watch the great event in complete privacy. A ragged line of flame flickered briefly along the shore where the Confederate batteries were dug in. With a demented howling, the shells hurtled across the sky and threw up spouts of water in an irregular pattern about the walls of Fort Sumter. The colonel beckoned Katrina Frederiksen to him.

"Kneel down facing my chair, Nina. Just sit on your heels a minute and watch while I unbutton."

Another flash from the guns was bright enough to illuminate the pentagonal walls of Fort Sumter standing above the slack water of the bay.

"Is it such a big one for such a pretty little mouth? A

refusal, Nina? I hardly think so! Must I give you to half a dozen strapping negro slaves for the night and ask them to teach you better manners? Imagine the size of a black tool in your bottom, Katrina Frederiksen. Those hips of yours are very demure but still rather narrow. And those prim little bottom-cheeks, Nina. A pert little arse but not quite a young lady yet! A black buck who went deep in your backside would burst you with his force, Nina. Be a wise girl and serve me as you must."

Another star-shell from the east of the harbour burst high above the scene. Katrina Frederiksen's soft little switch of pale blond hair tickled the colonel's bare loins as she bowed over him. Beyond the island, the outline of a Union supply ship might be seen.

"Let it lie on your tongue, Nina, just like a big toffee apple for a good little girl. Close your lips over it. That's excellent. Such a soft and warm little mouth. I'm sure you can suck like a greedy little girl if you choose. That's the way, Nina. Your instincts tell you what to do."

Now the harbour echoed to a muffled thunder and there was a spouting of flame as the guns at the loopholes of Fort Sumter replied.

"Don't draw away, Nina. It's bound to make you gag a little when it goes close to the back of your throat. No need to alarm yourself. You must get used to that. Use your tongue much more actively now."

The shells from Fort Sumter burst in a scattered detonation among the reeds and flat shorelands at either side of the harbour.

"Lift your hips from your heels now, Nina. Kneel on all fours while you use your mouth. Excellent."

The colonel reached forward and pushed down Katrina Frederiksen's little white shorts. Pressing her soft blond head into his loins, he was also able to lean forward far enough to fondle her hips and backside. The quick and hard little sounds from her throat as he thrust a little too far indicated how gorged the stiffened male flesh had become. It was impossible not to sense her urgency, while he pressed over her and fondled the taut silky flesh presented by the demurely rounded cheeks of Nina-Katrina Frederiksen's bottom-cheeks as she knelt on all fours and served him.

The Charleston gunners had now opened up on both sides. Fort Sumter disappeared among the drifts of black smoke and the plumes of water. Flame ran on the very walls of the fort itself.

"It's coming now, Nina. . . . Over your tongue and down your throat. . . ."

He held her blond head firmly and gave her no chance of refusal. A single muffled squirt was followed by a wild shrill mewing from Nina—and by a gasp from the colonel. Then, after a pause, came an irregular salvo of squirts. Little Miss Frederiksen was called "Nina" and "Katrina" alternately. She was also alternately called a darling or a beauty and a young whore or a little bitch. The colonel's hand smacked down on the prim little bottom-cheeks, one of which he called "Nina" and the other "Katrina."

At last there was a long breath from Colonel Randolph and a chuckle, as he pressed her face close.

"No drawing back, Nina! Do you feel it getting hard again! What a fretful little girl! Dear me, is it such a very big mouthful for you to hold? Flicker your tongue round it, Nina—or does Miss Katrina Frederiksen really want her prim little bottom-cheeks skinned by my whip? No? Then Nina must do as she's told . . . Excellent . . . A nice big helping of 'tool sausage' for a little girl's supper every evening . . . in a few weeks Nina will think nothing of having a mouthful every night and some thick juice to swallow . . ."

A star-shell burst high above the sea again. To the east, the first pale light of day was parting the clouds above the southern ocean. Then the bombardment of Fort Sumter resumed, this time in greater earnestness, by men who would settle for nothing less than unconditional surrender and the end of all resistance.

3
Helen Wong

It was as if the Old South had been restored in the middle of the modern world. The occasion was a private entertainment to be enjoyed by a select group of men and women, the best society from the steamy heat of the Mississippi delta or the aristocratic drawing-rooms of London and Paris. A slave-girl or two was to dance before us. These and a dozen other girls were to be enjoyed as slaves for the night in the old style. Whether it was debt or inclination that brought them to this, I cannot tell you. It would not be possible in our time for such a girl to be used as a slave in New Orleans or any place of its kind. Law and custom now forbid it, though methods still exist to take her to places where men of influence may hold not just one pretty girl but an entire harem in absolute bondage. No doubt this would be the destiny of Helen Wong.

The evening promised a storm. Lightning, like the flash of a whip, cut the heavy clouds, somewhere far off above the Yucatan. Its radiance glimmered and died on the sleek surges of the Mexican Gulf. On such nights in the city you feel the approach of the storm long before it breaks. Thunder will roll distantly through the elegant streets at dusk. A warm moist breeze across river and swampland will flutter the auction bills on the French Exchange.

Behind the iron latticework of balconies and verandahs, the sufferers fan themselves in the heavy humid darkness, impatient for the relief of the storm. But it will be long after midnight, when all but the lamps in the cajun cemeteries are extinguished, before the first heavy drops of the tropical downpour begin to fall. Then, in a few minutes more, the bursts of rain will sweep the darkened river wharves and the graceful wrought-iron balconies of the French quarter.

When dinner was over that night, the invited guests of whom I speak, strolled along Chartres or Bourbon Street, across the lawns of Jackson Square by the cathedral and the cabildo. In the warmly-lit cafés of the old city it was the hour at which the scent of grilled trout or crayfish gave way to coffee *brûlot,* spice and flaming brandy.

The gentlemen in velvet trimmed evening jackets had a common destination. To avoid betraying a secret or causing a scandal, let me call the scene of the drama the Rotunda of the St. Louis Hotel. That is, in truth, what the world used to call it once. The elegant circle of its floor is paved with concentric lozanges of Italian marble, black and white. The roof rises to a magnificent glass dome whose adjacent ceilings are picked out in white and gold. The grandeur of the place comes partly from Paris of the Second Empire and partly from the dreamworld of the Arabian Nights.

For the refreshment of the guests, there is a bar-counter of polished mahogany that stretches half-way round the circumference of the concourse. A man may be served by the white-jacketed attendants. He may choose the finest vintages of Burgundy or Bordeaux, Alsace or Moselle, and the most exotic liqueurs. Above the bar an ornamental gallery runs round the edge of the circle. This is reserved for ladies invited to watch the public performance. The private sequel is not for their eyes. Because the gallery communicates directly with the diningroom and ballroom of the hotel, the female guests are able to peep in at the proceedings without any danger of the scandal that might be caused if they were seen on the floor of the Rotunda itself.

By nine o'clock in the evening, the marble floor is thronged by bidders in velvet-trimmed coats and tall hats, which they have worn to add an illusion of the past come to life again. The murmur of voices and the grey-green spirals of cigar smoke carry up to the graceful dome in a perfume of finest Havana. All eyes turn upon the so-called "auction block." This is not literally a block but a rostrum raised at the centre of the room with a walkway of the kind that a fashion-model would parade upon.

When the gentleman whom I shall call "Monsieur Vignie" took his place to begin the sale, a silence fell on the murmuring crowd. Several girls were to be auctioned, either outright or for the purchase of their favours. I make no apology for confining my revelation to the appearance of one of them, a girl of nineteen or twenty. She was brought on to the dais when the sale had been in progress an hour.

At first glance, Helen Wong had a half-caste prettiness. She might have been the daughter of a Chinese slave from the Pacific trade matched with a white-skinned lover. On the orders of her master, Helen's black hair was worn in a stylish shock of slight curls, framing her face and trimmed short above her shoulders. Her high-boned cheeks showed a trace of rouge. Above the slant of her dark eyes, the arch of her brows had been darkened a little by a touch of the cosmetic brush. Helen had a graceful young figure. As a young woman on the verge of her twenties, her smooth limbs showed the light saffron tan of her mixed race.

The conditions of the sale were made clear. The man who made the winning bid would have his way with her that very night, if he chose. Or he might choose to have her put through her paces in front of the others. And if she were to leave him dissatisfied, she would find herself sold again on far worse terms. But first she was to improve the bidding by doing her slave-girl dance for us upon the dais.

In the case of such a girl as Helen Wong, she appeared on the dais in the skimpiest little beach-outfit so that the bidders might see at once what they were being offered. The pants were cut brief at front and rear, suggesting that Helen Wong must have had to razor-trim the dark little bush in her loins to accommodate it. The Chinesey tan of her lithe young hips was sexily nude. Men and women alike were keen for her to turn and show the seat of her white bikini panties. Men wished to enjoy the sight and women to compare her figure with their own. The pale ivory smoothness of Helen Wong's bottom-cheeks in their trim oval beauty was enticingly presented in her swimwear. She had pretty little breasts and their skimpy covering left little to the imagination.

As she stood on the dais, Helen Wong had a natural look of the graceful and the submissive, though with the hint of a mischievous smile about her pretty little mouth. Her dark hair was brushed into its slightly curled and perfumed shock, just touching her shoulders as she twisted her head. The face with its high-boned cheeks and demure little chin was animated by the gentle slant of her dark eyes and the high brows arching over them. The light yellow beauty of Helen Wong's figure was slim and lithe.

Her maiden youth was seen in her pert little breasts, the pattern of her ribs under silky tan skin, her small waist and flat belly. Her legs were graceful and slender. The taut rounds of Helen Wong's backside were neat and smooth.

A woman moves with charming awkwardness when she tries to run, her breasts and hips swaying a little too much to be truly athletic. The same is true when she teeters in high heels. In high-heels of the kind that Helen was wearing, her movements are even more charmingly constricted.

She came forward and stood barefoot at the centre of the marble floor, the auctioneer and his guests at its edges. By now, Helen Wong was naked except for the white nylon bikini briefs and bra. She twirled before the men, as if for their approval. Her tan-skinned thighs were sensuously agile, beautifully rounded yet so slim that they looked almost frail. The scandalous little panties were no more than a white pouch at the front, covering the pretty triangle of dark hair that crowned her sex, thinning to a mere strip of material round her waist to leave the flanks of her Chinese saffron hips bare. At the rear, the white swimwear panties had been cut outrageously tight and brief, arching up on either side of her agile young backside, so that the pale ivory smoothness of Helen Wong's bottom-cheeks was mostly bare. By their tightness and brevity, Helen's panties made her young body appear more sexually suggestive than if she had been entirely naked, which was no doubt what her master intended.

The unseen musicians began to play, the flute's wail rising in quarter-tones and the tambourine beating out the rhythm of the dance. Helen twined her arms above the collar-length shock of her dark hair. She began to round her hips gently and squirm her knees together. To one side of the Rotunda she showed the passionate gaze of her dark eyes with their hint of an Asian slant, the breathless parting of her lips, the supple arching of her smooth young belly. To those behind her, she offered the rounding and cheek-to-cheek writhing of her ivory-tan bottom-cheeks.

Vignie and his guests alike watched her keenly, as if anxious to miss nothing of Helen Wong's self-arousal. The girl turned with gliding steps, arching back and shaking her bare shoulders in a vigorous breast-bobbling rhythm. Gently she went down on her knees, head back and pert little breasts still thrusting in the tight white nylon of the skimpy bikini-bra with the energy of her movements. The men sitting near her leant forward a little for a closer view. She held herself like this, eyes staring almost sightless at the high Rotunda dome above her, shaking and shimmering, tensing and writhing. Then she bowed forward, as if to lick clean the marble tiling, hips raised from her heels. The tight brief seat of the white bikini panties was no more than a twist drawn deep and tight into her anal cleft, offering the lithe ivory tan of Helen Wong's backside quite bare in its spread-cheeked vulgarity.

Writhing to her feet like a snake, she bowed the shock of her dark hair as her hands went up between her shoulder-blades and she undid the clip of her white bikini-bra. Then she hooked her thumbs in the waist of her panties and drew them down. Standing first on one leg and then the other, she hooked her knickers off with a prettily awkward gesture, so that she now danced entirely naked before the men. It was to be an excitingly lascivious tribute and submission by the girl to her master for the night.

With a controlled writhing of her hips and a flesh-creasing roll of her firm young belly, Helen passed before the men on each side. She hung her head back and widened her knees, arching back to show the intimate dark-haired folds of her sex. Coming forward again, she bent tighter and tighter. Her forehead went down level with her knees, until she looked back at the men through the arch of her firm tawny thighs. The pert little cheeks of Helen Wong's bottom were tightly rounded and parted, offering unashamedly to her admirers a full view of her forbidden rear cleavage. Though she would not be given to any of them to use in this way, the girl's dance acknowledged the forms of submission that she knew she must make.

Helen Wong's Chinese-tan bottom rounded towards the auctioneer in charming innocence. She arched and writhed the lithe innocence of her young buttocks, the sweat of exertion shining on her yellowed-ivory nudity in the humid air of the delta evening. She bent forward a little and the slippery wet perspiration of the humid delta night shone like silk on the trim resilient cheeks of her young arse. Even without being told, Helen Wong was also squirming her bare slender thighs upon her own sensitivity in a squeezing rhythm. The men licked their lips, looking up and down to admire her slim bare arms, her young belly taut and flat, the demure beauty of her tense young thighs. As she squirmed her rear cheeks the feminine promise of Helen Wong's bottom was perversely offered.

After that she sank to her knees and drew herself at full length on the floor in a suggestive twisting and writhing of her legs, as if simultaneously fawning before them and bringing herself off in the excitement of her slavery. Whether it was finely acted or simply genuine, only the girl could say. But there followed a shuddering spasm, scaling the heights of ecstasy and falling back into contentment at last, as Helen Wong came to the climax and release of her passion.

The sight of such a girl dancing in this manner was profoundly stimulating, but it was curiosity rather than lust that roused most powerfully. Having made my bid for her, I chose my pleasure. It was merely to watch her. I wished her to be left waiting in her present state in the hotel room—but it was a room whose mirrors were windows enabling one to watch her in every detail.

Helen was innocently employed. There was an alcove in her room with a long mirror, a basin, and a bidet. She stood before the glass in her white glamour costume of diminutive breast-halter and the white cache-sex which was no more at the rear than a string between her hind cheeks tying to her waist-band. Watching herself, as if it were another girl obeying her commands, Helen Wong drew up the shock of her dark hair with her hands behind her head, looking more coquettish and flirting with her own reflection. Her face in the mirror was demure and pretty, the dark slant of her eyes meeting their own reflection with a heathen she-devil's prettiness. She held her own gaze for a moment longer, perhaps admiring the neat prettiness of her slant-boned cheeks, the narrowing to mouth and chin. Yet it took only a little softening of her playful devil-mask to show a natural beauty in the firm lines of Helen's face.

To see Helen Wong standing almost naked before her washroom mirror like this was to find the qualities of her mind reflected in her figure. She was a delicately-built girl, her back and shoulders sleek with the almond tan of oriental beauty. Her little breasts had a pert upward thrust. The bone pattern of her ribs was clear in her slim figure, her belly flat and narrowed. Her back was slender and silky. The pale ivory tan of Helen Wong's bottom-cheeks had a lithely rounded and prettily lascivious look. Her thighs had the same slim prettiness.

She watched herself for a moment more, then reached for the soap and ran some water. Beginning at her shoulders, she spread the sheen of wet soapiness over and down her body. Her hands fondled her breasts until, as she drew them away, the mirror betrayed the erection of her nipples. Her fingers returned to these hard yet sensitive buttons of flesh, which she excited further without a change of expression on her face. There was no shame in Helen Wong, only a frank curiosity about her own body and the pleasant sensations of such caressing.

Holding the soap in her left hand, she smoothed her right palm down her belly in a slow circling rhythm of comfort. When the lather shone upon it she began to work it into the dark triangle of hair which crowned her sex. At that point she looked away from the mirror. Was it embarrassment at what she was doing to herself? Or did Helen prefer to imagine that it was the hand of some boyfriend, or even some idol of the movie screen, doing this to her?

Still looking away from the mirror, head down like a little girl just scolded by her teacher, Helen shifted her knees apart a little. Her fingers slowly spread the sheen of lather up the inner surfaces of her thighs. A warm-blooded Oriental girl of nineteen or twenty masturbates impetuously —and so it was with Helen Wong. As I watched her, she used her second hand. It spread the wet sheen of soapy slipperiness over the delicate yellowed tan of Helen Wong's bottom-cheeks, the small of her back and the rear of her thighs. Then it seemed that she needed that hand to support herself as she manualised the flesh-folds of her sex with a muted resonance of wet flesh between her thighs.

As last she looked up, the black hair just long enough to touch her shoulders as it spread along the top of her spine. Her knees were pressed tight and the prettily rounded swell of Helen's ivory-tan buttocks clenched together, as if to imprison a delicious surge of erotic excitement. I waited a moment to see what she would do. Without bothering to reach for the towel, still sleek with moisture from waist to knees, she stretched out on the bed. She lay there naked, on her side, facing one mirror and with her back to the other where I stood.

Even had I not been able to see her face in the far mirror, as well as the way she plagued herself with her busy fingers between her thighs, the rear view of this naked Eurasian girl would have betrayed her guilty self-indulgence.

The sleek and soapy-wet seat gave a smooth and flawless gloss to the paler tan of Helen's rear contours, making her show the impish cheekiness of her backside most suggestively. On the curve of the Anglo-Chinese girl's smooth rear cheeks the film of moisture caught the light with a sheen like silk. Wet and sleek, the olive-skinned gloss gave a prettily fuller and fatter look to the cheeks of Helen Wong's sallow-tanned bottom-cheeks.

The moist gleam was like a pair of translucent tights or panties on the erotic double-cheeked swell of the girl's backside. It exaggerated their lascivious writhings and glistened soapily in the suggestive anus-crack between them. Now the tan-skinned cheek-swell of Helen Wong's arse began tensing and slackening in a slow, languorous rhythm. Her firm lazy thighs whispered together. A girl of Helen's kind, thinking herself alone in such a wanton mood, innocently offers the most intimate glimpse between the rear of her legs as she writhes with languid self-indulgence. I saw her fingers working back, rubbing and squeezing, stroking and fondling. There was a sense of conquest in being able to enjoy her most private erotic moments, unknown to Helen, as this demurely-shaped Eastern beauty caressed herself. Helen Wong masturbated out of pure need, reflecting the passionate and yearning trait in her character. But the society from which she came afforded her no other sexual expression than this. Even Helen Wong's masturbation was morally forbidden. Had Helen been caught at home, making love to herself, the most vindictive punishments would have been devised for her. These would not have been mitigated merely because she was nineteen or twenty and her natural passions well-developed.

Grinning with delight my companions craned forward to get the best view of Helen Wong's fingers running and twiddling, tickling and teasing herself, for she lifted her upper leg clear of the other a little to enjoy herself more. Regular sex on her own or with a man, since she was in her early teens, had taught her all the tricks and thrills that such fiddling and fondling of her most sensitive feminine flesh could devise. She lay with eyes closed as if she dreamed of a lover's caress. She breathed more quickly through her open mouth, turning over a little more on her belly, arching her lithe young backside out more fully as she pleasured herself harder between the legs.

She had no idea that anyone was watching her, believing that the ceremony in the Rotunda was still in progress. So long as she was under my supervision, Helen had no need to fear the consequences of being spied upon. I was determined to let her continue for my own instruction as well as for her own pleasure, wanting her to get tantalisingly close to her climax before I would think of intervening. In such a state, Helen would have little choice but to submit as she felt another hand covering her own. Glossy and suggestive, the sleek wetness of the soap endowed the tan-skin cheeks of Helen Wong's bottom with that more fully seductive appearance. This made the swelling and rounding of her young backside extremely seductive as she squirmed and panted softly. She was a lithe and agile girl who now abandoned all restraint. I could not help smiling as I tried to imagine what her response would be when she discovered that she had offered this display of self-caressing between her thighs and that the men who watched her had greatly enjoyed the swelling and writhing of Helen Wong's bottom-cheeks, the urgent tightening, the trembling and whimpering of pleasure, the desperate riding of her loins upon her own busy fingers. I doubted if she had the equanimity to accept the grinning and vindictive satisfaction of the voyeurs as a man's natural response.

Her movements gained speed and vigour. It seemed that Helen was now frantic to finish herself off. I heard the hard and rhythmic creak of the bed's wooden frame as her hips bucked hard against the mattress. There was a pause as she turned on her back, knees hugged up to her breasts and fingers playing rapidly on the exposed underside of her sex. At last she turned her face aside and bit the pillow hard between her teeth. The fingers went faster. The bed creaked in a quicker but erratic rhythm. There was a shuddering, a muffled groan. Her hand fell limp to one side and she extended the fingers as if to ease the strain in them. Her legs slid down and she let them lie apart. The stillness in the room was all the more potent for being so sudden. Helen Wong had had her orgasm at last.

I cannot say what lesson the others learnt from this innocent display. I went in alone to her at this point and, as a gentleman does not reveal the details of his own pleasures, you must allow the door to close upon us. I may tell you, of course, that I greatly enjoyed the hours remaining to me that night. But when I look back upon the occasion, it is the dance on the floor of the Rotunda that I remember—and that other horizontal dance to which Helen was excited by the first.

4
A Travelling-Man in the South Country

I doubt if you would care to change places with me, supposing you were to see me on the train or in the diningroom of a commercial hotel. A travelling-man with a leather bag and a portfolio of documents. A face with spectacles and moustache that you might change for a thousand others and never know the difference. A dull fellow on his way to perform some tedious duty for a mean employer. That is how I should appear to you. Journeying late at night in ill-lit draughty carriages. Sleeping on starched and unfamiliar sheets. Lodging on lonely beds in rented and fly-spotted rooms.

You see? I cannot lay claim to the make-believe of romance. The secret I share with you now is an episode in the most ordinary life.

I doubt if you would spare me a second glance before turning home to the arms of your warm plump Janet, or your squirming little Jacqueline, or your dreamily lecherous Michelle. Perhaps you have a fluffy young wife with a round and agile bottom who will carry in the supper and precede you lasciviously up the stairs to bed. Or else, in a private apartment when the city grows quiet, you enjoy an almond-eyed and tawny-skinned young mistress with a touch of the perverse about her as she waits for your ring at the bell.

How you must pity the poor travelling-man! But I do not envy your private moments with Michelle or Louise. I might give my reason in many words. For the moment I choose only a few. Kathy Jones. Trudi Simpson. Linda Sadler. And, of course, Maureen.

To you, the name "Maureen" evokes nothing. Or, at least, it summons up an image that has no resemblance to the one I see now. Picture her, if you will, at about twenty years old. She is no more than medium height, dressed in a thick cream sweater and blue jeans. Though she has a fair creamy skin and a slight blush of rouge in her cheeks, Maureen's face and profile have a rather calm and Grecian look. She has lustrous dark hair which falls in a fine sweep, sometimes pinned up in a short plait and sometimes worn as a loose collar-length pony-tail but in either case tied by a red ribbon.

The long oval of her face is made beautiful by the slight ellipse of her dark eyes with their fine brows and mascara'd lashes. Her chin is firmly moulded and her mouth well-shaped. In profile, she has a rather bold nose and long slope to her face, which adds to the Grecian look of her. Her figure is trim and youthful. From time to time, as she bends over quite tightly to arrange the books, the loose-fitting jeans tighten. Maureen's bottom is tautly and perfectly rounded, trim enough for the cheeks to be suggestively separated as she bends tighter still. She wears very tight briefs underneath and nothing is seen of these but a faint hem-line from the rear parting of her legs when she is bending right over.

Let me tell you how I first encountered her.

I know you will expect me to be discreet in the matter of concealing my employer's name. Nor can I reveal the title of the worthy charity whose patron he remains. You know as well as I that there are young women who fall by the way and are reclaimed under a regime of moral authority by wholesome toil. No doubt you have dropped a coin in the box from time to time for such worthy cases, while secretly envying the stern guardians who have such young females under their command. But one dare not entrust such girls to the strictest moralists—male or female—without some further supervision. Who will guard the guards themselves, as the wise old Roman asked?

That is my profession. In me you see what the Russians once called an Inspector-General of the institutions founded by my employer's generosity. I am the man whom their directors dread. They know I watch keenly during my visits and write my secret reports. So long as I exist, the public ignores the rumoured scandal, how a hardened slut like Maggie Turnbull had her front and rear approaches widened by the gaoler's stiffened resolve. How Denise Wilson, a cheeky urchin beginning her teens, was bent over bare-bottomed in the master's room one night. How he used her bottom to ease his stiffness before he whipped its slim bare cheeks with a pony-lash. Because I am trusted, no attention is paid to such mischief-making stories.

I had followed my calling for about two years before I first set eyes on Maureen. I drew up my reports neatly and exactly because I am an exact man by nature. Those who know me would vouch for this. And so I remained until the warm November day when I set out to visit Waterton, the country residence near Richmond where Mr. Milsom and his assistants apprenticed delinquent beauty to useful trades.

The railroad does not run to that remote and wooded

plantation among the hills of a deep river valley. There are no chance visitors. You leave the train at Richmond and wait for the driver who is sent by appointment to collect you from the station yard. Mr. Milsom arranges these things well. Waterton is scarcely more than one of his "hobbies," for he is a man of many commercial interests in the city.

It was my own fault that there was no driver to meet my train. I had decided to set off early and arrived two or three hours before the time appointed. I might have stood there in the station forecourt with my leather bag and waited but I preferred to explore the city a little, examining the red brick warehouses of the commercial quarter and the fine shops of Main Street. Mr. Milsom's name appeared above several of these.

There was a bookshop belonging to him which drew my attention. I thought I might spend half an hour browsing there. As I glanced at it, I saw that its window was in some disarray and that a new display of books was being set out by a dark-haired girl of twenty or so. I recognised her as the type whom he would have under his guardianship at Waterton. This did not surprise me in the least. I would expect a man of such enterprise to make use of the girls there for his own profit. I drew closer, just as she stepped back into the bookshop window from the wide and well-lit body of the shop itself. So it was that I first saw Maureen. I assure you that I stood watching that window, my attention drawn entirely to her and that the volumes of wisdom that waited in neat stacks to be set out received not a second glance.

I should have stopped to admire Maureen, even had it only been for the appeal of her face. Her dark hair was drawn back from her tall fair-skinned brow, its length plaited and worn up at the rear of her head by the aid of the red ribbon. Her constant labours, carrying the piles of books and stooping to arrange them, gradually displaced the elegant coiffure and, by the time I left, she was wearing her dark hair in a loose pony-tail, just brushing the top of her back.

Maureen was no more than medium height, dressed in a thick cream sweater and blue jeans. How one longed to feel that fair creamy skin and a slight blush of rouge in her cheeks, as she rubbed them obediently against the knuckles of one's hand like an obedient young puss. True, Maureen could look rather a hard-faced young bitch when she chose but there was wide-eyed beauty in those bold young features. Her chin was firmly moulded and her mouth well-shaped, able to perform whatever lip-service her master might command.

Her trim and youthful figure was easy to admire above the waist in the cream wool of her sweater. But it was from the waist down, where she was tightly clad in the thin worn denim of her jeans, that Maureen drew most admiration. I watched her for a while, admiring her slim straight thighs and the maiden tension of her hips. When she bent over to arrange the books, the cheeks of Maureen's bottom in the tight-fitting jeans were presented to the street in a way that caused most men to slow down as they passed. The cheeks of Maureen's arse were neatly but saucily rounded, showing her as a girl who had not yet acquired that extra rear swell which a young woman often boasts in the course of her twenties! Because of this, Maureen's buttocks parted as she bent right over and the stout central seam of the jeans-seat was drawn deep between them. The eyes of the men who passed told one what they would like to do to the girl if they had her in their power like that!

From the papers in my briefcase, relating to Waterton, I

recalled that there was a girl with the name of Maureen who was described as undergoing reformation by working out her "apprenticeship" in Mr. Milsom's shop by day and returning to serve her sentence at Waterton in the evening. I gave her my close admiration as she bent over to pick up several more books for display. I promised myself that I would be most exacting in my demands upon Maureen and that she would soon be one of the best-disciplined girls in the house.

Having spent an hour or two in the town, I went back to the station yard and there found the driver waiting to take me to Waterton. He was a burly taciturn fellow who spoke little during the journey. From main highways we turned on to tracks that led through woods of spruce trees, where you might still imagine the shots of some blind Civil War encounter echoing from opposite patrols. Our way followed the ridge of a valley whose cliffs dropped to a dramatic river-gorge. Its grim-looking ferry-town on the opposite bank was served by an iron railroad bridge on stone pillars, about which the rapid current from the hills broke and washed. There was nothing much to the brick settlement beyond half-a-dozen tall industrial chimneys and a drab street with a hotel and a general store.

It was getting dark by the time we approached the estate at Waterton, ten or twelve miles from town. A light but stinging rain was in the air, blown up the valley from the sea. The lane that we followed dwindled into an unmade track that kept us bumping and swaying for the last ten minutes of the drive.

The gabled mansion at Waterton was not quite the House of Usher, though its situation among the woods made one think of the possibility. A paradise in summer, it would turn to gloom with the first dank November days. I had arrived there an hour or more ahead of Mr. Milsom and the girls who paid the price of their misconduct by working for him in the town. Each morning they were escorted to their tasks and every evening they were brought back to the secure captivity of Waterton.

Mrs. Hamley, the mistress of the place, received me kindly and showed me to the library where I was to wait. A glass of malt whisky and a box of cigars were placed on the table beside my leather chair. I was invited to choose a volume from the shelves, if that would help me to pass the time more agreeably. I could not help noticing that the top shelf of the handsome break-front bookcase contained a row of finely-bound volumes whose subject was the chastisement of delinquent teenage girls and wayward young women.

I suppose there was nothing remarkable in this. Certainly there was nothing to prevent me choosing one of these for my reading while I awaited the arrival of my host. So I diverted myself to browsing through tales of fourteen-year-olds like Linda Jennings and Valerie Bishop brought to obedience by their teacher's cane across their bare buttocks. I studied the accounts of self-satisfied young women like Deborah Cameron and boyish thirty-year-olds like Trish Mitchell sadistically marked across their bottoms with a training-lash to teach them respect for their masters. For the best part of an hour I drew wisdom out of these curious pages.

Mr. Milsom arrived at his usual time and we renewed our acquaintance. He remarked, quite rightly, that institutions of this kind were much more easily run in the sympathetic culture of the south country. He smiled as he assured me that the authorities in the area fully supported his work. Several law-officers were regular attendants when punishments were inflicted, a custom which dated from the old days of slavery and the whipping-houses. On the few occasions when one of the girls under his rule had absconded, she had found not a single person to run to in the surrounding area and had infallibly been returned to face her penalty at Waterton.

It was my duty to report on the house and the way it was run. To that extent, I suppose it was in Mr. Milsom's interest to exaggerate his success a little. But in the year that followed, I grew more familiar with the place and I assure you that there was no exaggeration at all in his claims.

"And do you have a difficult case at present?" I asked him. "A girl who is to be given particular attention?"

He thought for a moment, perhaps feeling uncertain at how I would react to an exhibition of that kind.

"We give that attention wherever it is needed," he said at length. "I do not say we should do it often."

"There is one in the list given me by the director," I said at last. "Maureen. I do not find she has committed a serious offense but there is an accumulation of petty disobedience for which she ought to be disciplined. If you wish it, the matter can be settled during my visit. By that means, there will be no question that you have acted without authority in the matter."

It was not the strict truth, but I could not resist the thought!

"By all means," he said. "While you are here, we have approval from our benefactors."

Without telling me, he chose Maureen at once to serve as my chambermaid. When I discovered that it was she who was to attend me in the days before we settled accounts with her, I felt all the more pleased.

I woke the first morning in the room that had been allotted to me above the sunlit courtyard. Any misgivings that I might have felt the evening before about what I proposed to do to Maureen were dispersed. They had faded as a nightmare does in the strong light of the new day. Already the sun was warm on that finely weathered brick outside the window. The walls were fragrant with climbing stock in yellow and pink, while a light dew sparkled on the neat lawns. Further off, where the stately trees rose from the surrounding pasture, I heard the raucous crows in their high nests and the plaintive calling of doves.

I mention these things to show you how far removed the world of the house at Waterton seemed to be that morning from the worst reputations of such institutions or from the heated fantasies of sensationalism.

As I lay in bed and gazed up at the old beams of the ceiling, there came a gentle knock at the door. It was opened by the girl of about nineteen or twenty who had troubled my dreams. I saw the bold features, the smooth creamy skin, the trim figure in jeans and sweater. What a contrast she was to the fourteen-year-old schoolgirl-blonde, Linda Jennings, with her sly and sensual sniggering, about whom I had been reading before sleep.

"They call me Maureen, sir. I am to be your servant."

She had far more grace and better manners than such young minxes as Linda Jennings or that other girl from 3B, the gamine auburn-cropped friend Valerie Bishop. I wonder if you would have thought her beautiful? There was an air of suggestion in having her in my bedroom like this, even as a servant-girl. My stiffness grew until I thought she must see the shape of it under the sheet.

Whether she would prove to be a creature of moods and sulks I did not know but it was evident that a certain passion animated her looks. The light rouge on her cheeks heightened this. Her dark hair was drawn back from her tall pale brow and pinned up in its plait at the back of her head.

"Come in and show yourself, Maureen," I said, teasing her a little already.

She obeyed and entered the room, carrying a tray upon which my morning tea had been set out. She placed this on the table and stood there, as if waiting for a command. I was pleased that she had not changed from her costume of woollen top and tight jeans, which encased her almost skin-tight from waist to ankles. Not needing to add to her height, which is the case with some of these girls, Maureen had chosen shoes whose heels were flat and comfortable.

So you may see that my attention was drawn early to this dark-haired Venus of nineteen or twenty. I made her stand there a moment more and allowed my eyes to wander up and down the length of her lithe and agile young thighs in their tight faded denim.

"May I fetch your shaving water, sir?" Maureen asked in that quiet voice which added to her seductive qualities.

I dismissed her to attend to this errand at once, watching her as she turned and walked away. Her trim young figure was well displayed, the wool of the cream top shaping her breasts' firm tilt and the tight smoothness of her faded jeans showing her rear view from the waist downwards. Maureen has a slim firm line to her thighs. Firm and supple, they branched out and up from the knees. Her buttocks were tautly rounded and the young bitch swung them and swayed them with the energy of her walk. Usually it is the tilting of the tall heels on a girl's shoes which makes her do this. But Maureen does it from habit, as it seemed to me then. I smiled as I watched her, wondering if this young tart was unaware of the rear prospect she was offering me as she walked or whether she was doing it deliberately to provoke me and encourage my interest. I think, on the whole, that Maureen did not realize the sight she presented.

How could I resist certain imaginings, as I lay back on the sunlit pillows and waited for the hot shaving water? It is common enough for a man to indulge himself in a fancy or two when confronted with such a girl in such a situation. But my prospects were somewhat better. It was half way through these waking dreams that I experienced a shock of recollection. I sat up in bed, astonished at the thought which had just crossed my mind.

Perhaps for a man in my position, Maureen was not my servant in the ordinary way. She was to obey any command that I might give her. My power over her was absolute as a visiting inspector in a house like Waterton. If I chose to find some fault with her, I might order her to take down her pants and lie over the bed, as soon as she returned with the shaving water. My hand should become feelingly acquainted with the bare cheeks of Maureen's bottom and her thighs, even lightly touching the intimacy which peeped between her legs.

Of course, I should have to give Maureen a soundly smacked arse in order to account for her undressed state but that would hardly be disagreeable to a man who felt towards such a girl as I did towards her. After that, I need only report to the master that the girl had shown impudence or some inattention to her duties. Far from earning a reproach for what I had done to her, the spanking of Maureen would inscribe my name in Mr. Milsom's respect that very first day.

Have no fear, it was only a daydream. I was not to subdue the girl by an assault so lacking in subtlety. However, when Maureen returned, I saw no harm in testing my powers a little. It was not that I wished to embarrass or humiliate the young brunette but I meant positively to know how she would respond to my authority and command.

I was dressed in shirt and trousers by the time that she

entered with the can of hot water. Against one wall there stood a low chest of drawers, no higher than a table but too heavy to move. Between the back of the chest and the wall there was a gap about two inches wide. It gave room for a girl like Maureen to slip her hand down there.

As soon as she had put down the hot water on the marble washstand, I beckoned her across.

"Over here, Maureen! There is a collar-stud missing from my box. I believe it has gone down behind the drawers. Find it for me, if you please!"

She looked at me with the intensity of her fine eyes, all the more beautiful for their slight ellipse that suggested a fair-skinned Grecian maid. I think her cheeks may have coloured up a little under their light application of rouge. Whether the tones of the paintbox are smuggled in or improvised, such young ladies confined at Waterton also contrive to darken their eyelashes, brighten their lips, and powder their cheeks!

"May I change into my skirt first of all, sir?" Maureen asked in her quiet voice.

"By no means! I do not propose to stand here without my stud while you change your clothes. It is quite absurd. Find the stud at once!"

Do you see what I had in mind? Maureen was a quiet and thoughtful girl, superior in many ways to teenage sluts who were serving their time at Waterton. She was even dismayed more easily than tawny skinned young madams of the harem like Pabi Das. So I wished her to present herself in the most vulgar manner for my contemplation and to see how she responded. With a slight heightening of the blush, she faced the chest of drawers and bent forward over it in order to delve into the space behind.

What a pretty picture she presented to the room! As she bent forward, Maureen's hips in the tight denim of her jeans were nicely rounded and the material strained taut on her graceful young thighs. She tried at first to hold her left hand over the seat of her jeans as she searched with her right. But she could not reach properly without going right forward and using both. I sat on the bed a couple of feet away and smiled at the sight. The smoothly tightened denim shaped the two firmly swelling cheeks of Maureen's bottom. There was a slight intimate bulge, the hint of soft pussy-flesh between the rear of her legs.

"I shall make you search until you find it, Maureen! You may depend upon that!"

Need I tell you that all this time the collar-stud was safely enclosed in my hand? Once or twice she twisted her head, the plait of dark hair falling and untwisting until it was disordered into that loose pony-tail tied by the red silk ribbon.

"I can't find it, sir! Really I can't!"

Her alarm was something more than the unease she felt at having to show me her young backside in such a tempting posture.

"Continue to search for it, Maureen!"

She did so, twining her legs a little and pressing one knee into the back of the other as if she thought this might show me less of what nestled between her thighs. As she moved this way and that, delving behind the drawers, her hips shifted one way and another, the cheeks of Maureen's backside rounding and tensing in a subtle variation of curves.

"I'm not dressed properly yet, sir," she murmured presently without turning to look at me. "They make me put my hair up properly. And I haven't put my pants on under my jeans yet. I'll be late for work. Don't make me late, please!"

I got up with a smile and stood just behind her.

"Do they punish you for being late, Maureen?" I was sure that they did. "How do they do it?"

For a moment she could not reply. Then, her voice muffled by the way her face was turned from me, she murmured,

"The strap."

I studied the rear view of her as she still bent over and searched for the mysterious collar-stud.

"Do they use it across your behind, Maureen?"

I had no doubt of this, but the girl could not bring herself to reply.

"Is it your bottom, Maureen? A young woman of nineteen or twenty spanked like a little girl?"

This time she uttered an affirmative, most reluctantly and in a doleful voice. I was her master for the moment, however, and I would not for the world allow her to escape such a penalty. I determined that this morning Maureen was going to be late.

Standing right over her I shaped my hand upon the two rear cheeks which the thin denim seat of her jeans presented so conveniently. Her bottom-cheeks tightened a little nervously. When my fingers lightly touched the strained denim between her legs, I thought she was going to straighten up in defiance. A flash of her beautiful eyes and the heightened colour in her face was soon subdued, however.

"Continue to search until the stud is found, Maureen. I believe you pretend that you cannot find it because you like the feel of my hands. Is that it, Maureen? Even if they use the strap on you later, you think this is worth it!"

There would be no complaint at what I was doing to her now, I reasoned, for there could be no evidence. My fingers smoothed the insides of her thighs comfortingly and then I felt the tightened curves of Maureen's bottom-cheeks once more. Wanting her to feel that she had been intimately explored, even while still wearing her jeans, I drew a finger deep in the warm cleft between the cheeks of Maureen's arse. She gasped at this for I do not think that even her boyfriend had ever ventured there. And yet it is an area which any man would want to explore when presented with a dark-haired and fine-featured girl of nineteen or twenty who possessed Maureen's beauty and presented her young backside in this tempting position.

"You shall be late every morning of my visit, if I choose, Maureen," I said quietly. "I warn you, however, that if I suspect the least defiance in you, I shall also make a report to Mr. Milsom himself. And you would do well to remember that one of my duties while I am here is to assess the sentence that has yet to be carried out upon you. I shall not be here when that happens. But it might please me to know that you were first caned and then had to lie bare-bottomed over the study sofa for a taste of the stable lash!"

I enjoyed letting her know my true feelings in the matter. The first advantage of a house like Waterton, in my own opinion, is that it does away with all hypocrisy. The system is so arranged that one's power over a girl like Maureen is absolute. She herself is never in a position to tell tales of what is done to her. No protests ever pass beyond the walls of the institution and the frenzy or screams are silenced by the massive stonework of the vaulted cellar where discipline is inflicted. Even after two or three years of her "apprenticeship" here, Maureen would only be permitted a release upon license. She must live under the roof of Mr. Milsom or some other worthy gentleman, just as if she were a slave.

There is, then, no need and no purpose in concealing from a girl the pleasure one has in doing certain things to her. But one restriction cannot be too strongly insisted upon. For a girl to acquire a swollen belly while she is prisoner in such a place risks scandal. The master and justices who had her in their power might ensure that nineteen-year-old Maureen saw plenty of "masculine gristle" during her residence and that she was obliged to take ample helpings of it. But there were always certain discretions to be observed.

At last I allowed her to straighten up.

"Very well, Maureen. You shall go and put your underpants on now. And you shall put your hair up like a proper young lady. Perhaps we shall resume the search for the collar-stud tomorrow morning."

She left in a great hurry, no doubt hoping that she would still be in time not to delay her master's departure for his work. I had, however, taken care to detain her until five minutes after the hour when she should have appeared in his room.

Any man of sense, reading these words, will see that I had established the proper attitude and manner of dealing with such a girl as Maureen. The excitement of the sport in such situations lies in never knowing quite what the outcome will be. Yet I was in the unusual situation of having every advantage of authority and discipline on my side, while Maureen was unable to appeal against my decisions. Show me a man who says he would not like to change places with me and I will show you a liar. Or perhaps worse, I will show you a cringing and self-doubting creature who will be treated with contempt by most of the female sex and by every member of his own.

But I was too busy that day, checking inventories and accounts, to give much thought to Maureen. At dinner, Mr. Milsom explained that he had taken the girl on one side. Maureen was no longer in doubt of my power over her. Mr. Milsom had gone so far as to tell her that I should pass judgment on her misconduct—a serious case of defiance and insolence shown to her social superiors. If I chose, she might be warned to be on her best behaviour for the rest of her time at Waterton and then no more be said. But if a vindictive mood should seize me, then Maureen must scream and twist in her straps, bare-bottomed under the judicial lash. Against my decision, whatever it might be, she had no appeal. Indeed, I was the one to whom appeals were made.

This caused me a good deal of private amusement as Mr. Milsom and I sat over our wine after dinner and watched the fireflies among the trees. I did not make too much of it, though I sensed my host might have a surprise in store. It is my habit to retire about an hour before bed, so that I may read a little and smoke a cigar. In due course, I made my excuses and left Mr. Milsom, who smiled in a most significant way as we parted. I went to my room, lay back in the padded leather chair, lit a Flor Rothschild and opened a volume of *Finishing School,* which I had chosen from the private shelf in the library.

The narrative wafted me to another room where the curtains had been closed. Broad green school grounds were concealed but the scene in Croydon's room was also hidden from prying eyes. From chapter headings, I saw that the softly seductive young blonde, Linda Jennings, and the auborn-cropped gamine Valerie Bishop, were the first subjects of the account. After that I was promised the charms of Sandra Williams, a pleasant and helpful tomboy of fifteen. At the centre of the drama was Croydon's sly and sensuously soft little blonde, Linda Jennings, the Beauty of Form 3B. With her knowing blue eyes and sniggering manner, she was worth attention. Her pale blonde hair was worn forward in a little mane upon her lapel. She had a habit of pressing its silky softness to her mouth, as if for comfort while she was scolded. But as I turned the page, the scolding ended. In her blouse and school tie, her navy blue skirt, she was receiving commands. Linda dropped her skirt and stepped out of it. There was a heavy padded leather chair of the sort I was sitting in. They made her kneel astride on the arms, bending forward from the waist, head pillowed on the back of the chair, arms drawn down by wrist-straps. Linda shook aside her soft blond mane and looked back furtively under her shoulder.

Linda Jennings's school knickers, white briefs of stretched cotton web, had already been taken off. The tail of her white blouse was tucked high above her seductively pale little bottom-cheeks with their glamour-girl promise. Kneeling astride on the chair and bending forward, Linda offered a stimulating view. The assistant strapped her ankles and pinioned her wrists, her arms at full stretch. The mistress chose a supple bamboo. The air sang as the first of three dozen strokes smacked agonisingly across the pearl-pale softness of Linda Jennings's fourteen-year-old bottom-cheeks. Linda Jennings was a sly, mischievous, and sexy girl whom her teachers enjoyed punishing. When they took her knickers down for an after-school punishment-lesson, it was a long one.

I read to the point where the assistant's hand was over the girl's mouth to quieten her as she received the first stroke of the third dozen. It landed with sadistic energy across the twenty-four raised cane-weals already smarting dreadfully across Linda Jennings's sensuously writhing bottom-cheeks. The naked agony of it was more than even this sexy little blonde could bear. Her tear-brimming eyes turning up languishingly and her head drooped, as Linda Jennings drooled helplessly through the master's fingers clamped across her mouth, as if in sensual abandon. I did not get to the conclusion, nor to Valerie Bishop, let alone to the similar chastisement of an eager fifth-form hoyden, Sandra Williams. But I confess that the picture of Linda Jennings being thrashed for her impudence had caused my manhood to stiffen resolutely.

Just then came a knock upon the door. I slid the book under a cushion. I arranged my dressing-gown and pyjama trousers, so that the weapon should not poke its swollen head out. Then I called upon my visitor to enter.

The door opened and there stood my brunette chambermaid. I was still sitting in the leather armchair by the tall window with its curtains closed. It was just ten o'clock, and she was dressed in her jeans and blouse as usual.

"Come in, Maureen," I said, indicating the hearth-rug in front of me. She walked across and seemed in doubt as to how to explain her presence. She stood before me, the dark tresses combed aside on her forehead from a central parting, a rather pudding-faced dullness on the oval pallor of her face.

"Mr. Milsom sent me, sir," she said, turning her firm young profile away, as if she could not endure my gaze. "He wishes you to give the overseer his orders tomorrow. I am to be inspected by the overseer tomorrow evening."

Now this could mean only one thing. Next day, Mr. Milsom wished me to give the hard-hearted overseer details of what penalty and what degree of severity I judged suitable for Maureen's misconduct. I favoured her with a smile that she could not endure, teasing her a little as I kept her waiting.

"Then I shall make my decision tonight, Maureen."

To my amusement, her bravado gave way to a look of despair. She bowed her head showing the pretty tail of dark hair done up with its red ribbon. She looked up once at me with the most self-pitying expression in her dark-lashed eyes, while I considered her fate.

Before I could give my decision, she sank to her knees on the rug, buried her face in my lap and emitted a whimpering sigh. I drew aside the folds of my dressing-gown and my unbuttoned trousers. The girl looked uneasily, even with consternation, at the stiffening tool! But she did not draw away.

I later understood why. Maureen shared a bedroom with Kathy a tall, well-built, and firm-figured brunette of thirty or so with a fair-skinned face of clear, wide-boned appeal. I had admired the long well-exercised thighs of this young Amazon in her smooth-fitting jeans. The tight blue denim also showed the mature womanhood of Kathy Jones's backside as being quite big-cheeked but without undue fatness. The mature seat of beauty at thirty gave Kathy Jones's arse this appealingly Amazonian look. Because they undressed for bed in front of one another, Maureen had seen the pale cheek-swell of Kathy Jones's bottom darkly bruised and purple wealed for a week or two after the older brunette had been thrashed by the overseer's leather riding-switch. Kathy Jones, bottom-cheeks firm but full-swelling in their nudity as she was strapped down over the trestle, had a hard time from the vindictive overseer. A young woman of Kathy's maturity and experience can bear far more than a girl like Maureen. With the full-cheeked maturity of a thirty-year-old woman's backside at his mercy, he thrashed the bare cheek-pallor of Kathy Jones's bottom sadistically with his riding switch. Maureen dreaded the whip's naked agony across her own backside and thighs, the screaming and frenzy, the torture she might undergo.

I did not—and do not—regret that she suffered such fears for they spurred her on to relieve her feelings. I sat with Maureen's red-ribboned tail of dark hair tickling my thighs and her face still buried from view. I stroked the dark gloss of her hair where it was strained back from the tall fair-skinned nobility of her brow. In a moment more, I should have found the words to bring her to her senses. But that was not to be.

Maureen was more frantic than I could have imagined. The threat of a leather whip across her bare backside held such terror for her that she would do anything in the world to avoid it. That is quite proper. What is the use of such punishment otherwise? But before I could reassure her she placed a hand on my thigh with another sob and drew wider the vent of my trousers.

It is foolish to resist when a good-looking working-girl of nineteen or twenty helps herself in this way. Maureen drew out the warm sleeping serpent, whose bulk stirred into stiffness at the gentle and cool touch of her fingers. She raised her head and the loose tail of dark hair slid from her shoulder-blades and fell about her face as she gazed down at what she had done.

I looked down, so that I could watch what Maureen was doing. I had no intention of interfering with her submissive mouthing of stiff masculine gristle. It was sensible to enjoy it to the full. She turned her head on one side, holding the stiffened truncheon of flesh in her hand and I stroked the hair back from her face so that I could watch more clearly still.

Maureen touched her lips to the swelling head with a timid little kiss, not yet quite bold enough to open her mouth, take it on her tongue, and close her lips. Then she settled her head on my lap, kneeling up with her hips raised from her heels. Maureen studied the penis thoughtfully and with a sudden courage. I do not know if she had already been married or lived with a boyfriend. But she was a fully-grown young woman and any pretense of blushing innocence would now have been pure hypocrisy.

Again she kissed the knob and, holding the stiffness up,

kissed it along its length. But still she was not quite ready to abandon herself. Then she paused, drawing her face back, her eyes looking steadily at the hardened object. As if committing herself before she could have any further doubts, Maureen opened and rounded her lips and took the first inch or two into her mouth. I felt the wet satin warmth of her soft tongue upon which the stiffness lay. Despite the books she had read so furtively, Maureen needed no instruction nor education as to what to do next. She had certainly had a boyfriend or two, if not a husband.

Maureen sucked up and down its length with the eager but awkward skill of a little girl with a lollipop. Even if it was not her first time, Maureen would not have done it now, had it not been for her dread of the torture with which the whip threatened her. That thought of the whip across her bare bottom and the back of her legs had driven her almost wild by its intensity. She would do anything to escape it. She paused and drew back so that only the knob was still in her mouth. Then she moved her tongue and used its tip to tickle the vent and the foreskin rim. All her feminine self-regard was put aside. Her lips and tongue did what she imagined would give me the most prolonged and penetrating spasms of delight.

One has no conscience in a situation of this kind. As her head moved rhythmically forwards and back, and her tail of dark brown hair fell to and fro, I was determined to make Maureen go to the conclusion in one way or another. There was a particular excitement in the thought that I might oblige her to suck until passion boiled over her tongue and she was obliged to swallow her pride. It was important for Maureen that she should make her submission in this way.

I stilled her from time to time, laying my hands on her head in its sleek swathing of hair. I wanted Maureen to suck for as long as possible and, if it could be prolonged, for the better part of the night. By no means was she to spend half an hour kneeling before me and then go to bed in safety.

I cannot say how long it was before I made Maureen pause again and drew myself from her lips.

"Stand up," I murmured. "Stand up and take your jeans and knickers off, Maureen."

She pushed herself to her feet, glancing at me uncertainly once or twice. But she pulled off her jeans and her cotton briefs. I tucked up the hem of her blouse above her waist and made a gesture which, I suppose, was ambiguous.

To my surprise, Maureen walked across and bent over the table in much the same position as if I was about to birch her. The reason was simple enough. She knew that it excited the master of Waterton and the overseers to have girls like Jayne Webb and Kathy Jones in that position when those young women were punished and she thought that I would enjoy it now. I walked across and stood over her. I circled her waist with my left arm and bowed my face to her rear as she remained bending over the table. I kissed the backs of her soft pale thighs and Maureen gave a little quiver. I coaxed back the flesh of her sex to the rear of her parted legs and fondled it gently. By doing this firmly and certainly I quietened her tremors. All the same she gave a little involuntary shudder when I kissed it and trilled my tongue against the warm humidity of the sensitive flesh.

I did not hesitate to let my lips browse in light kisses on the firm pale cheek-swell of Maureen's bottom. She seemed a little tense at this, as if feeling a greater indecency. But I held her firmly, parting the cheeks and even imparted a light kiss to the tight little bud of Maureen's anus. I felt her check her natural tension at this, so that I should not think she was resisting me.

I pressed her gently to her knees on the carpet and told her to strip off her blouse. I had many plans for her that night but it would ruin my professional reputation for Maureen to have a swollen belly and produce an infant nine months after my visit! She turned on to her back, drawing her legs up and parting them widely so that her feet hovered in the air like pretty white birds.

I knelt down and entered her very gently. It would have been more difficult had she been a virgin. But Maureen had surrendered the pleasures of her loins to a boyfriend or bridegroom. As I toiled over her, I also kissed her bare breasts and teased their nipples with my teeth. Maureen was gasping and squirming. The sweat ran on her pale flanks and in the small of her back. It gathered in the hollows of her body on that warm night, as if she had hard labour to reach her climax.

She yielded to the rhythm of love, pressing and relaxing alternately so that she felt it more deeply and with greater vigour. I hoped that I might bring her off, for it is important that such a girl should associate her first proper experience with ecstasy of that degree. I could see from the way she fluttered her eyes and drew breath through parted lips that Maureen was floating high with the delicious and dreamy feeling of being ridden by a man. I think she had been denied this during her months at Waterton. Now it was necessary to prolong it so that she might have time to conquer her misgivings and join in the fun properly.

It would have been reckless for me to come within her. There was a point at which I withdrew and heard such a forlorn and bereft little cry from Maureen. She had been parted from the thing she adored most in the world! The beloved object without which she could not live! Had you told Maureen that if the penis completed its course she must have the whip then and there, she would have turned her firm pale bottom-cheeks obediently to the lash. I had driven her beyond reason or restraint.

But I would not deny her the release she sought. I turned her over gently on her side and lay behind her. The red-ribboned tail of dark brown hair just touching the top of her spine. I slipped my stiffness between her thighs from the rear, not entering her but ensuring that the rod stroked along her sex as I moved to and fro. She shuddered and moaned at this for she found that the sensitive lips and clitoris thrilled to such caresses. At the same time I slipped my arms round her so that my hands fondled her breasts and her belly.

Maureen was in a dream of bliss as all this was done to her and I had not the least doubt that she would come off in a moment more. I was more concerned about my own torrent, for the pressure of it was building fast. So I drew back to avoid the mischances which sometimes follow from releasing it between a girl's legs. I laid my erection along the hot humid valley between the rounded pallor of Maureen's bottom-cheeks.

"You shall feel it there in a moment, Maureen," I said breathlessly. "Will you mind?"

She shook her head. My right hand descended and slipped between her thighs from the front as we lay clamped in this posture. I fiddled and tickled and stroked, feeling her shiver and gasp with the excitement of it. A mad idea seized me. As my own spout boiled over, I directed the first jet of it to moisten Maureen's tight rear entrance. At once the knob pressed for admittance and, thanks to the preparation, I felt the yielding and the exquisite tightness of her rear muscle gripping me.

I believe we came almost at the same time. Maureen was gasping and crying and shuddering, keening in ecstasy, spiced by alarm at the feeling of the monster that filled and stretched her behind. My own instinct was to press in as far as I could and make Maureen take the spasms of warm passion in the depths of her bottom. As I did so, she seized my hand which had played and fiddled between her legs, kissing and tickling it with her tongue.

We lay for a moment with my manhood still in her behind and Maureen kissing the beloved hand. I realized that my stiffness was not diminishing, thanks to the tightness of Maureen's bottom and the excitement in my brain. She lay very still. Indeed, she was watching us in one of the mirrors, in which I was also able to see that firm beauty of her face with its dark hair strained back by the red ribbon.

Maureen could feel me inside her and was well aware of the continued hardness. After a moment, I sensed the unmistakable movement of her haunches. It was not the act of a girl expelling such an intruder. Maureen was encouraging me to continue.

"Do you want it again in this way, Maureen?" I asked, smiling at her in the mirror.

She nodded quickly. But I sensed from a certain flinching and sensitivity that Maureen was going to have to make a speedy exit to the bathroom after a further spouting in such a place.

I smiled and held her steady with a hand on each flank of her bare hips. Then the movements began. Maureen folded her arms and buried her face in them. This time she was purely submissive, receiving but unable to yield any more. She leant forward a little so that the smooth pallor of her bottom-cheeks rounded harder and she opened her backside more fully. While she was getting it, she held her buttocks rather tense and uneasily, which added to the appeal of the situation. At last I warned her gently to expect her reward, which flooded her quite as much as the first had done. This time she squeezed me out, turned into my arms and thanked me for what I had done.

I raised her gently and led her across to the hearth-rug, on which lay her fallen jeans and knickers. I sat down in the same chair and pressed her to her knees before me, allowing her to admire the cause of her "ruin" more closely. She held it in her hand and turned it this way and that, until it began to stiffen again. To my astonishment and delight, she lifted her hips from her heels, bowed her face over my loins again and once more cocooned it in the sensual delights of her young mouth.

I no longer had any intention of using discipline upon her, it would have been absurd. But Maureen knew she must make her departure soon. The result was that she worked her lips and tongue much harder than on the first occasion. When the moment came, I whispered to her, reminding her that she must not shrink from the tribute. I came almost as profusely as before and watched Maureen consume such love obediently.

It was past midnight. She got to her feet, looking a little confused. She snatched up her jeans and briefs.

"I must go upstairs," she said breathlessly, not even waiting to put her knickers on, for I guessed they would only have to be taken off again very quickly in a moment more. And so she rushed from the room, Maureen holding her other hand over her bare bottom in a gesture of apprehension.

I got up from my chair and adjusted my pyjama trousers. I was glad that matters had been resolved. There are those, I daresay, who will stand aghast and deplore my adventure as Maureen's lover. But let me say this. Maureen needed a man to do some such thing to her. She required an escape from the prison of her pent-up feminine emotions in a place like Waterton.

It was on the following morning that I was required to pronounce judgment on several girls whom Mr. Milsom paraded before me. No doubt Maureen expected to be treated with special favour. After the passion I had shown her the night before, she thought she had earned it. But when her turn came, a sudden excitement seized me at the notion of putting her under discipline by a skilled overseer.

"And what of Maureen?" Mr. Milsom asked.

The girl dropped her head a little, as if she could not meet my gaze.

"I should like her presented to the overseer over the stool and left to his discretion. He may punish a little, not at all, or a great deal."

At this she raised her face to me. The expression upon it was beyond the genius of all but the greatest painters to recapture.

Next day, as I made my little tours of inspection through the house and gardens, where the girls were put to work, I could scarcely keep my eyes off Maureen. The incident of that other evening had given her a new significance for me. I found that I loitered to watch her as she bent to one task or another in the house or she busied herself weeding and seeding among the flower-beds. I studied the bold young profile with its creamy complexion and the lustre of the dark hair strained back into its loose tail by the aid of the red ribbon. I considered the taut firmly-spread rounds of Maureen's bottom-cheeks in her tightened jeans as she stooped to her work.

Of course she looked back quickly from time to time and there was unease in her glance as she saw the way I was studying her. By quiet smiles and indications with my eyes, I made sure the girl knew what I was looking at and what my thoughts were. I guessed that Maureen, in her imagination, felt the ghosts of my hands roving over her thighs and rear cheeks in the thin tight denim, my fingers slipping into the seat of her pants, delving and running, parting and probing. The charm of the situation was that Maureen dared not protest at what I had done to her with her pants down that other night unless she wished to be punished for entering my room in the first place.

That evening, the fortunate overseer withdrew to the examination room where Maureen awaited him. It was his privilege to be alone with the culprit as he judged her fitness for chastisement and so I can only give an "outsider's" impressions of what went on between them.

The door of the room was open just long enough for me to see Maureen. The young brunette was wearing nothing but the short white woollen top in which I had seen her arranging books in the shop window. She was lying upon her belly on a high couch. Her arms were stretched down tight against the wooden legs, strained into position as if straps at her wrists held them like this. The pillows were not under her head but packed under her loins to raise her hips and make the pallid cheeks of Maureen's bare bottom swell fuller and broader. Her face was turned to the door to watch the overseer enter. The hem of the woollen top was drawn up to her waist at the back, so that her firm young thighs and the taut rounded pallor of Maureen's rear-cheek swell was suggestively presented.

Before the door swung to on its automatic hinges, there was time to see the overseer sit at an angle on the couch, level with Maureen's hips, looking back towards her feet. He circled her waist with one arm to steady her and bowed his head to study the elasticity of the young woman's buttocks. One heard Maureen gasp and fret at such a suggestive inspection.

From the next room, where the stool and chairs had been arranged, it was possible to overhear some of the overseer's words as he murmured to the girl. The springs of the couch shifted under the urgent pressure of her knees as the man's fingers mapped her rear contours. Then there was a smack to make Maureen turn her backside this way a little and another smack to make her keep still. There followed a bottom-smack to make Maureen lie forward more tightly and a double rear-cheek smack to make her behave herself.

The promises that I overheard were fragmentary but they were enough to make me smile with pleasure at the thought that I had put Maureen into safe hands. A sounding seat-smack preceded them, and then another.

"Every Saturday night from now on, Maureen . . . strapped down over the stool . . . backside properly bare . . . obedience lesson with the bamboo cane to begin with . . . your bare bottom marked wickedly, Maureen . . . hear you scream, Maureen, but sometimes use the gag . . . chastiser naturally excited . . . snakeskin pony-whip later . . ."

There was no doubt that the overseer's examination was conscientious in the extreme. He studied Maureen's firmly-rounded rear-cheek swell in every attitude of tensing and slackening, every shifting and rounding. He observed closely the line of its cheeks, fatter and softer in the lower curves. He steadied the bare flanks of her hips with his hands and fondled the smooth double contours of the cool twin cheek-mounds. His fingers parted and his eyes gazed at the incurve of the girl's rear crack where Maureen's skin-tone darkened a little from pearl-pallor to yellowed ivory. By the time he had finished, he had acquired a knowledge of her rear anatomy that Maureen's boyfriend or bridegroom would have envied.

It would be indiscreet of me to say too much in describing what happened when he brought Maureen into the room where we waited. For the rest of the evening she viewed the scene behind her through the arch of her own legs as she bent tightly astride over the tall stool, the red-ribboned tail of her dark hair falling askew. During the next hour, the bare pale cheeks of Maureen's bottom danced to the tune of the overseer's lash. She heard the walls ring with her own frenzy and drank her own tears from her lips. But the sequel to this drama was still more diverting.

On the following morning, Maureen was changing from her denim skirt to her jeans, ready to leave her work in the house and begin her labours in the garden. Two of the worthy women who supervised the girls, Mrs. Hamley and Mrs. Shire, were in charge of her. As she took the skirt off, Maureen wore only the tight cotton briefs of her knickers below the waist. These panties were cut high and tight at the rear, the elastic hem arching up on either side to leave bare the lower part of that bottom-cheek. The two women smiled at what they saw.

Turning to Mrs. Shire, Mrs. Hamley said that she now understood why Maureen had looked so sorry for herself earlier that day. Mrs. Hamley confessed she had no idea that the severity of the judicial whipping, to which Maureen had been condemned, had been carried out on her the night before. Mrs. Shire smiled as well, knowing that Maureen heard every word that passed between them. She explained that Mrs. Hamley was under a misapprehension. The judicial punishment was a far more solemn occasion and would not take place for another fortnight. It would be more formal and severe than anything Maureen had yet known. The present weals of bamboo across her twenty-year-old buttocks were no more than a casual bottom-smacking, given the night before to curb her impertinence. What lay in store for the girl, two weeks hence, was a ritual of much greater intensity.

Seeing the dismay with which Maureen looked round at these words, Mrs. Hamley caught her eyes with a smile. Mrs. Shire added that Maureen would be told the date and the details several days before. The torment of waiting would precede that of the whip itself. At night, the guardians would hear the sleepless gasps and sighs of Maureen's self-pity. She might be glimpsed lying awake with the light on, looking back over her shoulder and examining her backside in the mirror as if to catch a final view of it in its unblemished state. In her sleepless apprehension, there would be touchings of herself in that area, fretting and squirming, as Maureen's bottom-cheeks itched with the dread anticipation of naked agony under the whip.

Maureen had thought her ordeal of the previous evening settled the score and that she had paid her price. Now she stood aghast. And then the glances of amusement which the two women had exchanged were turned upon the girl herself. As if mesmerised by the horror of her predicament, the young brunette seemed unable to turn her eyes from the vindictive smiles of the two older women.

It was on the following day that I left Waterton, so that I cannot give you an account of the reckoning which Maureen was called upon to pay a fortnight later. But in one respect, science has reduced the miles to naught. Even a travelling-man, spending a night in a fly-spotted rented room, may be everywhere at once. The telephone by his bed may ring. Let him pick it up and he will hear the voice of Mr. Milsom. If the receiver at the other end is carefully placed, he may also hear what happens within several feet of it. Mr. Milsom has a voice that is calm and clear.

The high clear echoes in that invisible room assured me that they have taken Maureen far beyond anything that it would be prudent for me to describe. And in this there is an advantage. Such a girl may complain at casual or orthodox discipline. But let it be of a kind to include incidents she cannot think of without a blush, and the secret is safe. What happened to her after that, I cannot say, except that she was apprenticed to an intimate friend of Mr. Milsom's.

For myself, I had many more establishments to visit and many more instructions to give before the year's end brought me back to Waterton again. I travelled far and wide in dimly-lit carriages on little railroads at all hours of day and night. I am the man you pity as you get down from the railroad car with home and comfort waiting for you. I am the companion who travels on to towns and wildernesses of which you may know little more than the names. I am the man alone in hotel diningrooms and bars, retiring unaccompanied at night to his hired room with its ancient porcelain and narrow bed.

I am the travelling-man, the poor devil who is pitied by all those other folk hurrying home. And yet, if truth were known, how many of them would like to change places with me after all!

5
Monnelia

It is the boast of Charleston that it represents the elegance of the old world beside a southern ocean. The blossoming season enjoys a perfect setting of white mansions and graceful carriage-drives. The sun's brilliance shivers through the fronds of palmetto trees and splashes on the living gloss of mauve and scarlet blooms. The gorgeous petals are soft and lush as the satin pallor of white-skinned beauty glittering with diamonds or the silky limbs of a dusky-sheen slave-girl moving lithe and easy through the twilight.

The night of Colonel Ashbee's dinner in the fine house overlooking White Point Gardens marked the opening of the spring season. The live oaks of the public promenades, with their veils of Spanish moss, were already in leaf. The tall pillared houses, their elegant verandahs shaded by magnolia in full bloom, had become the retreat of fashion and sophistication. In a little while the heat of the lowland plantations would prove insupportable to the ladies of those country estates. And then the world would move to the ocean. But even here in Charleston, the waves of the evening tide seemed to lie enfeebled and panting on the shore of White Point Gardens and the East Battery by the time that the sultry day was done.

The expanse of White Point Gardens, where the canopied carriages rolled along the wide and shady gravel drives, was the grand parade of the old colonial quarter. Inland from this park, down narrower and more winding vistas, azalea and bougainvillea blossomed crimson and purple over private walls along King Street and Church Street. Here stood those handsome brick dwellings with their white pediments and porticoes, their famous masked piazzas, built a century before by the lawyers and physicians, the land agents and shippers, all those who grew rich upon the backs of the great plantation lords.

Colonel Ashbee was the lord of Chelsea Landing, a fine plantation in the tidewater country. But he was also the possessor of a stately waterside mansion on the South Battery at Charleston, convenient for business with his factor and the diversions of town life. The cream-painted elegance of this villa suggested the home of a Spanish grandee or a colonial governor. All summer long, its open piazza-verandahs caught every light Atlantic breeze in the stifling months of July and August. Even in this, Charleston society proved singular. What the rest of the world called a verandah, the Charlestonians called a piazza. Behind tall railings and palmetto trees, these open and shaded retreats ran the full length of the great houses on every floor.

Perhaps the colonel was not a great deal richer than his plantation rivals. Yet the Grecian pillars of his loggias seemed more graceful and the ornamental balustrading more airy. Colonel Ashbee was a man of leisure, able to make his fortune and still have time for the handsomely bound volumes of his Corinthian columned library. He was the first gentleman of White Point Gardens.

When the hot sun had set and evening came there would be an agreeable dinner, at home or elsewhere, with the finest society of Drayton Hall or the East Battery. The latest virtuoso of the keyboard would send the arpeggios of Chopin skimming into the warm night. Or perhaps a young daughter of fashionable birth who fancied she had a talent for opera would warble a little Rossini or Gounod. The colonel smiled and tapped his hand in time to the music.

But a man who does so much in public is the more entitled to private pleasures of a lavish kind. He has done his duty and must now be the man he wishes to be without interference from the world. Sometimes, as the sun sank golden beyond the Cooper River and the mangroves, turning the quiet sea to Prussian blue, the colonel dined at home with his cronies and their women. These were not occasions that the town heard about. Much went on behind the door of his elegant white-and-gold diningroom that was not fit for the ears of polite society. Such pleasures required the attendance of his most beautiful slave-girls. It was the custom that his guests should stay the night in the cool and airy bedrooms of the upper floor. His companions in pleasure must not be seen driving away at two or three in the morning. After such excitements, breakfast was served late the next day. It was often noon before the last guests emerged to join the others in the shade of the piazza which looked across the live oaks of the gardens to the glittering calm of Charleston Harbour.

In company with his friend Colonel Johnson, he agreed to try the pleasures of a white girl from one of the Elliot Street houses and a graceful black beauty of his own. In order to be clear of prying eyes and wagging tongues, they were to dine and take their pleasure with the girls on

Colonel Ashbee's yacht, anchored for the night off Fort Moultrie. They would be attended only by the two chosen girls and by the colonel's footmen and his valet, Hargreaves.

Colonel Ashbee's girl, Monnelia, was an exquisitely-formed slave-maiden, a creature of natural poise and lithe figure. She seemed the daughter of African grace or darkest Caribbean elegance tempered by the southern genius of Louisiana or Mississippi. She was just nineteen years old and had the seductive loveliness of a heathen warrior-princess. When she was brought on to the auction dais in New Orleans, they had made her pose naked to show the deep bronze smoothness of her body. The long lines of her dark-skinned thighs and legs had a satiny gloss as the strong lights were directed upon her. Her thighs were trim and her hips rounded, her shoulders sleek and her breasts carried high. Her warm-toned face was animated by eyes that seemed wide and soft. Her nose and chin were perfectly formed in their African beauty.

There was nothing gross or coarse in her looks, she might have been a model of refinement and elegance. But she promised sensual pleasure to the man who would master her and her lips had a desirable fullness. Her short hair was brushed up from her face, the better to expose her delicate ears with their thin gold rings. At the back its cropped length was tailed and ribboned to leave her neck and shoulders quite bare.

On the evening when Colonel Ashbee entertained his friend Colonel Johnson, the valet and footmen had made Monnelia strip down to a single garment and a pair of shoes. Her warm dark body was covered only by a brief corselet of thin white silk. Her legs and thighs, her arms and shoulders, even the upper half of her back, were completely bare apart from the two shoulder-straps that helped to hold the corselet in place. How easily the shape of her spruce young breasts was seen through the thin silk! The nipples were erect, a tribute to her natural animal vitality. The satiny-bronze of the firm globes bobbed a little in their youthful elasticity as she walked.

The hem of the white silk corselet was cut above her dusky hips on either side. At the front it narrowed between her legs, just covering the little bush of dark hair that crowned her sex. At the rear, the seat was deliberately cut too small to cover completely the sleek ebony smoothness of Monnelia's bottom-cheeks. Her long African-tan thighs were slim and willowy in their supple grace. Best of all, the valets had made her wear smart white shoes with tall heels, so that the rounding of her hips and backside, the sinuous squirming of her thighs, were seductively exaggerated as she walked—whether or not she wished it.

Colonel Johnson was amused at the way in which Colonel Ashbee had chosen to curb the disdain of this beautiful nineteen-year-old negress. Yet he was frankly admiring of her supple figure, the self-possessed beauty of a tribal princess in her face, the primitive warrior-girl appearance of her upward brushed hair and its ribboned coiffure at her nape. Her brief-cut waitress-costume not only made Monnelia expose her beautiful legs and hips, and her seductive dark-tanned bum-cheeks, but was designed to make her feel she was doing so.

When the meal was over, Johnson watched her approach with the silver tray of decanter and glasses. In the prim movement of her haunches there was a natural sophistication. Her long and elegant legs moved with controlled ease. She set down the tray. Then she went to fetch the silver cigar-box.

When she turned, he had a view of the proud young negress-skinned swell of Monnelia's bottom-cheeks and the supple curving walk of her bare thighs. Where the white silk of the corselet emerged between the rear of her legs, its seat was cut to arch up high and tight so that the dark oval smoothness of Monnelia's hind cheeks was suggestively half naked. She did not suffer a big-buttocked and heavy-thighed look which mars some girls of her race. A native grace of shape and movement made Monnelia's backside worth studying. Its cheeks were tanned as silken ebony as her other surfaces. Colonel Johnson, admiring her elegant and youthfully trim hind curves, thought that the dusky gloss of this rear cheek-skin suggested Monnelia wet-bottomed from sitting in dark and bitter coffee sludge.

Colonel Ashbee showed his mastery of the girl by the little services he made her perform in this state. Still with her back towards them, it was necessary for the elegant young slave-girl to bend right over to find the cigar-box. The satin-smooth and African-ebony cheeks of Monnelia's behind swelled out temptingly from the drumskin tightness of her white silk panties as the search for the cigar-box detained her in this lasciviously inviting pose. The curve of her hips as she bent over soon strained the thin white silk of the corselet seat into the slave-girl's rear cleavage, so that her warm-toned buttocks were quite bare and temptingly offered. It was not hard to understand why the overseers longed, in vain, for news of misbehaviour by this beauty of a savage culture and for a command to discipline the velvet-dusky cheeks of Monnelia's bottom with the cruellest stable-whip.

There was no hypocrisy in such matters. It was acknowledged that to whip Monnelia's backside would be extremely enjoyable for men of their kind. Even now she was obliged to hear the colonels' laughter from behind her and the suggestions of what they would like to see done to her. Then she turned with the silver cigar-box and came back towards them, bare legs moving with maidenly restraint and her eyes downcast to avoid meeting the smiling gaze of Colonel Johnson.

While their dark-skinned warrior-maid stood before them with the box, eyes demurely downcast, they agreed that Monnelia thought too much of herself for a mere slave-girl. She must be cured of this pride by a reminder of the more vulgar aspects of her femininity, which even a daughter of equatorial beauty possesses.

Johnson kept her standing by his chair as he smoked his cigar. He ran his hands up and down the sleek dark velveteen gloss of her thighs, which were level with his eyes as he lounged back in his chair. Bowing his head, he kissed her just above the knees and then allowed his lips to browse upwards on her dark satin flesh. Monnelia, looking modestly away from him and with her fine brown eyes still lowered, straddled a little in obedience to his orders. He kissed the inner surfaces of her willowy negress thighs. His lips feasted on this warm silken texture as high up between her legs as he could go, his tongue touching the faint mineral taste of her there. His fingers meanwhile felt her sex through the thin silk of the corselet, fondling her and stroking, stroking and fondling, until Monnelia released her pent-up breath in a gasp and her body shivered. This barbarian nymph needed a good milking between her legs by a skilled hand, he thought, and she had been too long without it. He continued until he felt that Monnelia had wet the silk of her panty-crotch a little with the natural lubrication of her erotic excitement.

The colonel turned her to the table and made her bend forward across it. Smiling at the sight she presented, he tugged the seat-hem of the corselet higher so that the material was gathered and cut tight in Monnelia's arse-crack. He was determined to have Monnelia's satiny blackamoor buttocks temptingly bare. Though she squirmed a little from what he had been doing to her before, he now gave his attention to the negress-skinned cheeks of Monnelia's dusky arse. He fondled her elegant young backside, caressing the slight flesh-creases under the shapely swell and softness of Monnelia's bottom-cheeks.

He began to kiss the bare native tan of those cool and dusky rear globes, which caused the girl to hide her face by leaning her forehead on her folded arms. He insinuated a finger under the twist of silk and explored her bum-cleft. He felt her flinch as his fingertip touched Monnelia's arsehole. Gratified by this, he stroked and tickled her there for a long time to make her accept what she would instinctively have rejected. Gradually her hips and her shapely dark-skinned legs in the high-heeled white shoes relaxed.

Even the dignity of a maiden-warrior like this could be overcome by caresses. The natural sensitivity of Monnelia's behind had begun to welcome the finger's teasing and tickling. Through the thin silk he fondled her young breasts with his other hand. The slave-girl could not conceal her natural and instinctive excitement. It amused Johnson that while Monnelia's behind tightened against the caressing finger, her dark nipples grew hard as berries at the excitation of that sensitive place. Her natural animal excitement was stirred by the thought that he was prepared to be so perverse with her.

He made her perform little tasks, picking up crumbs or reaching for dishes. In each posture she was required to bend. Each time that she did so, he inflicted a vigorous smack on the bare ebony ovals of Monnelia's bottom, hard enough to make the very air sing. To spank such a beauty of Niger or the Congo, so tall and maidenly, was a considerable stimulus to a man of his maturity.

During these attentions which Colonel Johnson paid to Monnelia, Colonel Ashbee had prudently withdrawn to an adjoining stateroom to be waited upon by the treasure chosen for him. She was a white servant-girl of the coquettish kind whom Colonel Johnson employed in his Charleston mansion. What a contrast she was to the jungle Venus being spanked in the saloon.

Colonel Ashbee smiled and turned his attention to the white girl before him. Louise was the type of indentured maidservant who easily passed into the total possession of such a man as Colonel Johnson. Studying her, Colonel Ashbee thought to himself that the young bitch was not quite tall enough or slim enough to be a glamour princess but she had an impudent quality that made him want to enjoy her. Her coiffure had been carefully arranged for the occasion. The short cut of her dark hair with its fringe was drawn back tightly, straight and slick to show her ears and neck, trimmed off at her nape. She had used mascara to darken her lashes, emphasizing the round saucer-eyed cheekiness of her sexual flirtation. At seventeen her face still had the rounded quality of adolescence, a pert young nose and a firm chin. She was dressed as if to excite her bridegroom in a honeymoon hotel. And though the sleek pale softness of teenage flesh gave a slight plumpness to her shape, she was deliciously served up.

Her legs were sheathed to mid-thigh in translucent stockings of black silk. There was a succulent stretch of bare white thigh-skin between the stocking-tops and the lace hem of her short black knickers. Her still rather adolescent thighs had that sheen and softness which showed the perfection of Louise's body at seventeen. She wore a matching bodice and a pair of shoes with high heels to simulate a little of the height she lacked. Colonel Ashbee was pleased to see that she was a filly who had not yet been broken in and grown brazen. In the intervals of flirting, when she thought he was not looking, Louise's bold young face showed her to be tense and very ill at ease. She was like a little girl who comes for the first time under the command of a stern teacher.

He was content to have her standing by his chair and to run his hands over her legs in their sleek black stockings. Louise flinched a little as he began to caress the soft bare skin above her stocking-tops! Then he commanded her to pose before him in postures of calculated impudence. She squirmed her hips nicely and angled her legs as she imagined a girl would do when offering herself for sale. When he made her turn her back and bend over, the tension was evident again in the way she held herself. The face she presented as she stooped had lost its soubrette sauciness and was uneasily self-conscious once more. Ashbee preferred this to a girl who was insolently sure of herself. Though she still wore the tight knickers of thin black silk, her bending posture added a slight fatness to the vulgar swell of Louise Neville's bottom-cheeks. In this posture Colonel Ashbee found her suggestively exciting. He liked to see her pose as if she were asking for certain bedroom perversities to be inflicted. The apprehension in her young face warmed his enthusiasm.

He summoned her to kneel before his chair and unbutton him. From the slight hesitation, he guessed that Louise had probably mouthed some lucky boy on whom she had a crush. But to be commanded to use lips and tongue by a man almost three times her own age caused her a natural apprehension. She drew his manhood out, kissed the tightly swollen knob uncertainly several times and hesitated again. It required a peremptory instruction before she opened her mouth and began to behave properly.

Louise gave him several minutes of undiluted bliss with her lips and tongue. He wondered if she truly had done it before for a boyfriend, or whether a natural feminine instinct guided her in such soft and moist caresses with her mouth. He was content, for the moment, to stop her when he felt crisis draw near and then make her start again when it subsided. In this manner she held the root of the staff with one hand to prevent it going too far. Then, while she looked saucer-eyed under her dark lashes at what she was doing, Louise Neville drew more eagerly on his enlarged manhood. With timid inexperience, she mouthed it and trilled her tongue about its prow for the next half hour.

Colonel Ashbee and his guest each spent a pleasant hour or two with the girl of his choice. Yet next morning there was an indefinable air of female conspiracy in the staterooms. It was as if something had happened during the night, while the masters slept. What it was, neither man could guess. Nor could he offer proof that it was any more but a suspicion bred in his own heated imagination.

It was a week later when Colonel Ashbee received through the post a package from an anonymous well-wisher. When he opened it, he understood at once why there had been such a sense of female conspiracy in the air. He and Colonel Johnson had slept soundly after their indulgences. They would not have heard a regiment of infantry marching on the deck, let alone a girl slipping softly from the bed and gliding to another rendezvous. The postal package, wrapped in blue paper, contained a dozen photographic prints. They showed Monnelia and Louise together, sprawling on the wide dining-table in the light of dawn, among the debris of the banquet.

That in itself was nothing. But as he looked at the photographs, Colonel Ashbee knew that he was the victim of a plot. Monnelia and Louise had seemed to offer themselves for the pleasure of the two men on that evening. All the time, the cunning young bitches had used this occasion to contrive a passionate meeting of their own. Louise and

Monnelia were secretly in love, he was sure of it. Monnelia would never be permitted the freedom to visit the Elliott Street house. Louise would find it difficult to gain access to the slave-girl's bed. But they had met somehow, previous to this, and consummated their love. Now they had used the men's desire for them to meet again. The photographs were proof of it.

With an uneasy sense that scandal might be gathering round him, Colonel Ashbee studied the photographs. Who had taken them? Who else had seen them? He shuddered at the thought that they were now in the hands of General Beauregard, Miss Amanda Stevens his young mistress, the Honourable Judge Sprange, and the leaders of Charleston society. But then he told himself that blackmailers did not work in that way. His hands itching for vengeance upon the pair of girls, he studied the first photograph of the black beauty and white sprawling across the banquet-table.

The two girls were as nearly naked as made no difference. The sole garment remaining was that pair of Louise Neville's knickers in thin black silk which still dangled from one of her ankles. Black and white beauty sprawled in a most ungainly attitude, Louise with her head thrown back, biting her lip gently with the intensity of her pleasure. All the soubrette cheekiness had gone and her face was racked by the exquisite pangs which betrayed the true sexual passion of a woman for a lover.

Monnelia had one arm round Louise's fair-skinned waist to curb her writhing of pleasure a little. Her other hand was busy between those soft young thighs of purest pallor that relaxed and opened innocently to her expert caress. The negress with the warm-skinned nudity of her smooth shoulders and back, her graceful young thighs and regal bearing, was conditioning Louise to pleasures with a woman that the victim would soon be unable to renounce. In any city as cosmopolitan in its tastes, there were fair-skinned girls of her own age who would enjoy giving Louise lessons in the art of lesbian love. Ashbee thought of Jane Truman the pert little blonde whom he proposed to cure of her infatuation with her own sex, even the two pert little adolescent negresses on his own plantation, Jenny and Jackie, the twins whom birching had failed to cure of their vices.

He looked at the photograph again. The naked waitresses had gorged themselves on the remains of the banquet. There was a smear of fruit sorbet on Louise's lip and a splash of wine on her breast. It was the latter blemish, just by the nipple, that Monnelia was licking off with her expert tongue. Her head was bowed to this task and she showed the camera only the short ribboned tress of her upward-brushed crop at the rear.

Colonel Ashbee saw nothing of the self-consciousness or apprehension in Louise's face now that she had shown when she was at the command of man. With her short dark hair slicked back, her bold young face with the long dark lashes of her blue saucer-eyes showed what a shameless little whore Louise Neville was at seventeen. The soft adolescent pupil lost all her fearfulness in the arms of her swarthy mistress. Louise appeared bold and insistent in her love-making with the supple and passionate young negress. There was a hard and demanding quality about her. Monnelia too had lost her demure and reticent air, the soft brown eyes now illuminated by desire and beseeching.

As Louise faced the hidden camera lens, so the other girl presented the rear view of her dark-tanned skin. Louise was tense with the surge of pleasure swelling till it must burst in her loins, while the ebony Venus was opening herself in the warm and yearning expansion of desire. Those elegant African-smooth ovals of Monnelia's bottom-cheeks were arched backwards towards the concealed photographer, as if inviting the camera to explore her backside more intimately. Even in anger, Ashbee felt a satisfaction that the slave-girl should have shown herself in a manner she would have shunned if she knew she was being watched. Monnelia's dusky-cheeked arse swelled seductively. Its dark moons were lightly parted, seeming innocently to invite the smack of a man's hand, a long session with a punishment cane, the fierce caress of the overseer's whip, the hectic assault of sodomy. She, at least, was his slave and must answer to him.

It was probable that the two girls had been making love together on the table for much of the night, as soon as he and Colonel Johnson had fallen asleep. The second picture showed, by the look of relaxation and fulfillment on the face of the fair-skinned partner, that Louise had climaxed on the expert fingers of the native girl. They were both in a gentler and affectionate mood now, playing with one another's bodies as little girls play with toys or dolls. Even for the most demure teenage girl there exists a fascination at the prospect of exploring every hole and corner of another young beauty, tickling a sensitive spot or intruding a playful finger.

Monnelia had used a blackened wick or a fragment of charcoal. With this she had made a flower of Louise's belly button, drawing petals on the pale skin round the charming whorl of flesh. Each breast had been patterned round the nipple. Bold-faced now, Louise was slyly smiling, looking back to the mirrors to see the handiwork on her own bottom. Its soft pale cheeks were signed with Monnelia's name, as the artist of this design. Colonel Ashbee scowled at the scene in the photograph.

Louise had also enjoyed some amusement with her companion, finding one of those brightly-feathered dusters whose rounded handle of three or four inches is the thickness of a thumb. By oiling the handle with butter, she had employed Monnelia's behind to give the black warrior-princess a fine peacock tail, sprouting from between her rear cheeks. There was another photograph, taken as the dark-skinned beauty paraded on the table, moving her willowy equatorial thighs, admiring herself in the mirrors. Monnelia's rear-bouquet of feathers was an adornment she evidently enjoyed and which it excited her to look at.

The next of the pictures showed that the playfulness had been only an interlude in their passion. Now the two lesbian lovers lay head to tail, each having her eyes and lips level with the loins and backside of the other. The charcoal was smudged and indistinct upon Louise's pale softness. Much of it had now been transferred with some wetness to Monnelia's lips! And still the peacock-tail of feathers sprouted from between the smooth satin-ebony of Monnelia's bottom-cheeks. There was no doubt from the photograph that the two girls were having fun with each other. They sucked one another's sensitive adornments, and trilled their tongues in places of excruciating responsiveness.

They did all this with an eagerness they had never shown to Colonel Ashbee or Colonel Johnson. Louise was running her tongue nimbly in the dark-haired paradise between Monnelia's thighs. At the same time, Monnelia had made Louise present herself in an upward squat. The tongue of the dark-skinned Aphrodite ran everywhere along the cleavage from the base of Louise's spine to the guardian clitoris at the portal of her sex. The seduction was cunning and remorseless, the tribal beauty playing in the sensitive dell and not even hesitating to insinuate her tongue-tip in the tight posterior dimple. The camera showed that Louise was squatting fuller, as if to admit the intruder as far as possible. Colonel Ashbee guessed that the saucer-eyed soubrette must have come to her climax with such cries of release that nothing short of drugged stupor could account for the two men being deaf to her.

In the final picture all passion had been spent. It was not long before the two men stirred from their sleep. Louise and Monnelia lay among the guttered candles and the debris of the banquet, still naked in their gentle embrace. If they were not asleep themselves, they were certainly lying with eyes closed in dreamy recollection of the love-making they had just shared. The light shone full on the blackamoor gloss of Monnelia's bare thighs and hips. Inspired by the joy of release she had shared with Louise, her dusky skin displayed a living sheen that only the excitement of gentle but cunning kisses can awaken.

The two girls had not drawn apart but now lay more gently together than in the fierce passion of their earlier embraces. Louise's dark lashes were closed over her blue saucer-eyes. The light caught the sleek short crop of her brown hair and her face had a childlike solemnity as she dozed. Monnelia's thigh was crooked lightly and possessively across the soft pallor of Louise's hip, as if to remind her prey how easily the act of sexual conquest might be repeated upon her.

Ashbee's footman had entered and smiled at the sight of the dark-skinned girl's back, the upward brushed hair and its short ribboned coiffure at her nape. The African-sleek ovals of Monnelia's bottom-cheeks were arched back towards him with innocent vulgarity. He saw the warrior-maiden's dark-haired sex between the rear of her open legs. The resilient ovals of her ebony-cheeked backside swelled seductively, its twin mounds drawn apart by the way she was sprawling, so that Monnelia's anus was shown. The footman smiled at this. It was not the smile of a simpering suitor but of one vindictive in his master's cause. He would not shrink from putting Monnelia's backside and loins to torment. His thoughts of Monnelia's swarthy-cheeked bottom envisaged a stable-lash and the long nozzle of a pair of serviceable bellows.

As the camera showed, he had slyly rewarded Monnelia, standing over the sleeping girl with weapon erect in hand. Exciting himself by watching the bare negress-skinned cheeks of Monnelia's shapely young bottom, he pumped up considerable passion, releasing it in short vigorous gusts of warm libation upon the dusky native cheeks of Monnelia's backside, trying to aim as much as possible where her dark bottom-cheeks curved in together. The photograph showed the shine of splashes and tell-tale trickles down the dark ovals of her buttocks, which she slept too soundly to feel. The footman withdrew, turning back to grin to himself at the state in which he had left the young blackamoor girl. She stirred soon and he peeped from the door to watch Monnelia wake and feel behind her in some dismay at the manner in which she had been used.

Even before this intrusion, there was evidence of the gasping and threshing frenzy with which Louise had undergone her first lesbian seduction. One of her soft pale breasts was stained by wine, when she rolled on to her belly where a glass of claret had been upset. A blob of grey candle-wax had fallen on one mocha-dark oval of Monnelia's backside, almost in her rear cleft. The sting of it was nothing to her as she laboured on top of the other girl. Louise had writhed against the butter-dish in her ecstasy, for a smear of it gleamed on one fair-skinned thigh. Convulsed by the action of Monnelia's fingers or tongue between her legs, she had also sat back in the dish of dead cigar butts. A powdering of the grey ash now smudged a bare and softly pale cheek of Louise Neville's bottom as she displayed it unwittingly to the camera.

The more Colonel Ashbee thought of the trick played upon him, the angrier he became. In wild flights of imagination, he devised ways of giving Monnelia and Louise Neville a hard time at the hands of a sadistic stable-groom.

But the colonel was too wise to resort to the private whipping-house or any other place that might start tongues wagging. In any case, there was little he could do to satisfy his anger just then against the softly-shaped pale-skinned seductiveness of seventeen-year-old Louise Neville. But Monnelia was his slave and must answer in whatever way he chose. Even so, Colonel Ashbee still declined to make his vengeance public. He was a cunning strategist in matters of war and passion. When Monnelia was called to account, it would be in the most perverse and vindictive manner.

It was the colonel's custom, during the Charleston season, to play host to a decayed old gentleman from Massachusetts. Captain Prince, as he was called, had been the colonel's commercial agent in Boston. His influence in the city was enough to secure ready purchase and speedy payment for each cargo from Chelsea plantation that passed through the factor's sheds at Charleston's East Dock. While the Bostonian was his guest, Colonel Ashbee supplied him with an obedient slave-maiden for his bed, as he would order the finest claret or burgundy to accompany their dinner.

For a proud young negress beauty like Monnelia, a month or so under Captain Prince's command was a penance. She would shudder at the very memory of it in time to come. The captain was not in his first youth. Though a natural sensualist in his desires, his powers as a lover had long since been on the wane. As often happens in such cases, he made more extreme and eccentric demands upon the girls chosen to serve him. Such was the case with Monnelia.

Captain Prince was wearied by his railroad journey and enervated by the torpid summer of South Carolina after the cool and bracing air of Boston. For several nights in the fine house on the South Battery he required complete rest and long hours of sleep. Then, at last, he intimated that he would be prepared to receive the chosen slave-maiden in his room that night.

The scene in the boudoir overlooking White Point Gardens and the sea was elegant and instructive, as midnight approached. Captain Prince had exhausted his youth and strength in voluptuous enjoyment. Now, as an elderly gentleman, he was unable to do full justice to the African-velvet beauty of Monnelia. For a long time he was content to make her walk up and down before him, as he reclined in the comfort of the basketwork bedroom chair. For this she wore the white shoes with tall heels, her short cotton bodice, and her tight brief panties of white silk. Captain Prince needed the leisure to admire the calm beauty of this tribal maiden's face, the natural uprightness of her figure and the lithe easy movements of her legs and hips. In the white silk of her fancy underwear, the dark gloss of the girl's body was still more suggestively luminous. At the front, her tight white panties came down in a sharp v-shape to cover her warm loins. At the rear they were cut quite high and brief, so that they left bare the lower and softer swell of Monnelia's African-tan bottom-cheeks.

Captain Prince watched the elegant movements of her bare dusky legs, the controlled writhing of her hips as she walked, the slight rounding and contorting of Monnelia's buttocks which she carried soft yet trim in the agility of her youth. Though his virility was in decline, he resolved to do whatever he could to her by way of pleasure. In order to determine what this should be, he made Monnelia lie on her back over the bed with her knees hugged to her breasts so that he might inspect the underside of her squat. Next he made her stand up and bend over to touch her toes in front of his chair so that he could admire her rear view. This more vulgar sight of her, the satin-sleek jungle-tan ovals of Monnelia's nineteen-year-old backside swelling out at him, excited this jaded old libertine the more strongly.

At last he resolved to begin, unbuttoning himself and reclining in the basket-chair. He had placed it so that it was at the correct angle to the triple mirror on the far side of the bedroom for him to watch the girl in the glass. Then he began his night's diversions.

First he made the swarthy young jungle Venus kneel before his chair. Captain Prince knew very well that slave-girls of Monnelia's warm-skinned kind are taught early to suck their masters when commanded and they are given to understand that refusal is not permitted. He ordered her to slip off her bodice and panties. She was to present herself naked to perform this homage to him, except for her white glamour-shoes with their high-heels.

With her eyes lowered, she knelt before him, sitting on her heels and holding the grey-haired member cautiously with one hand as she lowered her lightly parted lips. But he was not satisfied with that. He quietly reminded Monnelia that she must not sit on her heels while she sucked his tool but lift her hips, as if on all fours. He had adjusted the dressing-mirror so that he could watch her. Monnelia must lift her hips and keep her lithe African-dark arse-cheeks turned to the long glass. Her elderly admirer would excite himself by musing upon the reflected image. And so he did. But the touch of her tongue playing upon him and the sight of Monnelia mouthing and arching her bottom out at the same time was still not enough to stimulate him to do his duty properly. Only after half an hour did the sight and the sensation combine to cause a twitching and a slight suggestion of stiffening resolve.

He kept her busy in this manner for half an hour more, by which time he was more than ever in the mood to do something to her himself. He told her to stand up, turn her back to his chair and bend over again tightly. A little awkwardly in her white shoes with their tall heels, Monnelia obeyed him. The captain smiled at the vulgarly suggestive rear view that the graceful young negress reluctantly offered. He slipped a hand between her legs from behind. Monnelia shivered with mingled excitement and revulsion at his intimate caressing of her. Then he began to fondle the dusky African-velvet sheen of Monnelia's bottom-cheeks, ending with a sharp smack on each of them, hard enough to make the girl catch her breath.

Though Captain Prince might be despised by the girl as a used up old libertine who could not have his way with her, the truth was that Monnelia had more to fear from him than from some lusty young spark who could mount astride and ride her at full pelt. The captain's frustration would lead to more perverse and gross forms of submission inflicted upon this tribal beauty. He might do it in part as a substitute and in part to avenge himself upon the girl. But from the first moment when she shivered as he touched her between the legs, Monnelia knew by instinct the danger of being under the orders of such a man.

Presently he required her to lie on the bed, naked as she was except for the white high-heeled shoes. She was to lie on her side with her back to him, for he could see the front aspect of her reflected in the mirror easily enough. The captain then shed his own clothes and put on his cotton nightgown with its tasselled cap. Slipping down on the bed behind her, he stretched out adoringly as she lay on her side. Captain Prince, free from the restrictions of Boston society for a month, trembled a little with excitement at the extreme lewdness of what he was going to do.

Lying behind her and a little further down in the bed, he instructed the graceful young negress to begin by arching the dark brown satiny-tan cheeks of her backside out until she felt them touch his features, so that she was almost sitting on his face. He assured her that this gesture, which others might find impudent, would not offend him in the least, even though the elegant ebony ovals of her smooth buttocks parted and she revealed her rear valley to him. He kissed and tickled her most sensitive body-jewels. Despite her distaste for such arousal of the swarthy sheen of her smooth flesh, the tribal beauty squirmed and gasped over the bed with a grace of movement and a litheness of figure that a ballet-girl would have envied.

For an hour or two, Monnelia's arse-cheeks and the posterior opening of her thighs were the object of the captain's browsing, kissing, and tongue-tickling. He admired her so closely that Monnelia constantly felt his breath upon her dusky native-girl bottom and the rear of her thighs. He kissed her legs and between them, as well as between her swarthy rear-cheeks. After such little excursions, his lips and eyes always returned to the negroid-cheeked sleekness of Monnelia's backside. Small wonder that after a night with the elderly gentleman Monnelia surrendered gratefully to a release of her desire by the fingers of another young woman, either the impudent maid-servant, Louise Neville, or the new white mistress, Amanda Stevens with her fair tresses and slim undulating figure. Captain Prince ignored his slave-girl's feminine desire. It was as if he could not believe she possessed such urges and needs.

It was doubtful whether any master revolted her as greatly as this old gentleman with his lubricity. The dusky equatorial beauty with her ribboned tresses would much have preferred a possessor who demanded of her the fierce and vigorous passion to which she knew how to respond. The captain was content to turn her on her belly so that he might kiss Monnelia's bottom while she drew from him in her mouth the feeble sperm-tribute of his passion. Or he would content himself by laying his tool limply between her hind cheeks or the rear parting of her thighs and working it there for an hour or more, which was the time it took the captain's man of war to get up steam. Too irresolute to penetrate to the inner sanctum, Captain Prince drew himself up at last and released the thin volleys of his sperm in warm runs upon the sleek dark swell of Monnelia's bottom-cheeks and the backs of her thighs.

She must lie over the sheets in this state beside him until morning. In the light of the candelabra, the gilded mirrors of the room reflected the sleek and satiny jungle tan of Monnelia's bottom-cheeks, their elegant ovals splashed and dribbled by the thin passion of the superannuated captain. Fretting and resentful, the blackamoor Venus waited sleepless beside her master with her warm native passions unfulfilled. But she was not always as fortunate as that.

Sometimes the captain himself was not satisfied to leave Monnelia in this state without further testing her. He would cross to the cupboard and take from it a cane, choosing among the long and whippy bamboos kept there for his use. Though each bamboo had been fashioned as a punishment-cane, he made no pretence of chastising Monnelia. Instead he assured her that this was a bedroom caning, which he inflicted entirely for his own pleasure. He promised that he greatly enjoyed doing it to those slave-girls put at his disposal. His warrior maiden was not one to scream easily but the captain intended, as he promised her, to bamboo the dark brown sleekness of Monnelia's arse-cheeks very hard indeed. It was prudent that she should not be overheard and for that reason he had been given a room as soundproof as any gaoler's vault.

He adjusted the leather wrist-cuffs and waist-strap to prevent resistance and secured her face-down on the bed with the pillows under her loins to raise and swell out the negroid-brown sheen of Monnelia's graceful backside. Being a military man and therefore strong in his sword arm from practising slaughter, he wielded the bamboo with cruel panache and a sure eye. He spent a good while measuring the cane this way and that across the satiny African-tan of Monnelia's bottom-cheeks. She tensed those bare elegant ovals with instinctive fright at the light menacing touch of the bamboo. Long before the caning began, he had her squirming with a fearful apprehension.

Sometimes, before beginning, he seemed to grow amorous again. He would lay down the cane on the bed for a moment and stoop over her. The long willowy grace of Monnelia's negress thighs received his kisses. Moistening his lips expectantly with his tongue he browsed on the rear of her thighs. Then his kisses touched the delectably nubile rear cheeks, the smooth coffee-dark swell of Monnelia's bottom. He kissed Monnelia's bottom long and intimately, the same African-tan girl-bottom that he was about to cane so pitilessly. Monnelia tensed and squirmed a little under his attentions. Her wide brown eyes betrayed her fear at the pain of the whipping she was going to get and yet they also conveyed her timidity at displeasing the man who commanded her.

Captain Prince's amorousness had its reasons. Monnelia's fearful anticipation made her bottom and thighs, the areas to be bamboo'd, of great interest to him. He breathed deeply the body-warmed air from Monnelia's sleekly-dark brown-cheeked backside, as if savouring the perfume of her fright in it. His lips touched the tribal-dark smoothness of Monnelia's bottom-cheeks. He sought a finer silken excitement in the feel of dusky rear-cheek skin, inspired by the same fright. The negroid satin of Monnelia's bottom-cheek gloss yielded the electric thrill of her fright to his lips as he kissed her arse lingeringly. Indeed, his breathing and browsing upon Monnelia's arse sometimes delayed the ordeal of the nineteen-year-old negress for half an hour. But it never saved her from it.

Then, with the veins standing out dangerously on his forehead, he thrashed the sleek ebony beauty of Monnelia's backside and the rear of her thighs at their tops. Each night that he did so, he made it as much like a prison whipping as possible, though he still did it purely for his own pleasure. The smarting willow-pattern of the bamboo weals across her lithe and dusky rear cheeks—and the cuts here and there—seemed like a vengeance upon her for his own inability. Monnelia's arse was a gracefully seductive target for a man who enjoyed caning negro girls. He bamboo'd her with savage energy, often letting the cane thrash lower to catch the backs of her thighs as well.

He allowed no respite during the caning and, with such a man, the girl's own actions intensified her ordeal. Much of the time her face and the upward brushed warrior-maiden coiffure of Monnelia's black hair were twisted to him. The calm dignity of her African beauty was transformed to a wide-mouthed and wild-eyed frenzy. Because she was free from the waist down, the long athletic grace of her thighs squirmed as if making love. What Captain Prince called the nigger-girl cheeks of Monnelia's bottom rounded and writhed as if in an erotic dance. A less demented master would have strapped her down properly when she deserved punishment. But Captain Prince liked to see the sinuous native writhings of Monnelia's bottom-cheeks, as if she was riding on an invisible lover beneath her and was therefore randy for chastisement. Only once did she kick out at Captain Prince in her desperation. His mouth tightened with sadistic zeal and he promised to inflict "a real punishment-lesson on the bare cheeks of Monnelia's nigger-girl arse." To reward her misconduct, he took a short-tailed leather whip and skinned Monnelia's bare bottom until its cheeks were smarting raw, then smeared them with salted fat.

At no time did he show his swarthy young jungle Venus the least pity. During the course of one night he caned the graceful negress-skinned cheeks of Monnelia's bare bottom three times and broke several bamboos with the force of the strokes across the dusky beauty of her lithe African-tan rump.

The elderly captain spent one or two nights a week with the girl. He caned Monnelia's bare ebony-skinned backside and thighs every week or ten days, he was severe on the nights when it happened. He would thrash the elegant dark-brown ovals of Monnelia's nude buttocks bruisingly with the bamboo before going to sleep and sometimes wake her again to be caned during the night. The sight of raised bamboo weals from his first caning of Monnelia's nigger-girl bottom merely excited him to greater severity. This time he would also strap her graceful dusky thighs together tightly and wad her mouth with a gag.

When he did not cane her, he left her to lie beside him until the morning with her young desires unappeased, Monnelia's bottom-cheeks and the rear of her upper thighs splashed with his passion-juice. Only once did he order Monnelia to make love to herself in front of him, at which she froze, unable to obey. It was not shame alone but her revulsion at Captain Prince that disabled her.

This refusal, far from sending him into a rage, caused Captain Prince to smile. He was a thin and vindictive prude, for all his lewdness with the girl. It was perhaps his greatest desire to see her flogged or in some way punished for the natural and sensuous grace of her movements. Small wonder that those who knew him elsewhere spoke of Captain Prince as a moralist who had never known what it was to entertain a voluptuous thought. He was regarded as the sternest and most upright figure of authority by his family and his neighbours alike.

There was a certain truth in this. Though he enjoyed his weeks of indulgence with such slave-girls as Monnelia, he never seemed to develop a normal man's affection or desire for them. Perhaps it was the feebleness of his manhood that affected him. Perhaps it was a self-disgust at his tonguing and licking of their intimate parts, a revulsion for which he punished them.

Whatever the answer to the riddle, he now regarded Monnelia as an ebony-skinned young whore, richly deserving the worst fate that could be devised for her. It was not for Captain Prince to devise it. The girl was not his property but merely a creature made available for his pleasure on vacation, as Colonel Ashbee would have provided a horse from his stable or a servant to carry his portmanteau.

But Captain Prince had no intention of returning from Charleston without leaving Monnelia something to remember him by. Something that would cause her to wince and draw breath every time that she tried to sit down for the next week or two. That was to be his retribution upon her. And it would not cost him a cent. He had only to write a note to his friend Ashbee, while the colonel was absent at

Chelsea Landing for a few days, complaining of Monnelia's conduct. How the native beauty would wish that she could wear some other skin than her own for a few weeks after that!

On the colonel's return to the South Battery, his friend made a complaint of the girl's conduct. He insisted that "the young nigger bitch Monnelia," as he called her, was in need of a lesson in manners. Colonel Ashbee knew quite well that the captain merely wished for the excitement of seeing Monnelia dealt with in the private whipping-house. This was kept by the local "jumper" near the slave-market in Chalmers Street.

An appointment was made with the proprietor of this establishment—the so-called "jumper"—for three days hence in the afternoon. Monnelia was informed at once that she would be whipped there over the public trestle, so that those who wished might come in and watch at the rear door of the room. She was left in no doubt that the punishment would be inflicted on her bare bottom and that something like the short-tailed pony-lash would be used. All this was explained to her in advance so that she might have a few days of nerve tingling apprehension with flutters of panic in her young belly and, at night, the sleek ebony cheek-flesh of Monnelia's bottom crawling and tingling with horror at the dread of what lay in store.

Three days later, after lunch, a pair of closed carriages left the South Battery and drew up on the cobbles of Chalmers Street outside the market building. Very discreetly, the occupant of one was handed down and hustled quickly up the stairs by the jumper's assistants to the long room above the market. Colonel Ashbee and Captain Prince followed from the other carriage. At one end of the room was a heavy waist-high trestle whose top was padded by black leather and whose stout wooden frame was equipped with restraining straps. There was a table upon which lay a bamboo cane, a long slim riding-switch, a short-tailed training-lash, and a little green bottle of sal volatile. A few yards behind this, two chairs had been placed for Colonel Ashbee and his guest. Further back, the room was divided half way by a boarded waist-high counter, from which the idlers and the curious were permitted to watch. The door was not yet opened to them, however, when the colonel and the captain took their places. The jumper and his three burly assistants were ready to begin.

Captain Prince approved the way in which the jumper tried to curb the disdain of this graceful nineteen-year-old negress. He felt a satisfaction in seeing her supple figure, the self-possessed beauty of a tribal princess in her face, the primitive warrior-girl appearance of her upward brushed hair and its ribboned coiffure at her nape. Her brief-cut panties and bodice made Monnelia conscious of showing off her beautiful legs and hips, and her seductive dark-tanned bum-cheeks. Every one of the idle boys of Charleston who watched from the rear of the room had a stiffening muzzle in the front of his pants at the shapely ovals of Monnelia's bared African-brown bottom-cheeks squirming with self-conscious control as she walked in her white high-heeled shoes.

She was called forward to receive her sentence from Colonel Ashbee. Captain Prince watched her approach. In the demure rhythm of her haunches there was a natural elegance. Her long and graceful legs, bare and swarthy, moved with practised delicacy in the high-heeled white shoes. She came towards them, long thighs brushing with maidenly restraint and her eyes downcast to avoid meeting the gaze of the master who would determine her punishment.

The colonel kept her standing there, waiting to hear her fate, for much longer than Monnelia could endure without a shudder and a catch in her breath. Despite the sultriness of the afternoon, her flesh was chilled by apprehension.

"Now, Monnelia," he said at last, "for the true kisses that you spurned from an admirer, you shall receive fifty kisses from the pony-lash upon the bare cheeks of your bottom. The effect of such naked agony upon that dusky young arse of yours will improve your manners more than any words of mine. Go and place yourself over the trestle in the position that your chastiser commands."

When she turned to walk away, Captain Prince licked his lips at this view of the proud young negress-skinned swell of Monnelia's arse-cheeks and the supple curves of her bare thighs. Where the white cotton of her tight briefs emerged between the rear of her legs, its skimpy seat left bare much of the dark oval smoothness of Monnelia's nigger-bitch bottom-cheeks, as the captain thought of them, the gloss of her dark brown arse-cheeks suggestively half naked. A natural beauty of shape and movement made Monnelia's backside worth studying. Its cheeks were satin and ebony as her other skin surfaces. Like Colonel Johnson, admiring her elegant and youthfully trim hind curves, the captain thought that the dusky gloss of this rear cheek-skin suggested Monnelia wet-bottomed from sitting in coffee-coloured sludge. But the bare graceful swell of Monnelia's dusky arse-halves would have made any other jungle princess pine with envy and any hangman lick his lips and reach for a pony-lash.

They watched her approach the sinister trestle with controlled steps. Monnelia must have known that the white shoes with their tall heels made her hips more mobile as she walked and made her seem to flaunt her nineteen-year-old blackamoor bottom at her chastisers. Though panic was fluttering in her young belly, dark-skinned Monnelia was made to seem as if she was truly asking for a whipping. But seeing the lash coiled ready on the table, Monnelia was fearful of making matters worse by such voluptuous roundings of her backside as she walked. Those white high-heeled glamour-shoes made the supple-figured warrior-maiden seem to flirt her hips and arse at the very men who were going to give her a thrashing.

"Bend over the trestle, Monnelia! Right over it!" the jumper said smiling.

The satin-smooth and jungle-brown cheeks of Monnelia's behind swelled out temptingly as she bent over cautiously and the jumper's assistants held her forward over the padded trestle. They strapped her down in this lasciviously inviting pose. The swell of her hips as she bent over also strained the thin white cotton of her knicker-seat into the slave-girl's rear cleavage, so that her warm-toned buttocks were quite bare and temptingly offered. She was obliged to hear the laughter of the idlers in the public area behind her and the suggestions of what they would like to see done to her.

The jumper's assistants had Monnelia bending over tightly along the trestle, its leather-padded top supporting her from her pubic bush to her throat. Her dusky bare arms were pulled down at full stretch either side and strapped to the supports by leather wrist-cuffs. They also used a broad harness belt round her bare waist and strapped her down very tightly on the padded frame.

The jumper himself took the waist of her briefs, drew them down her legs, and made her step out of them. He used intimate fingers to free them where they caught under her legs or in her rear cleavage as the humid warmth of the room made Monnelia sweat a little in these crevices. He took a length of stout cord, tightening a loop round her bare brown waist and the padded trestle-top to hold her down. The remaining length he drew tight down on her lower belly, straining it back under her legs and up deep and taut between Monnelia's swarthy buttocks to knot it firmly in the rear of her waist. Bound tight over the trestle like this, all surging or twisting of her hips and backside was prevented. By tying her in this intimate manner, he ensured that the double-cheeked ebony swell of Monnelia's arse-target remained properly presented for the whip. It was almost more suggestive than complete nudity. As she bent over, the cord was just visible, straight and tight between the dark skin-gloss of Monnelia's bottom-cheeks. Indeed, its thickness kept her cheeks apart a little and in that way actually exposed her to more searching discipline.

The jumper's assistant had pinioned the slave-girl's ankles together to the upright of the trestle. He also strapped the dark willowy grace of Monnelia's thighs together, very firmly to the trestle, just above her knees. There was a last precaution. It was not possible to see clearly, from behind, the precise manner of quietening her. But in the afternoon of discipline that followed, Monnelia's wild shrillness never rose above a trapped and energetic mewing. Colonel Prince smiled to see them gag a beautiful nigger-bitch like Monnelia.

With a figure that the Three Graces might envy, Monnelia bending over tightly with her legs strapped together at the ankles and round her lower thighs, displayed a delectable rear-cheek target to the jumper. Other men whose disciplinary zeal knew only the pale buttocks of reformatory girls of fourteen or fifteen, like Sally Fenton and her elder sister Jane, would envy him the chance to whip the satiny equatorial tan of Monnelia's elegant bottom-cheeks.

For almost half an hour, the jumper heightened her ordeal by delaying the punishment that Colonel Ashbee had ordered and insisting on the native beauty presenting the velvety dark cheeks of her backside fully to his satisfaction. He was not easily satisfied. First he spat in his hand for luck, then murmured a command. Not seeing it obeyed, he aimed a ringing cheek-smack on Monnelia's bottom and then another. The onlookers smiled, seeing from her tensing and pressing of her thighs how much it stung her. He smacked the swarthy flanks of her hips side to side. He smacked her legs hard from her hips to her knees. She would have twisted her face round but it was the duty of an assistant to prevent this by standing astride at her far end of the trestle and holding Monnelia's head between his legs. Moistening his palm repeatedly, the jumper gave Monnelia a really well-smacked bottom to begin with, the echoes of the spanking ringing hard and sharp, until the cheeks of this warrior maiden's backside shone slinky wet from it.

"I shan't hurry with you, Monnelia," he said at last, a little breathlessly, "with a good-looking black girl, I prefer that it should last all afternoon."

He was as good as his word. Presently he picked up the whip with its stout handle and its thin tail of woven leather that dangled about eighteen inches. He cracked it sharply in the air and the onlookers saw Monnelia's buttocks and thighs flinch at the report. Then he trailed the cold menace of the leather lightly over the swelling dusky ovals of Monnelia's bottom-cheeks and round her thighs. The murmuring among the spectators at the back of the room fell silent in expectation.

The thin leather snake caught the light as it came whistling down and landed with a pistol-crack sharpness across the sleek ebony swell of Monnelia's bottom-cheeks. Her legs went tense with the anguish so that the muscles appeared in contour. From the public area of the room there was a sharp intake of breath in admiration and excitement of what the chastiser had done to the shapely young negress. The whip had marked Monnelia's buttocks with a fine curlicue and a red-hot kiss of leather. He caught her again, the whip curling so that it just touched where one cheek began to curve in towards the other. A wild mewing was heard and the knee of one shapely negress-skinned leg tried to jam into the back of the other as if to contain the torment.

"This is just practice for a while," he said quietly, leaning over the native girl. "Just so you get to like the feel of it before we start counting up to fifty."

This caused a certain amusement from the loafers and loungers. Then the murmurs died away again. Tight-lipped and keen-eyed, the jumper stooped a little and looked closely at the native-tan ovals of Monnelia's bottom, as if to see where she would feel it worst. With the suggestive length of cord drawn tight and deep in her arse-valley she could not clench her rear cheeks together, which made it possible to catch her a little more intimately than would otherwise have happened.

The lash sang out again and caught her beautifully low across the swelling equatorial tan of Monnelia's bottom-cheeks. It made her toes curl with the agony of it and her hands clenched into fists. They saw her strain against the broad strap that pinioned her graceful dark-glossed thighs tightly together. In doing this she surged back a little so that the hard-stretched elegant ovals of Monnelia's African-satin bottom seemed to stick out as if she was really asking for more whip-kissing.

"Now the fifty strokes of the whip across your nigger-girl arse, Monnelia," the jumper said with a smile at her.

The stable-whip printed the first of its fifty kisses, leaving another searing loop of fire across Monnelia's young backside. These loops and curlicues remained, printed in raised weals across her satiny dark bottom-cheeks. The whipping began in earnest. Though only her buttocks and the rear of her thighs made up the target, Monnelia was flogged like a hardened criminal. The man who held her head between his legs had restoratives at hand. If her endurance failed her, there need not be a long interval before she was enabled to take what punishment remained.

When the fifty had been given, the jumper turned to Colonel Ashbee to ask if he was now satisfied with the state of his recalcitrant slave-girl. No doubt he was. However, etiquette required that he should pass the question on to old Captain Prince. The captain walked forward and looked at the swarthy whip-tapestried cheeks of Monnelia's behind. He went and sat down again.

"I should like to see her receive a further measure," he said to the jumper, "the amount to be at your discretion."

There was no mistaking the excitement among the other onlookers at the torment to which he had condemned Monnelia. When her blackamoor-skinned bottom was under his orders, he would explore and pursue the possibilities it offered for punishing her until the afternoon waned and dusk turned into night. Even under Captain Prince's commands, the sun was low when at last Monnelia was unfastened and carried out, still naked below the waist. She was dumped into the colonel's baggage-cart by those who carried her. There she sprawled, face-down and bare-bottomed over an old straw-mattress, eyes brimming over as she lamented her condition. In this sorry state, the grooms drove her back to several days' isolation in the attic room on the South Battery.

Monnelia might have fared worse, had not the jumper been afterwards engaged to thrash a pretentious young black bitch, Mandy, eighteen years old, who had answered back to her master. The bare and fattened negress cheeks of Mandy Drummond's bottom were flogged at sunset with a cart-whip. It was an engagement for which the jumper was well paid and which he was obliged to honour. The spectators pressed at the counter and watched enthralled. Her shrillness was not muffled, so that Mandy Drummond's screams added an edge of drama for the voyeurs. Even Colonel Ashbee and his guest idled there to see the black slave-girl taught a lesson in manners. Then they went home, well contented with all that had happened in Chalmers Street during the past few hours. In the company of Captain Prince, the colonel ordered that two bottles of his best claret should be opened and aired to accompany their dinner.

A few weeks after this, Monnelia's fate was decided. It happened on a warm evening after dinner when a good many gentlemen from the lowlands of South Carolina gathered in formal dress at the Chalmers Street market. It was almost a private occasion, an auction to which only genuine and confidential bidders were admitted. Mr Roberts, the auctioneer, took his place upon a dais in the upper room. Commonly used as a place of public chastisement for errant slave-girls, it made an agreeable venue for the private sale.

The light shone brightly on the auctioneer's rostrum and the roofed market before it, the white shirt-fronts and jewelled stud-buttons, the gold links and silk coats of the bidders. In the whole of that summer, it was the only auction of fancy-girls to take place in Charleston. The belle of the evening was Monnelia, put up for sale by "a gentleman of the first rank."

It is easy to imagine what brightening of their eyes and licking of lips there was when this dark-skinned gem of young womanhood was brought forward. The auctioneer beckoned her and Monnelia moved with maidenly reluctance into the light. On such an occasion, when the purchasers must see what it was they bid for, she was naked apart from the white tall-heeled shoes, which ensured the exaggerated squirming of her hips and thighs, the fuller rounding of Monnelia's swarthy bottom-cheeks as she walked.

This equatorial beauty approached her destiny with the same elegant and controlled walk, her lovely young face lowered as if to watch her feet and the ribboned tresses of her hair bound back. Mr Roberts, the auctioneer, stood her well forward, raised her chin upon his hand and made her show the beauty of her dark-skinned face fully to her admirers. Her spruce young breasts and flat belly called his attention next. Then it was the long elegant line of her young thighs and calves.

Turning her, he made her bend so that the mocha-brown sheen of Monnelia's bottom swelled more suggestively. He was frank as to her amorous pedigree, admitting that she was no longer a maid between her legs and that even Monnelia's backside was not quite virgin. Yet he assured his audience that such use had woken her passions thoroughly and that the man who mastered her now would have reason to thank those who had trained her so well. He added that Monnelia's bare arse had had the whip and that she had learnt several very painful lessons in this manner. Yet it was visible that she had not been marked indelibly and that Monnelia's bottom bore no little brand of the circular marking-disc between its cheeks as yet. The purchaser might commission the jumper to print that mark at some future time, if he chose.

The bidding began and soon developed into a duel between a Charleston merchant and a Savannah trader. At $800 dollars, victory went to the trader, the owner of a fine house near Oglethorpe Square. All who witnessed the contest were satisfied by its outcome. That such a master was the best for this Belle Sauvage was universally agreed. There was some amusement at the final glimpse of the tribal Venus. She was required to remain bending while her new master and the jumper talked earnestly of the design of a little disc to establish his ownership. Its mark would be made in the traditional place. In other words, the positioning was to be intimate upon the negress sleekness of Monnelia's bottom-skin. So placed, it would be concealed while she stood upright but displayed when she bent over tightly and her rear cheeks parted.

As was proper, Colonel Ashbee's name was not mentioned. Nor was that of the lucky purchaser. When the graceful dark-skinned beauty was displayed, the auctioneer remarked several times that the young slave-girl was the property of a gentleman who had trained her as was necessary for the pleasure of those who might command her. It was a matter of honour that this claim should be believed and that it should prove true. The bargain was thus sealed on both sides.

Both the colonel and his successor were present two weeks later when the jumper placed the coin-sized disc in the brazier. A low stool was necessary to support the beautiful jungle Venus, secured on all fours over it. The swarthy gloss of Monnelia's graceful nineteen-year-old bottom was thus presented full and spread-cheeked to the room. Though the weals were hardly discernible now, it seemed that she had been early taught a lesson by her new master. The swarthy-cheeked swell of Monnelia's backside had been soundly thrashed with a cane, probably on the night of her purchase.

Her former master was a connoisseur of rare and curious occasions. He now made a final close inspection of that posterior view. No less than Captain Prince he was intrigued to sniff for an air of panic round Monnelia's blackamoor arse. He must test with his lips the African-gloss of her rear cheeks for the electric tension of fright that gave allure to the ebony-tan satin of Monnelia's bottom-skin. Though this was his last sight of her, Monnelia's behind occupied all his attention as the part to be embellished.

Her masters past and present took their places. The harsh panting of bellows heated the disc in the coals until it shone cherry-bright. Monnelia's backside echoed the menace of the bellow rudely with panic of her own, as she saw the metal grow bright. The little disc was oval in shape and about an inch long, its open-work forming the name "Monnelia" and the description "Slave." The jumper could not resist the chance of placing the mark as intimately as possible between the dusky rear cheeks so that the glowing rim almost touched the tight rear hole. As the young negress watched in panic over her shoulder, he approached with the bright disc on its spindle. His lips moved in a smile and he made no attempt to hide from the ebony-skinned beauty the excited stiffness of the tool stretching the front of his pants.

He bowed his head, watching the chocolate-brown skin-silk of Monnelia's bottom-cheeks closely where they curved in together. He chose the most intimate inward slope of the girl's behind. He pressed the glowing disc to that inward cheek-curve of her negress-skinned arse and exhaled his tension as he held it there for ten long seconds. While the jumper exercised his skill, slowly and lovingly, the colonel breathed the air of Monnelia's wildness, as if it were a fine bouquet. When the disc was pressed in place, the jungle-tan sleekness of Monnelia's bottom-cheeks assumed that very tension of ecstasy or torment which was so exquisite to the lips or to caressing fingers. It was necessary to torture Monnelia in order to achieve that dusky silky tension in the bottom-skin of her rear cheeks which the electric thrill of the agony produced in her. The jumper leant over her, his bulk weighing down on her hips to add to the restraints holding her in position. He pressed the red-hot disc to its place long and firmly, his tongue running on his lips in the excited air of her shrillness. If he tortured Monnelia as his duty required, his free hand fondled the dark gloss of her bare hip-flank at the same time.

Colonel Ashbee turned to his successor, remarking that the curving in of two cheeks offered the possibility of the first print of ownership being reflected upon the other side. The Savannah trader nodded to the jumper, whose assistant fortified the dusky beauty with sal volatile. By this means she was enabled to undergo the second part of the ordeal, the bright glow of the disc pressed firm and long to the coffee-tan cheek-skin on the opposite inward slope of Monnelia's swarthy-satin bottom.

She passed from public slavery into a far more private kind, exercised in another country, in the colonial enclave of Cheluna. In Cheluna the possession of a slave-girl— black or white—was the privilege of any man wealthy enough, as it remains to this day. By such means, Louise Neville and other pale-skinned teasers found themselves sisters in bondage with Monnelia again in a most unexpected way. There were protests and little rebellions of the sort with which every harem is familiar. And, as usual, they died away when the captive realised that her fate was absolute and irreversible.

On this estate in a remote area of Cheluna, the tall and graceful negress was examined, from the rear as well as from the front, by her new master. The little disc-marks that were revealed when Monnelia bent over or knelt forward, spread-cheeked, excited him greatly. It was not enough for him that they should show their own identity and status to the world. Next to that must be his own name and claim of ownership. The trestle was set out and the negress-skinned beauty was made to present herself bottom-upwards.

It is an intriguing comment on modern men of all ages who possessed the girls that they became more tyrannical in places where absolute possession of their slave-maidens was possible without any fear of tales being told or reproaches levelled against them. On their travels to Arabia or Africa, they were guests of European regiments at the colonial barracks when an Arab girl was to be punished for some reason and those who had ordered it came to enjoy the drama. Cheluna's new master was to witness the humiliation of one such proud young female rebel before coming home to command Monnelia's ordeal.

Shaida's tousled black hair clustered down between her shoulder-blades and over her forehead. The strong full curve of her young face was marked by the directness of her brown eyes, the black arch of her brows, the bold line of her nose and her brightly-painted lips. She was dressed in the blue cotton of her short jacket and pants. The slight voluptuous weight of her hips and thighs was well suggested by this costume. Shaida's body-skin was a dusty Asian gold. As the curve of her chin and her face suggested, there was a somewhat heavy look to her breasts and thighs, hips and backside. Those who watched her standing there were now confronted by the sallow Eastern tan that emphasised the rather slack voluptuousness of Shaida's bottom-cheeks.

Bare from waist to heels, Shaida was strapped on all fours over the block. Standing back, no longer mocking or smiling, the trooper drew a short lash through his fingers, raised it behind his shoulder and flashed it down across the full swell of Shaida's buttocks. The walls of the yard rang with the sharpness of the stroke as the fierce leather tail cracked and clung round the sallow-tanned and slightly fattened cheeks of Shaida's bottom. She tossed her tousled black hair, trying to crane round, and screamed into her gag.

The rails above were crowded with officers watching justice done. Again the whip caught the light, kissing the fattened tawny cheek-swell of Shaida Ali's bottom again with the naked agony of skinning leather. She tensed her buttocks desperately but there was nothing she could do to ward off the worst of the punishment she had earned. Some of the onlookers were there from a sense of righteous indignation at the girl's misconduct. Others had come to enjoy the sight of a native girl like Shaida barebottomed and to feel the exhilaration of seeing the whip smack agonisingly across the full-cheeked suggestiveness of Shaida's olive-skinned backside while they heard the muted frenzy of her screams. Seeing the tousled black hair fly this way and that, the wildness in her firm young face assured them of her torment.

There was no dismay among the onlookers. They watched and listened like connoisseurs. Even during judicial discipline the sallow Asian tan of the voluptuous and rather fatly presented cheeks of Shaida's bottom had a vulgarly sexy look. It was a bottom that European disciplinarians, with vindictive lechery towards Asian and Arab girls, would enjoy punishing. The writhing and cheek-creasing of Shaida's seductive and full-cheeked Arab-girl arse was like the squirming of an erotic dance. The suggestiveness of her bare bum-cheeks, rather than the girl's crime, ensured that the whipping was severe and prolonged. As the lash made her tawny bottom-cheek flesh quiver with the thirtieth stroke, Shaida contorted and yelled wildly, spicing the excitement of the voyeurs and making them determined to prolong the drama after the allotted number of whip-lashes. This command pleased the trooper who had the task of whipping her and was greatly enjoying it, envied by all his comrades.

Such masters enjoyed themselves perversely with white girls like Louise Neville, as well as with tawny-skinned girls of subject races, like Shaida. Old Mr Hardacre was greatly intrigued by the ingenious pleasures he might enjoy with a white-skinned slave-girl on a sub-tropical estate like his at Cheluna. He ordered a garden-carriage to be prepared, a light and daintily-built vehicle to carry one person. It had been adapted so that a stout wooden bar joined the two shafts at their tips and another joined them further back.

Louise Neville at seventeen was half-schoolgirl and half-woman. Her round impudent face with long-lashed saucer eyes, short slicked-back hair moulded to her head, seemed impudently bold. She stood in her underwear, the black silk of her showgirl knickers tight on the seductive double-cheeked swell of Louise Neville's bottom, the adolescent puppy-flesh softness of her hips and thighs.

Louise was made to stand between the shafts with her back to the driver's seat. Though she struggled in the grasp of the two assistants, they bent her forward and secured her over the bar that was screwed to either shaft. She was bending tightly over this rear bar, held down firmly by a fixed black strap that was drawn hard round her bare waist. Her arms were pulled out at full stretch before her and her wrists held in leather cuffs fixed to the tips of the two shafts. The impudently soft cheek-swell of Louise Neville's bottom tensed with alarm in the tight black sheen of her thin panties. At seventeen years old, Louise had tarted herself up to provoke the male sex. She was like a pretty painted doll who invited them to have fun with her. The round firm-chinned face had an insolently pretty look with its lashes darkened by mascara to give her a saucer-eyed cheekiness. But this appeal would now work its excitement on the sadism of the man who commanded her. The realisation of this gave her impudent young face a frightened look, which merely heightened its prettiness.

She was wearing a white waist-length singlet. The pale adolescent softness of her thighs was sheathed to mid-point in the sheer black of nylon stockings, drawn up tight by the elastic straps of a suspender-belt. She was also wearing the black translucent knickers that ended in a frilled hem just at the top of her thighs. Drawn glossily skin-tight at the seat and smooth as drumskin when she bent over the bar, Louise Neville's panties made the soft swell of her bottom-cheeks in this posture look extremely sexy. But it was impossible that she should be allowed to wear her knickers for the session that was about to begin, however much she hoped he would not undress her.

Though she tensed against him, it was easy enough for the overseer to take the elastic waistband of Louise's knickers and draw these slinky black panties down her pale squirming thighs. As he did so he smiled to himself, leaning over to watch her seventeen-year-old backside as the pale bottom-flesh swelled fuller a little, freed of the restraining panty-silk. Her glamour-panties soon hung in an untidy tangle round her knees, then fell to her feet.

"Imagine you've committed the worst offence in the school calendar, Louise Neville. You're in the head teacher's study now about to get your punishment. That should help you to understand what's going to happen presently."

The round impudent face of this seventeen year old with her blue saucer-eyes and dark lashes, her bold looks and slicked back crop of dark hair was a study in dismay. Her chastiser naturally wanted to cane the soft pallid shimmer of Louise Neville's bottom-cheeks far more sadistically than any teacher would have been permitted. Samson took his seat in the carriage. The bamboo cane rattled lightly as it was picked up.

He reached forward with one hand and Louise flinched and tried to tighten herself as he fondled the warm feminine cunt-flesh peeping back between the soft pallor of her bare thighs above her stocking-tops. He fondled the flesh back a little more so that he could work it rousingly with his fingers, while the bending seventeen-year-old girl gasped and squirmed her pale thighs.

"A nice warm little nest, Louise," he said teasingly. "You'll be more responsive to discipline if you're worked up a little first of all by having it fondled."

"Not too much," Mr Hardacre said presently with a laugh. "She's making the inner surfaces of her thighs slippery-wet. We mustn't let her go too far."

Samson moved his hand, his fingers now exploring the forbidden rear valley between the soft puppy-flesh pallor of Louise Neville's bottom-cheeks. The heat of the day and the exertions of her struggles against the men who had positioned her had left her warm and humid in her teenage bottom-crack. As she uttered shrill protests, the impudent prettiness of her face turned towards him. Louise was writhing over the bar, not realising how the swelling and contorting of her hind cheeks excited him all the more. He fiddled knowingly with the tight-petalled bud of Louise Neville's arsehole until the girl could scarcely contain herself. At last he drew his hand away.

"Pull forward, Louise. Draw the carriage forward. Keep your back straight and your bottom facing up towards me."

However completely she obeyed him, Louise must have known he would not be able to resist using the cane when she moved seductively in this posture.

"No!" she cried urgently, frightened of what was to come. "No!"

Samson smiled at this. Down flashed the slim cane and the pallor of Louise Neville's bottom-cheeks quivered briefly at the impact. Samson's smile broadened. Half rising from the seat, he gave her a second and third stroke, the bamboo landing across her soft-fleshed backside with a smack like a whip.

"Don't keep us waiting, Louise," said Mr Hardacre with quiet amusement.

She let out a wild cry as the cane caught her again. Louise was straining every muscle of her black-stockinged legs and her bare hips. Smack! went the cane again. Whip! . . . Smack! . . . Whip-smack! . . . Round went the wheels at last.

Samson had no eyes for the beauties of the garden. His gaze followed the squirming nudity of pale teenager hips and backside as the girl pulled forward. This seventeen year old had tarted herself up in the belief that it was to be a more glamorous occasion. Even now she tried to twist her head round, as if to implore him. But she invited punishment even by the way in which her short-cut dark hair was slicked back to give a bolder look to her rounded young face with its blue saucer eyes and pretty ears, the firm chin and tempting mouth. The lashes of her eyes had been darkened and the mouth carefully lipsticked. Her effort was not wasted. By emphasising her impudent prettiness, Louise had ensured that he would enjoy whipping her all the more.

At each step, Louise's hips swelled fuller and went further over the crossbar. She was beautifully positioned for him at that moment, black-stockinged teenager legs squirming, the puppy-fleshed softness of her bottom fattened out in a seductive double-swell of rear cheeks. The groom thrashed the pale swell of Louise Neville's bottom-cheeks with a cane as she sprawled arse-upwards over the bar. His mouth tight and the veins standing out on his forehead, he bamboo'd Louise with vicious energy. Stirred by the natural impudence of her round-faced saucer-eyed impudence, the bold slicking back of her short dark hair, he left a fine tapestry of bamboo prints across the soft cheek-pallor of Louise Neville's arse.

As she lay bottom-upwards over the bar with each forward pull, her buttocks were drawn apart in a seductively full rear view. The soft pallor of Louise Neville's bottom-cheeks tempted punishment like any delinquent schoolgirl over the teacher's desk. But no school punishment would allow the lucky teacher to see Louise Neville's bottom-cleft drawn open as it now was. She seemed to be asking for a crack shot, her anus the tight little bullseye at the centre of the intimate target. Samson's mouth tightened at the sight. He laid the bamboo down and chose a finer implement. The short snakeskin lash threw a flash of black light and caught Louise expertly between her soft rear cheeks.

To get the better of a seventeen-year-old girl like Louise Neville was a great satisfaction to her master and to Samson. Once she bore the bamboo imprints of her obedience training, and once she had seen for herself in the handmirror that it was so, there would be no more dispute. Louise Neville wept prettily a little for the state of her soft-cheeked young bottom. But then she accepted her fate and served her master, seeking consolation at the same time in the arms of Monnelia.

She was by no means the last white-skinned girl to be added to such collections of beautiful captives at Cheluna.

In modern times, not far away, a descendant of Mr Hardacre, on his visits to northern climes, chose other beauties for his amusement and spent freely to arrange their abduction. This was the case with Tania, a well-spoken and rather self-regarding girl of nineteen whom he noticed while strolling through the shopping parades of his vacation city.

He walked past the shop window and caught his first sight of her. She was alone in the shop, standing behind the counter, leaning on her elbows and reading the newspaper, spread on the surface before her. Young Mr Hardacre noted a soft but sly prettiness of face and a rather tomboyish figure. She appeared to be at the end of her teens, her thick brown hair curled and cut short at her collar, worn forward a little so that it clustered over her forehead. When she looked up from the paper and glanced in his direction, there was a pert prettiness about her lightly olive-skinned face, a tendency to dimples. Her nose was neat and straight, her chin well tucked-in. The cheekbones seemed high under her light blue-green eyes, making them appear deeper set and more shadowed. This gave the girl a sleepless and enervated look. Young Mr Hardacre thought it would not be surprising to discover that Tania Nicoll masturbated a good deal, as she lay restless in bed.

There was certainly a look of self-loving and self-indulgence about her. He could see from the window that she had a softly appealing figure, though she was perhaps no more than medium height. He imagined cuddly breasts under her woollen top and quite a broad young seat. With his usual circumspection, the young Hardacre walked round to the side window, so that he was able to look at her a little from the rear. The girl continued to lean forward over the shop counter with her chin in her hands, reading the paper. To Mr Hardacre's amusement, the young tart was wearing a pair of jeans, the thin denim having a pale washed-out look and drawn skin-smooth as she leant over the shop counter, chin in hand, and read the paper. Moreover, her posture pulled the jeans still more taut over her buxom and rather tomboyish hips and buttocks. Mr Hardacre drew breath sharply and studied the view that the girl offered, for she could have had no idea of the way she showed herself or even that anyone was spying through the side window of the shop. The fullness of her rear cheeks was clearly separated by her pose with a well defined cleavage between them. Tania Nicoll stood like a young pavement whore, slack-hipped, one cheek of her rump higher than the other.

Still not realising the view that she offered, Tania hollowed the back of her waist downwards, causing the swell of her behind to be thrust out further in the most exaggerated and full-cheeked manner. It was this, Hardacre thought, that caused her rear cheeks to be so seductively separated.

A day or two later he walked that way again. A small dark-haired girl with a pretty and vivacious face was serving in the shop. Tania, in her short sweater and tight jeans was lying on the rear counter. She lay propped on her elbow, for all the world like a harem odalisque. She had turned on to her hip, crossing one leg over the other at the knee, so that the voluptuous swell of her young hips was exaggerated by the pose. By turning on her side like this, her backside in skin-tight denim was offered to passers-by in all its suggestive cheeky fullness.

This modern Hardacre, who had his camera with him, contrived to take several photographs of her in this pose through the window for his private collection. When the shop had closed, he watched her clearing up. Moving a pile of papers, she bent over and presented to the window the seat of the faded blue jeans, shaped by a pair of rather tomboyish and ungainly bottom-cheeks. Mr Hardacre could not resist taking a photograph of this suggestive rear-view of Tania Nicoll as well. He naturally wondered whether she had yet had her boyfriend's hand inside her knickers or his tool between her legs. Passing that way in the early evening, he had noticed that she was sometimes called for after work by a young man of her own age who no doubt drove her home.

Determined to discover more about her, young Hardacre bided his time and then entered the shop to buy some trifle or other. His dealings with the girl convinced him that she thought a good deal too much of herself and needed to be taught a lesson in manners. She spoke with a semi-educated twang. It was clear that she was stand-offish or indifferent in serving her customers. Mr Hardacre persisted with her and found that a little coaxing brought out a slyly evasive smile.

He went in a day or two later to buy string and sealing wax. While awaiting her attention, he heard one of the other girls call her Tania. He studied her again as he cooled his heels. Tania had quite a small or delicate face and features when seen from the front, her eyes a very light green and the whites remarkably prominent. It seemed, after all, that she felt a sense of responsibility for her job and that she became quite eager to please her customers when pressed. Hardacre noticed that she wore a gold ring with a stone, possibly an engagement ring. He noted that her skin seemed paler, apart from the light olive tan of her face, and that her mouth was quite brightly painted. She wore rings for display on three fingers of her right hand. Her curly hair was quite a light brown with a central parting.

He made his arrangements for Tania. This buxom and curly-headed tomboy of nineteen found herself on that Cheluna estate where her pale skin did not excuse her from slavery. But she was a still self-centred and off-hand girl who must be taught obedience and good manners. In this case Mr Hardacre decided that Tania Nicoll must be broken in like a rebellious filly. It was easily done. In the paddock there was a yoke-bar, running out horizontally at waist-height from a central capstan. It was intended to be driven round in a long circle. The device was equipped with straps riveted to the bar.

There was the usual vain resistance on behalf of outraged feminine dignity as three of the overseer's men brought Tania out and secured her bending over the bar. The pale blue jeans were strained tight over her full tomboyish hips and backside as she writhed her legs, while her waist was strapped down firmly and her wrists buckled into leather cuffs. Then, despite her writhing, Tania's jeans were undone and drawn down.

Tania Nicoll's panties were the ones that showed their shape through jeans denim when she bent over in the shop, they were plain stretch-briefs of white cotton worn by so many girls of her age and type. As she bent over the bar she wore only these and her short woollen top. As Tania had her panties taken down she revealed a slight heaviness in the pearly cheeks of her bottom and her thighs. She tensed herself instinctively. There was a pale vulnerable look to the cheeks of Tania Nicoll's backside, laid bare to the cool air from the warmth of her underpants and also laid bare like this in the open air of the paddock.

The overseer was a true tyrant in dealing with Tania and had chosen a slim leather switch that had a spring like a rapier. As he touched the cold leather gently across the bare pallid cheeks of Tania Nicoll's bottom, taking aim, the fattened curves of her rear cheeks tensed together in alarm, compressing her anal cleavage to a thin tight line.

There was no reason for him to restrain himself. Moreover, as the girl strove forward, bending over the bar, the suggestive squirming of the bare cheeks of Tania Nicoll's bottom in their full-swelling pallor looked extremely sexy. As she laboured to turn the yoke-bar through its long circles, he walked behind her, whipping her savagely across her behind with hard measured strokes of the black leather switch. The pulses of the watching men quickened as Tania Nicoll screamed, the shrill rising cries ringing out and fading across the empty landscape. Though Tania screamed for an end or at least a pause in this discipline, her master ignored her wildness and answered her with peremptory commands.

"Keep your back straight, Tania Nicoll . . . and your bottom facing the overseer properly, Tania Nicoll! . . . Bend tighter over the bar as you push it, Tania. Show a more sexy rear view to the overseer. He's going to whip you anyway, Tania. You might just as well make it enjoyable for him . . . Don't try twisting your bottom aside from the whip, Tania Nicoll! If you try tricks like that, I'll have you put through your paces again tomorrow! . . . You've got rather a fat bottom, Tania Nicoll, haven't you? A nice target for the man who disciplines you!"

Tania had been brought there to be broken in and the way in which she was presented, strapped bare-bottomed over the bar, naturally excited the overseer's severity. But presently it was judged prudent to quieten her shrillness by means of a gag, which held the cotton web of her panties in her mouth as a wad. Those who witnessed her ordeal considered that Tania deserved it.

It was good to have Tania completely at one's disposal in this way and to make her pay the price for her indifference and off-handedness to those she served. Sometimes the overseer was content to walk behind her for a while, merely gazing at the smarting and crimson willow-pattern of bamboo which the riding-switch had printed across the bare double-cheek swell of Tania Nicoll's arse. Then the sight of the tomboyish pallor of Tania Nicoll's bottom-cheeks squirming and flesh-creasing as she laboured to push the heavy bar made him restless again. The air rang to the whip! . . . whip! . . . whip! . . . of the supple leather switch, thrashing across Tania's firm-swelling buttocks with every step she took. He was determined to teach the young tart a lesson she would remember always. And so he did, with every reason to justify him.

As the hours of the afternoon passed, Tania's pallid thighs strained and her hind quarters surged with the effort of driving the bar round its circle. Much later in the afternoon, when she had been whipped soundly but was still under his discipline, there was a moment of drama. The whip caught the full cheek-swell of Tania Nicoll's backside agonisingly. It was as if the torture of it immobilised her in mid-stride and she tried vainly to tense herself. As she posed for a second or two, writhing arse-upwards over the harness-bar, the pallid swell of her buttocks was drawn hard apart by her tight-bending posture. No wonder Tania was desperate to preserve her feminine self-esteem. Her body was tense as if on a rack and the short tousled crop of her curls was lowered. The halves of her young backside were stretched hard apart in this posture. The onlookers saw that Tania Nicoll's arsehole had gone urgently small and tight. Driven beyond endurance by Samson's whip, she was struggling to contain herself in front of the smiling voyeurs.

Samson did what the spectators hoped. He ordered Tania to keep moving and warned her that the preservation of her feminine dignity was no excuse for halting. He reinforced this command with a vicious stroke of the supple leather switch across the bare and pale cheek-swell of Tania Nicoll's bottom. Immobilised by the searching smart, she lay there over the bar, squirming and tensing to control her urges. She had shown such a high opinion of herself and such indifference towards the men and women she served that all those who watched her now drew a certain satisfaction from Tania's predicament. They watched keenly, hoping to see Tania Nicoll humiliate herself and learn the lesson of her slavery.

After Tania had had her first afternoon of obedience training, she lay limp over the bar to which she was still attached, as if the labour and the sweat, as well as the ordeal of the whip, had drained all energy from her body. While she dropped over the bar, the tousled light brown curls hung down and the rather heavy swell of Tania Nicoll's arse-cheeks faced up, flame red from the whipping and with a suggestively lewd blemish or two. This suggestion of little-girl rudeness which the nineteen-year-old tomboy presented gave a sluttish but also a wantonly sexy look to Tania Nicoll's backside.

As her master remarked, a girl of Tania's kind would not accept her slavery as easily as old Captain Prince's negress slave Monnelia, not even a girl with a voluptuous olive-skinned bottom of Arabia like Shaida. There was an attempt by her to escape from Cheluna. It was easily frustrated but in the white slavery of such places, attempts of that kind are traditionally rewarded by the placing of the master's mark upon the treasured object, so that it shall not stray again. Such precautions, already traditional when employed upon Monnelia, were the prerogative of Tania's master. A stable-groom was given instructions that the usual prints, each the size of a small coin, must be placed on the inward sloping surfaces of her nineteen-year-old buttocks, where they joined in Tania Nicoll's bottom-crack.

The groom could scarcely believe his good fortune,

knowing that he would be permitted whatever other rewards he chose to take. A few days later he entered the cellar vault where the culprit was bent forward tightly over a trestle with her thighs braced astride a little. Straps attached her in this posture and she was naked but for the short white singlet, its hem tucked up above her hips at the back. With her tomboyish thighs braced astride as she bent, the pallid cheeks of Tania Nicoll's bottom were presented in a firm full swell, just as young Hardacre had photographed her bending in her tightened jeans while she cleared up the shop after work. The groom was looking forward with considerable excitement to what he was going to do. But he did not hurry himself and made his preparations with care. He leaned over her, one arm steadying her round the waist and examined Tania's behind close enough for her to feel his breath on her pale rear cheeks.

No boyfriend nor even a medical examiner had ever studied Tania Nicoll's bottom-crack and this rear view of the flesh-folds of her sex so long and intimately. The slightly heavy pallor of Tania's bottom-cheek skin-tone turned a little sallow between those rear cheeks as she was made to show the dark-petalled body-jewel of her desperately tightened arsehole. Though the mirrored vault showed the groom her crop of clustering brown curls and the high-boned slyness of her face with its deep-set blue eyes, he never took his gaze from this close-up view of her backside.

He bottom-kissed Tania Nicoll for half an hour and tongue-flicked her between the legs, which served only to heighten her panic. Gasping and tensing against his kisses, the nineteen-year-old girl twisted her crop of curls and tried to look back at what he was doing to her. He drew away at last. Then there was a soft and not ungrateful cry from Tania as he took her between the legs from the rear.

After a pause, the sound of a jar being unscrewed was heard and the slipperiness of the vaseline smeared between her rear cheeks. A wilder cry from the girl signalled the brutally hard stretching of Tania Nicoll's arsehole on the hardened penis-muzzle of the groom. After he had finished with her in this way, there was the sharp hiss of supple bamboo cutting the air to try its flexibility.

"Fifty across your bottom, Tania Nicoll, while the disc lies in the coals. Just like a prison-farm boy of fifteen or sixteen being punished for trying to escape."

He murmured to her a moment more, advising Tania to forget her femininity for a while and to try and excite herself by imagining that she was such a prison-farm boy whose bare backside was being thrashed by a sadistic prison-farm warden, in his study with her pants down. He urged Tania to join in the pretence for half an hour that she was such a boy in such a plight and to surrender to the excitement and drama of being a bare-bottomed culprit strapped down over a sadist's study-sofa. Fifty times the air sang with the sharpness of the prison bamboo across the soft pallid cheeks of Tania Nicoll's bottom, the walls ringing like the yard of a stable to the trainer's whip. The groom's excitement quickened as Tania Nicoll kicked and screamed under the bambooing, her mouth wide and eyes brimming under her tousled crop, the swell of her wealed and fattened bottom-cheeks surging and tensing seductively. But in reality a sadistic prison-farm warden presented with Tania as a delinquent lad, bottom-upwards over his study sofa, would not stop there. Nor did the groom. It would be seemly to draw a veil over the rest of the proceedings. Yet it was hard to blame the groom for enjoying himself. Indeed, it would be illogical to do so. He had been given his instructions. Since he was ordered to punish Tania, it was better that he should enjoy doing it than perform his duty unwillingly.

As for the present master of the estate, Tania and many others have passed through his hands. Cheluna remains a place where self-regarding and self-centred young women of the modern type are brought to learn their lesson.

Like a true connoisseur and master, the possessor of Tania and so many of these other white slaves has added to his collection from time to time. At length it occupies so much of his attention that he seldom leaves the secluded and well-appointed estate where he keeps his interesting harem. Despite the generation separating him from the ordeals of Monnelia, his passion is a standing proof of the manner in which the values of mankind remain constant and resolute in the face of intellectual fashion. He smiles at the hang-dog air of guilt assumed by those men who live in fear of their womenfolk. He believes that only the most contemptible male hypocrites would pretend that they do not sometimes dream of the pleasures and excitements of being the master of Cheluna.

Part Two

THE TROPIC OF VENUS

6

The Captives of Cheluna

South of the border means many things to many people. In this case it was Cheluna and the captivity of Brigid, a red-haired nymph; the extremes of passionate arousal and sexual tyranny with Lesley, a boyishly cropped Venus in her late twenties. Though it is far from Spain, the city has all that you might expect to find in the plains below the north-west Pryenees. The wide perfumed avenidas recall Pamplona or San Sebastian. They converge upon a fine ornamental fountain with its inward-arching sprays. But Cheluna is modern as well as ancient. There are castellated apartment blocks in caramel or white stucco. The stucco is peeling a little and the ornamental battlements are roosting perches for the gulls from a sluggish tide and a humid coast. There is a concrete bull-ring that would make a true follower of the art despair.

One walks after lunch in a vast square at the end of the Avenida Carlos III, the Plaza Andalusia. There is a mournful sound to the street names of Cheluna, for so many of them mourn a lost and distant homeland. But the Plaza

Andalusia is a vista of arcading and cafés, bars and moviehouses. At the centre of its wide presidential space is a bandstand, a forest of green wooden chairs, and a white finger-monument to forgotten colonial wars. It may be that the enclave of Cheluna—a few hundred square miles only—enjoys nominal independence. However, a "nation" of such size must be dependent upon its patron for the expertise that officers a police and a civil guard.

The Captives of Cheluna, as I call them, were under sentence as surely as any delinquents brought before a court. They were those girls and young women who had inspired a vindictiveness rare in the male sex by their malice towards certain of its members. They were prisoners of that most unusual and dangerous lust, sexual vengeance. How they had been abducted from the place in which they lived and brought across an ocean I cannot tell you. It was not my business to know. I believe it was by ship and my guess is that a well-paid captain carried this cargo from time to time in a securely locked cabin and with each pair of wrists strapped behind its owner's back or handcuffed to a bunk. Once in Cheluna, the captors would have no difficulty. The Chelunese officials smile upon the fate of such young female rebels and secretly approve it. To interfere or encourage open scandal would be to risk rebellion among their own womenfolk, which no sensible man will countenance.

After a few days, the captives were transported from a secure house near the waterfront of Cheluna to a large and private estate in the foothills, some miles beyond the little provincial town of Camba Real. There were never many young women under discipline there, I daresay not more than six or eight at any one time. Some of them were girls of great beauty who had attracted the admiration of a man rich and powerful enough to have whatever he desired.

Upon this estate, when their resistance to all demands had been overcome, they were trained by their mentors to provide the pleasures of their master's choice. Most of them were young women against whose conduct such a man had a justified complaint. If he was resolute enough and his purse long enough, he might taste the rarer satisfaction of seeing these contemptuous and self-opinionated young creatures broken in like rebellious fillies. Then they were at his disposal, to serve him or be sold to those who would know how to enjoy them.

Certain negotiations preceded these dramas. It was customary for a girl to be photographed surreptitiously before she was abducted, so that the man might identify her beyond doubt. There were recent photographs of Brigid, a girl of twenty-two or twenty-three who was to be escorted from Cheluna to the estate outside Camba Real. They had been taken of her in a sunlit garden where she was working. She was a pretty girl with a fine figure. Her pale red hair came down in a sheen of gentle waves to fall forward on her lapels. It was cut in a straight fringe, parted on her forehead. Her fair-skinned face had a resolute line to the chin and a straightness of the nose. Her mouth was firm and the points of her cheek-bones gave a good width to her face.

The young redhead was dressed in a dark-blue sweater and a pleated yellow skirt that was short as a cheerleader's. Indeed, she had the look of a lithe and agile young creature. I saw from the short skirt that her legs were firm and lightly-muscled, tanned a gentle pale gold by the sun. Her figure was firmly developed and at the same time supple as a dancer's. Brigid had the look of a healthy and active girl, though marred by a certain indolence in her expression. I imagine that her leisure was swimming, riding, or tennis.

As she worked, the short yellow cheer-leader skirt left bare most of her silkily sun-kissed legs. The long red hair that framed her face was spilling charmingly forward as she stooped to her task. She did not know, of course, that anyone was watching her, let alone photographing her, as she weeded the long flower-beds. As the young redhead bent down, she showed that the white elasticated briefs of her cotton knickers had ridden up at the seat with the heat and exertion of the past hour. On one side, the proudly rounded pallor of Brigid's bottom-cheek was laid seductively bare.

The easy carelessness of her movements suggested a well-exercised girl with outdoor interests and a healthy sensual appetite. She was no pale-cheeked virgin, nor a virgin of any kind. Even at college, she would have had a boy up between her legs at full length. Brigid attracted men, as girls of her type do. She was a self-absorbed young creature who walked slowly—almost languidly—with her thighs bare under the little skirt, her red tresses clustering forward on her collar and hiding the firm set of her face as she brooded on her present situation. The camera caught her as Brigid looked up without expression from the steady eyes under the fringe of her red hair.

It was good to see the change in Brigid while she was held captive in the humid waterside city of Cheluna itself. It persuaded her that there was no point in a pretence of maiden bashfulness. The journey to Camba Real and the estate lying beyond was at night in a fine black Astra limousine with leather upholstery. I rode with the driver in the front while the girl was locked in the back, her wrists strapped together and cuffed to a steel security ring, set in the frame of the car at one side of the back seat. Next to her sat Manrique, the warden of the estate.

As the young redhead walked to the car in the closed

courtyard at Cheluna, her head was bowed and the glossy tresses of pale red hair clustered forward like a well-scolded child. Under the fringe her eyes appeared clouded with doubt and the firm mouth was turned down forlornly. The dejected casting down of her glance almost hid the self-possessed features of her fair-skinned face.

Camba Real, the first destination, was several hours away. It was a place of villas behind tall hedges of laurel or ivy, public gardens with sandy gravel paths among lawns set with magnolia, camellia, and almond trees. A French physician from Evian-les-Bains had founded the Centre Climatique de Cure. It was set among wooded hills and a rich syrupy smell of warm pine, a place of violets and yellow butterflies.

The province of Camba, alone among those of the colony, had been the scene of civil disorder and banditry from across the frontier. Several years before a state of martial law had been declared there. It had never been strictly enforced and, for that reason, had never been rescinded.

Visitors from Europe or the United States would shiver at the delicious thrill of being for a few days in a city that was surrounded by the guerrillos, who might at any moment overrun Cheluna, ransack the cool hotels, cutting the throats of the husbands and raping the wives with satyric zeal. The promise of such fiery excitements contributed much to the tourist trade of the old colonial enclave.

The truth was that the guerrillos, bandits, resistance fighters, or what you will, were none of them bad boys at heart. Indeed, they were the children of the agricultural poor who came to town to clean boots or stayed at home to harvest the maize and the rice. Not for the world would they have cut the throats of those who brought dollars and pounds sterling to their meagre trade. The bourgeoisie of the world returned home with tales of ambush and ransom, when the children of the revolution did little more than shake their begging-boxes angrily on the verges of the country road, perhaps throwing a few fire-crackers under the cars and carts of the unwilling philanthropists.

All the same, it would not do for a traveller of Manrique's standing to have his pockets emptied by these mischievous waifs. So the car that took us to Camba Real was preceded by a lorry with a dozen conscript riflemen and followed by a flat truck with two machine-gunners and their old-fashioned Lewis gun on display. The terrain would have favoured an attack. The road ran like a raised causeway through the fields of maize towards a green haze of distant hills. Such a convoy was lifted above the surrounding land like a target in a shooting gallery. But the sight of the Lewis gun and the riflemen would be quite enough to deter the childish banditti. Why should they go to such trouble when there would be easier and move valuable prizes?

We had hardly passed through the northern suburbs of Cheluna on the start of our journey when Manrique began fondling Brigid, doing it in a manner that let her know he would be busy with her all night, until we came to the foothills at dawn. The mirrors of the car showed the girl's behaviour clearly. This was intended. We were both studying Brigid to see how she would respond to enforced sexual attentions.

Manrique began with her in the usual way. Brigid had had sufficient experience with boyfriends not to be shy and was sensible enough not to resist when her wrists were pinioned anyway. Though she said little, she shook back her tumbling red hair and turned her face up to be kissed by the stranger who commanded her, taking the tongue quickly between her lips. When his hands moved gently to the front of her sweater, she eased round a little so that he might work her sweater up, undo her bra, and feel the soft erotic promise of two resilient firm-tipped young mounds resting in his palms. Brigid liked that and the nipples of her firm young tits hardened at once. She was no virgin and was used to regular fondling by a lover.

They continued in this manner until the last of Cheluna dropped away behind. There were only distant lights across water and vast tankers at anchor. Brigid was a shapely but well-built girl. It took a little effort to place her over his lap so that he could work under the pleated yellow skirt whose hem ended well above her knees. She made no objection to this, having had it done before, no doubt. He smoothed his hand up and down and round the long firm curve of her thighs in their sleek honey-gloss panty-tights. The reed-grown waterway of the Iruna irrigation canal appeared briefly below us in lamplight.

He made up to her, kissing her firm neck that was left quite bare as the tumbling ginger-red tresses fell aside. On the northern horizon, a mountainous terrain had begun. Close at hand one saw only the dark spaces of rice paddies and the wind-breaks of Aleppo cypress.

Gently he pulled her further over his lap, running a hand up the firm and glossily sheathed calves of her legs, the skin cool in the freshness of the spring night. It required an effort to move her and position her conveniently for fondling in the cramped space of the car seats. She sprawled in a rather ungainly fashion, the silky red tresses falling aslant her firm young face. Brigid was lying face-down over his knees, like a naughty little girl waiting to be spanked. But spanking was the last thing she wanted just then.

Still kissing Brigid's neck and ears, which made her squirm with natural sensitivity in such a place, he ran his hand higher. Soon it was travelling over the supple cheek-curves of Brigid's bottom, the tights sheathing the paler ovals of her arse-flesh which were bare under their translucent veil. Perhaps she would have liked her tights taken off or his hand inside them but knew better than to be too eager with a man like Manrique. For his own part, he did not need to undress her any more for his present purpose. As the last stretch of the Iruna canal sank into the darkness, the satiny coolness of Brigid's hind cheek-swell came under his hand, gently fondling her backside and thighs.

A gentle pat on her thighs, a brisker smack on their backs to coax her a little. He landed another smack on the firm resilient swell of Brigid's bottom-cheeks, their contours tantalisingly presented by the translucent nylon. He studied her fullest swell, the slightly fatter fullness low down, the rounding out and curving in together. Another nuptial pat, some fondling, a light smack or two, more fondling, another affectionate smack. She lay there, presenting her rear cheek curves to feel the light sting of such familiarity!

The lamps and white walls of a little crossroads town sailed by beyond the window. A light bottom-smack and a whispered suggestion in her ear. Brigid was now being caressed where she surely longed for it most. She let out a long fluttering sigh. The young redhead was teasing and riding a little in grateful response to the stroking fingers.

He took the hairbrush with which she had been brushing her long pale-red tresses before the journey and gave her a bottom-smack with the back of it and then another. There was a gasp and an attempt at wriggling away. But Manrique wanted to see a true maiden's blush glowing through the filmy seat of her tights.

After that she lay quiet, displaying her seat of beauty. The translucent nylon still clung smooth and flawless to Brigid's hind contours, making her round the firm cheeks of her backside most suggestively. On the curve of the nylon seat, the sleekness caught the light with a sheen like wet silk. The honey-toned gloss was transparently tight on the pale ovals of the young redhead's buttocks. This gave a slightly and seductively fuller look to the cheeks of Brigid Price's bottom. But these rear cheeks still showed a taut controlled suppleness. An agile girl of twenty-two has a firm self-assured development of her backside and hips, most appealing in this way. The smooth sleekness of the tights obliged her to appear vulgar and suggestive over his knees.

He applied another smack or two of the hairbrush, on the pretext of reprimanding her. Brigid was gasping hard and writhing to contain the sting. This tensing and squirming of her spanked buttocks was profoundly exciting to him. The surging and contorting of her rear cheeks suggested Brigid with her lustrous red tresses spilling as she toiled bottom-upwards in some labour of honeymoon passion. The cheeks of her tights, fitting transparent and skin-smooth, showed a suggestion of strawberry cream blush which the hairbrush had brought to the firm swelling globes of her backside.

The seat of the tights still stretched like translucent skin on the erotic double cheek-curve of Brigid's behind. There was a slow and energetic swelling of her bottom-cheeks tensing and slackening in a languorous rhythm with Manrique's fingers fondling and fiddling with the folds of sexual flesh between her legs. Her taut thighs whispered together in the sleek mesh. Glossy and suggestive, the tights shaped the cheeks of her behind in that fuller swelling exercise. The tensing and rounding of Brigid's pearly-firm arse-orbs grew more lewd as she squirmed and panted. It was as if she rode an invisible bicycle hard up a steep hill. Her admirer was intrigued by this swelling and writhing, the ecstatic tightening, the lewd tremors and vulgar rounding of the cheeks of Brigid's bottom! As the miles passed the young redhead lay face-down over his lap masturbating quite openly by squeezing her thighs upon her sex and writhing her bottom, in a manner that showed she had had plenty of practice.

From time to time she would let out a long shuddering breath and lie limp. Brigid had wet the crotch of her tights with sexual lubrication long before Manrique slipped his fingers there and began to rouse her all over again. He gave her no rest during the night's journey. As soon as she had finished, he started her off again. Sometimes he spanked the softly-rounded cheeks of Brigid Price's bottom hard with the back of her hairbrush. Though she cried out a little at this, it was noticeable that after such spankings her orgasm was more tumultuous when it came.

As the sky above the mountains showed the first pallor of morning, she was truly exhausted, lying quite limply over his lap, her tights soaked by her efforts. Manrique stroked her face, coaxing her to full wakefulness. His fingers slipped between the rear of her thighs. He tickled and teased the sensitive sexual flesh, knowing that in a moment more Brigid would not be able to resist driving herself to another release. At last it came. She breathed more quickly through her open mouth, turning her head to one side a little. The ginger-red tresses slid away, revealing the firm young face with eyes closed and lips lightly parted.

The road to the estate in the foothills began at the centre of the little town of Camba Real, by an old imperial hotel with stone-columned pergolas, and a row of little art deco shops, a café terrace under trellised vines, and the Ciné Mirador. Behind its walls hung with purple bougainvillea and scented by lemon trees, the Ciné Mirador offered matinées and midnights of movie romance, languishing and vibrant with violins, that the rest of the world had finished with years before. Camba Real was an old-fashioned society, where secret and wicked pleasures might be enjoyed that would have caused scandal elsewhere.

The car entered a long driveway between pine trees and stopped at last. Brigid wrestled against Manrique's embrace and pushed herself clear. Though a slight hectic flush betrayed her a little, she was sitting demurely on her bottom in her seat, the short pleated skirt arranged, by the time that the chauffeur opened the door of the limousine in the walled stable-yard. It was as they led her away that the moist patch on the leather where she had been sitting revealed her state of arousal.

Manrique was pitiless in making a good-looking young redhead like Brigid endure a torment of pleasure during the long hours of the night journey. Cambina Alta, as the estate was called, removed all necessity for him to conceal his feelings. A young woman who had been brought there to learn her lesson would experience amorous lewdness from her mentor that was beyond anything imagined in her previous life. But she would also endure sadism that was as conscientious and earnest as any lover's attentions.

Because the young female captives were trained and punished on behalf of men of wealth or influence, whom they had somehow injured or offended, not one of them would be permitted to return the way she had come. Remote and guarded estates or princely houses of the East with Moorish arches and marble fountains would be their destination. Each had offended by wanton disregard for her marital duties or wilful promiscuity combined with arrogant self-determination or vindictive resentment towards male admiration.

There was one young woman, who had made charges of harassment against her admirer that would have destroyed a lesser man. She was photographed secretly before her abduction while her fate was dicussed with him. As in Brigid's case, the surreptitious photographs had been taken from a parked car while she was tidying a garden. It was a convenient method of using the camera. The photographs showed her high-crowned pudding-basin crop and fringe of straight fair hair, no doubt making her more boyish for her female admirers. Yet her captors would find a challenge in the firm fair-skinned features, the dismissive blue eyes and the sulky weight of her mouth and chin. Nor would they ignore the long trim legs, taut young hips, and the firming out of her bottom-cheeks in the fulfillment of youth two or three years short of her thirtieth birthday. But still the arrogant blue eyes looked a little away from the lens and the fair-skinned facial beauty of her clear features under the parted fringe was marred by that sullen air of a spoilt and peevish little girl.

Several views showed her standing in an appealingly thoughtful mood with a small child, gazing at some object in the distance. In several other pictures she stood alone, head bowed in contemplation of a garden task to be performed. Others were suggestive views on the next day when she wore a trouser-suit of thin black cotton. They were taken from behind as she bent tightly to clear the flower-bed. In bending over so fully, her posture drew skin-taut the thin cotton trousers of the black suit. Her legs were tensed astride and knees braced forward as she bent in the effort of garden-labour. The camera caught every detail of this pose. The photographer chose this view to show the mature firmness of her thighs and hips, the full broad swelling of Lesley's bottom-cheeks, which had an air of regular sexual experience and well-controlled childbearing. The parting of her buttocks, the inward slopes of her bottom-crack, even her vaginal flesh were clearly shaped by the thin black cloth, drawn skin-smooth on her hips and her backside. It was an important rear-view photograph of her figure, as she straddled and bent slightly, showing herself very fully. It gave quite a firm big-cheeked swell to the cheeks of Lesley's arse, showing the bold, self-assured manner in which a young woman of twenty-seven or twenty-eight moves her backside. The boyishly plain crop of her fair hair and fringe was combined with the mature feminine rear-cheek swell of a young woman with kids of her own. The effect was to make her perversely seductive.

At Cambina Alta, this urchin-cropped married Venus was informed that she would be trained to whatever degree of obedience was required by the man who had sent her there. She would be punished for arrogant promiscuity, her resentful assertion of her own rights to choose who might make love to her and in what way, her contempt for natural obligations. She would be seduced by cunning and passionate lewdness, then chastised with a sadism that she she would learn to dread all the more for its amorous enthusiasm.

She was called to account one evening as the warm breeze stirred the thick-planted firs on the lower mountain slope. They had stripped naked the firm pale maturity of her body, then costumed her in black restraining straps round each ankle and each wrist, round her waist and round the mid-point of each thigh. There was also a leather collar round her neck. It was not necessary to fasten her down yet but they pinioned her wrists in front of her. She was to lie waiting on a divan and they secured her to its frame by a light steel chain from her leather anklet.

There had been resistance and outrage, demands for them to stop and then a pretence of sulky indifference. But the contempt in her blue eyes was matched by the forlorn look of an overgrown waif with pudding-basin cut and fringe. Those who left her on the divan smiled at one another. Lesley had not yet had a taste of the punishment she would get later that night. She would be different after that. Young women of her kind always were, however disdainful beforehand. An emancipated and self-opinionated young woman of twenty-five or thirty needed only an hour of the training-lash across her bare bottom to be like a tearful little girl making up to her teacher again after a spanking!

It was just after eleven o'clock. A few minutes later, Manrique stretched out on the divan behind her as she lay on her side. But he was lying further down so that his face was level with her hips, the full-moon pallor of Lesley's bottom-cheeks and the rear opening of her legs, no more than twelve inches from her. The area of his interest lay between the black strap across the rear of her waist and the straps round the middle of each thigh. He could scent the faint tang of feminine arousal and knew that she had been fondling herself when she thought she was alone. He allowed Lesley to keep her folded hands pressed between her thighs under the pretext of shielding herself there. By this subterfuge, she might continue to fondle her sex with furtive pressing and touching. Manrique was no barbarian, knowing that a woman of her age, so used to coming on the stiffness of husband or lover, or on the fingers of another bored young lesbian, would want to finish her self-indulgence.

His kisses, beginning in the warm blue-veined hollows at the backs of her knees, travelled up until he was nuzzling cool smoothness on the rear of her long taut thighs close to their tops. The kisses grew more general. Though she pretended indifference to him, his lips browsed over her thighs and bare back, her breasts and shoulders. Between her legs he tasted the mineral tang of her arousal high on the inner surfaces of her thighs. Nor did he hesitate to nuzzle the proud pale cheeks of Lesley's backside, which had once squirmed humidly on honeymoon sheets and contorted urgingly in the spreadeagled pangs of labour.

Her sex in its excited state came next. He had made her curve forward from the waist and draw one leg up. Now he was taking her roused cunt in his hand like a fledgling bird, and was kissing its moist lips and slit deliciously with a skill that must have driven her frantic. The movement of the clock showed that she had endured more than ten minutes of such exquisite torment and that Manrique had brought her to a shuddering climax by such light pouting lip-touches and tongue-tickles.

The cool sleek moon-cheeks of Lesley's bottom were being kissed again. Her face was lowered as if in dismay and only her long parted fringe was visible. Like a randy bumble-bee he pouted over the cheeks of her proud young backside. His lips moulded a teasing kiss to Lesley Hollingsworth's arsehole. Her instinctive tensing at this caused him to draw away a little and view the area, smiling to himself. His fingers stroked her up and down her rear crack. He fiddled with the tight crinkling of the flesh petals of her anus, where even a mature young woman who has ridden the penis regularly and had a baby or two still shows herself so very small and tight. His lips touched the warm inward slope of one of her bottom-cheeks where the skin-tone turned from white to yellowed ivory. He settled down to give her a good long kissing there and then on the other slope of her arse-cleavage. The mirror showed him the sulky downturned line of her wilful mouth and the self-pity in her blue eyes.

He made a long study of this full close-up view of her

backside and pouted his lips lightly to the young woman's tight rear hole. There was a tension in the line of her bare flank that showed Lesley would have closed the way to him, had he not kept her rear cheeks firmly pressed apart. The clock-hands indicated that his kisses teased the young woman's tight and flinching rear hole for ten minutes more. It was a perverse and mocking tribute, not paid to her even during honeymoon passion or the courtship of her lovers.

Manrique ordered her to lie quite still, kissing and finger-stroking her bottom-crack. He was studying it very closely and intently. At twenty-seven or twenty-eight years old, Lesley Hollingsworth's arsehole was the anus of a young woman who had taken her pants down for regular sex in bed and outside it. She was no eager or nervous beginner but casual and practical in making love. Lesley took her knickers down with a male or female lover as indifferently as if she had been on her own in the toilet about to sit on the pedestal or in the shower. Manrique studied the rear hole of this young woman who had paraded a swollen belly and had given an infant or two to the world. Though it was still virgin-tight, her experience of the penis and of child-bearing naturally made Lesley's arsehole seem more sexy and lascivious to him than if she had been a self-conscious and fearful youngster of fourteen like Eleanor Hurst. His fingers were touching and fiddling with it, the tension in Lesley's buttocks showing how hard and in vain she still tried to deny him access. He ordered her to lie quite still, kissing and finger-stroking Lesley's bottom-crack. He was studying it very closely and intently.

"Lie forward a little more from your waist, Lesley. I want a bigger and fuller view of your backside."

She shifted reluctantly, obeying him. He brushed the rear of her legs and the peep of her cunt with light kisses.

Lesley was tense, her head bowed away from him as if to hide her face, her breath exhaled in self-pitying sighs. He kissed her cunt, testing it with pouting lips. He kissed the sleek pallor of Lesley's bottom-cheeks. They were drawn conveniently hard apart by her posture as he kissed Lesley between them. Her knees jammed hard together as he applied a teasingly suggestive kiss to Lesley's arsehole. There was nothing from which he would shrink with this wanton boyishly-cropped Venus-wife. He kissed each cheek of her bottom in turn, then the backs of her thighs . . . then Lesley Hollingsworth's arsehole . . . bottom-kissing over each rear cheek again . . . her arsehole . . . the peep of her cunt . . . Lesley's arsehole . . . her cunt . . . the backs of her thighs . . . the small of her back . . . her bare shoulders . . . her breasts. . . . more kissing of Lesley's bare bottom-cheeks . . .

They led her into the other room half an hour after midnight. There was soft wrestling and gasping, then a murmur of approval as the last of the straps was tightened. Someone remarked that Lesley lying bottom-upwards over the padded arm of the leather chair looked a mature pearly-skinned young Amazon, well-ridden by the male and, consequently, able to endure her punishment. Naked but for the black leather straps, the swell of her pale backside was raised and broadened by the padded chair-arm. She knelt on the chair-seat, lying forward on her belly over the padded scroll with her arms down at full stretch and each wrist strapped to a foot of the chair on that side.

The Moselle wine bottle with its long tapering neck had been drained. The man who had sent Lesley to Cheluna had drawn a line round the bottle-neck, three or four inches from the top where it was scarcely possible for a man's forefinger and thumb to encircle it. That was the precise extent of his vengeance. There was the scrape of metal on glass as the vaseline jar was opened. Lesley twisted her high-crowned boyish crop, shaking her parted fringe clear as she tried to see what was happening. There was a whisper of vaseline smeared on the tight entrance between her rear cheeks. Her thighs and buttocks tensed and she cried out in alarm. She turned the plain high-crowned crop of her fair hair, the sulky mouth and the arrogant look in her blue eyes now a study in dismay. Jason put the jar down and gave Lesley a sharp bottom-smack, hard enough to make her catch her breath. He laughed at her astonishment and gave her another rear-cheek smack. Someone else called her a snooty young bitch and there was another hard smack on one cheek of her backside and then on the other. Gomez said,

"Very well. Smack the young bitch's arse for her first."

Each man came forward. Some were content to give six or eight hard measured smacks on the bare cheek-pallor of the young woman's bottom. Others gave twenty or thirty. By the time the arse-smacking had finished, there was such a mournful wailing from Lesley as she lay over the chair-arm. It was just like the study of a strict teacher where a sulky little girl of ten or twelve lies over the sofa after having the punishment-strap with her knickers down.

"Never had a bedroom spanking, Lesley?" Jason asked with a smile. "Not even on your most passionate night with a new lover?"

There was an indistinct wail of denial from the young wanton. Jason perched on the front of the chair-seat with Lesley still strapped over its arm. He circled her waist with his left arm. The cool hard tip of the Moselle bottle touched tight vaselined flesh. Her first wild protest was prudently diminished by packed cotton web. A second muted outburst provoked a sharp smack on a feminine swell of bare rear-cheek flesh.

Five minutes later, her pale thighs were straining desperately hard against the wide black strap that pinioned them. Her behind was still so tight that no more then an inch of the intruder had entered. But the tension in the firm swell of her moon-pale buttocks showed her desperation. After ten minutes, the attempt to make her pay her penalty in this way was interrupted while they curbed her resistance. Jason cut the air with a hard swish of the bamboo to test its flexibility. The panic in Lesley's face was an exciting contrast to her former indifference, which had shown in those photographs of the plain pudding-basin crop and fringe of her straight fair hair framing a firm self-possessed face, the dismissive arrogance in her eyes, the sulkiness of her mouth and chin.

"Thirty-six this time, Lesley," he said calmly. "Fifty, if I have to do it again."

The air sang with the impacts of bamboo on her bare rounded rear cheeks, the strokes sharp as a horse-trainer's whip. Then the cane rattled on the table as Jason replaced it. He perched on the chair again and smiled at the smartingly-raised imprints of bamboo across the bare swelling cheek-pallor of Lesley Hollingsworth's bottom, which was tensing and squirming at the lingering anguish of the weals. He circled her waist again. The bottle knocked the table as he reached for it. He adjusted it implacably to its task.

He brought pressure to bear once or twice before he overcame the natural difficulty. The onlookers heard Lesley Hollingsworth fart at the forced entry of the intruder, perhaps unable to check herself as the ravisher stretched her so hard, perhaps because she tried to open herself and shorten the ordeal. But soon her keen-edged mewing rose in a wild uneven arpeggio. She strove to force her shrillness through cotton web. The assault was closely contested and prolonged. The outburst faded. The chair creaked as the pale gloss of Lesley's nude weight lay suddenly limp and bottom-upwards across it, while the plain crop of her fair hair drooped. Jason held the intruder firmly in place.

A pause and a pungent air of ammonia salts. Plaintive mewing on one side, amusement and rear-cheek smacks from the other. Jason gasped with the power of his exertions. Just after one o'clock in the morning the bare-bottomed scene over the chair-arm showed the high-crowned boy-cut of fair hair turned frantically and a frightened urgency in the aloof blue eyes. The fluorescent light caught a sheen of vaselined flesh between her rear cheeks. The line round the bottle-neck was lost to sight in the implacable perilously hard stretching of Lesley Hollingsworth's arsehole. The onlookers gazed at the raised bamboo weals across her bottom-cheeks and the tyrannical impaler between them. Jason's hand moved rhythmically, aiding the device to make love to Lesley in this way. The next half hour was one of desperation, amusement, and high drama.

Later on, Jason stroked the side of the young woman's face as her mouth formed a forlorn and howling oval while her eyes brimmed over under the long parted fringe of her fair-haired crop. The truth was that the injury to her feminine dignity and her fright at how far they might go proved worse than any slight damage to Lesley's rear anatomy. Jason spoke quietly to her, making her lie there over the chair-arm as she listened. He reminded her that the man whom she had tried to destroy by public accusations of his crimes against her sex was entitled to choose the penalties that she must endure. The punishment she had just suffered and the means of enforcing it had been specified by him to the last detail. He assured Lesley that this was not to be her only experience of it.

But even in this regime, the young women spent more

time making love than enduring the sentence passed upon them. There was a fine round show-bed with silk-covers in a master-bedroom. It served as an arena upon which girls made love together for their own pleasure and the amusement of those who watched. Their partners were chosen for them and the lesbian love-making, so far as possible, was enforced.

The girls appeared, as Lesley had done over the chair-arm, naked but for the series of black straps. They were made to lie on their bellies, head to tail, and were attached to one another by a simple but ingenious device. As they lay top-to-toe, heads level with one another's hips, a short strap from the front of each girl's waist-belt was drawn down her belly and back between her legs to the front of the leather collar worn by her companion. The result was that each girl's view was filled at a range of nine or ten inches by the bare bottom, the backs of the upper thighs and a rear view between them of the other girl's sex. Each slept with her head pillowed on the bare arse-cheeks of her companion but could not turn away from the view presented to her.

Mature young wenches like Mandy Worth or Jackie Green were partnered in this way, as were beginners like Eleanor Hurst with sexually experienced young women like Jenny Woodward. When Lesley's turn came, they found her a nymph of sixteen with long slim-thighed elegant legs, gracefully oval bottom-cheeks, and a fine fair skin. Judith's light brown hair was worn in a sweep from her high crown to her shoulders, framing a face of pale oval beauty with demure features and wide-set eyes. There was a certain resistance but presently the attachments were complete and the pair lay there on their bellies, each at kissing and fondling distance from the rear approach to woman's most secret and sensitive parts.

It was expected that Lesley must take the initiative with a girl a dozen years her junior. The hand of one of the female attendants therefore fondled the young woman's sex to encourage her.

"She's a young beauty, isn't she, Lesley? . . . A little shy but a real young lady! . . . Let's stroke and tickle your own sex for a while, Lesley, to get you in the mood . . . Is that nice, Lesley? . . . Look at Judith's slim graceful young thighs, Lesley. . . . Kiss the backs of them for a moment, near the top, where she's so sensitive . . . And kiss the inner surfaces of her thighs, Lesley. . . . I'm sure you'd like to, wouldn't you, if you were on your own with her? . . . Those warm flesh-folds of her sex, Lesley . . . Stroke them for her . . . Ah, you're beginning to get a little wet and slippery, aren't you, Lesley? . . . Do you like to see those bare nymph-cheeks of Judith's bottom curving out at you? . . . Can you feel what you're doing all over my fingers, Lesley? . . . That's better . . . Kiss Judith's legs again, between them this time . . . Reach up and fondle her nipples, Lesley . . . Are they hard with excitement now? . . ."

Soon it was unnecessary for the other woman to continue as Lesley began to seduce the graceful long-haired Venus of sixteen. There were protests and sobs from Judith at first, then sighs and fluttering breaths. Presently she bestowed her first uncertain caresses and kisses on the legs and backside of the young woman who was fiddling and playing with her so expertly. Judith's natural feminine instinct told her what she must do to Lesley. Each saw the other's thighs squirming and backside writhing with languid excitement. They slithered and sweltered with sexual exertion in the humid night. It was dawn before they lay exhausted on their bellies and fell into profound sleep until noon, each with her head pillowed on the other's bottom-cheeks, the silk cover of the bed dark with the sweat of their sexual labours.

It was not intended that a permanent romance should develop between two girls. That was to be discouraged. On each occasion of this kind, it was Manrique or one of the others who chose the partner for the girl who was to appear before him. Romance might lead to conspiracy. Apart from that, the ingenious method of attaching the two girls ensured that they saw little of one another beyond the immediate rear view from the back of the waist to the back of the knees. To Judith, Lesley was never more than a firm full-cheeked bottom, a pair of well-exercised thighs and an easily roused sex. To Lesley, a nymph like Eleanor was a pair of graceful young thighs and quite a ladylike bottom whose feminine shape was still in bud rather than blossom. There was hesitation but not refusal when the seduction of a beginner was required. Lesley was assured that any rebellion would have a double consequence. She would hear Eleanor's screams as well as her own ringing back from the stone walls of the vault, where the smacks of the whip across bare female bottom-cheeks were sharp enough to stun the ears of the onlookers.

It was part of Lesley's conditioning that they made her perform vulgarities she would have disdained and bridled at when still free to choose. To curb her pretentious self-importance was quite as necessary as to carry out upon her the discipline that had been agreed with her master. One morning with Pabi the Asian girl she was made to lie on her belly over a washroom stool, while Pabi took down Lesley's briefs. Then she must open her legs while a porcelain rim pressed between the firm pallor of her thighs. After chiding and warning by Jason, as well as a tickling of the little fountain-hole by Pabi, they heard the liquid whispering of her much-needed release.

They put the chamber-pot aside and kept her lying bottom-upwards over the trestle, legs closed. As Pabi masturbated her, Lesley squirmed on the fingers of the dark-skinned girl. Presently, a glass pencil-probe was dipped in the liquid-soap of the hand-basin. Jason slid it into Lesley's backside. For a moment he worked it in and out. Then he withdrew it with a sound of soapy suction and an urgent tightening of Lesley's anus. The porcelain rim was touched to the rear of her thighs high up. Lesley gasped and shuddered at the artful running tickles of Pabi's fingers on her sexual flesh.

"Don't keep us waiting, Lesley!" Jason said, patting her bottom sharply and significantly. Nor could she after such unladylike needs provoked by the soapy probe. Yet even as she did as he commanded, Pabi's fingers trilled and tickled between her legs. The pot was put where Lesley saw cause for a blush, had not Pabi brought this sulky pale-skinned wanton above all sense of shame or decency in the high air of sexual bliss. Pabi's free hand gathered the tissue and restored a questionable decency to Lesley's rear prospect.

The high-crowned basin-crop of Lesley's straight fair hair was turned aside, showing her lips parted for breath as she laboured with eyes closed in a dream of bliss. She was working herself hard on the Asian girl's fingers. In the moist heat of that climate, a sheen of sweat gave a pearly gloss to the full moon pallor of her rear-cheek swell, a fuller and seductively fatter look to the cheeks of Lesley Hollingsworth's bottom, as she ran with perspiration in the enclosed arse-heat between them. Pabi tipped a little of the liquid soap on to the sweltering and erotically squirming rear cheeks. Then with a delightfully lewd improvisation, Pabi reached to the chamber pot and took the discarded paper sheets that lay on top, uncovering the object of

Lesley's dismay. With the discarded sheets, she wiped over the pale sweat gloss of Lesley's bottom-cheeks and between them, then wiped over the rear cheeks again to leave this wanton young woman looking like a rude little girl.

There was no resistance, Lesley loving her masturbation by the skillful fingers of the Asian girl with such intensity that she would endure any rudeness rather than lose the climax of pleasure upon which all her thoughts were fixed. Jason studied the vulgar and suggestive appearance, the squirming and swelling cheeks of Lesley Hollingsworth's bottom as she toiled to a climax on Pabi's fingers. He walked to the cupboard and chose a supple bamboo. A visitor that afternoon was shown the young woman. Having seen the dark swollen weals across Lesley Hollingsworth's bottom-cheeks, he was surprised to hear that they were not the result of the boyishly-cropped young woman having had a proper prison whipping in the Almeida gaol of Cheluna itself.

On the following day, it was Brigid's turn over the trestle, her ginger-red tresses tumbling as she rode and writhed on Pabi's fingers. By that afternoon the welts of a whiplash showed across the gracefully-rounded cheeks of Brigid Price's bottom for the first time in her life. In tribute to his visitor, Manrique had invited the governor of the Almeida to exercise his skill.

Sun flooded the mountain firs in richer light that late afternoon. The black Astra limousine with leather interior carried the governor down the road to Camba Real and on through the night to Cheluna. The car that had brought Brigid left without her. The young redhead had put on her sexiest act for Manrique, as she lay over his lap on the night-drive, hoping to win his favour. But, like the other girls, her drive to Cambina Alta was a one-way journey.

7
Port Xantra: A Modern Adventure

My adventure, though recent enough, began some years ago in a dockland city of the more civilised and old-fashioned kind. It ended in a place I shall not call by its true name, a decaying imperial outpost similar to those refuges that men of wealth found after the overthrow of the Confederacy a century before. I did not become the possessor of a harem nor even of a single slave-girl. Yet what follows is the story of a modern odalisque, as I call her.

Since I first saw her at work in the fashion window, I have always thought of Miss Jolly as my Odalisque, though it would be hard to say precisely which blood ran predominantly in her veins. Was it perhaps a mixture of southern French and a dash of Greek or Egyptian? Could there be a little heat of Celtic temper and even a look of a shop-girl Cleopatra? Studying her at her shopwork, she seemed to match certain types of Asian or even Caribbean beauty.

The truth is that Miss Jolly was probably an appealing warm-skinned mixture of all these things. I knew her only by that name and would not have known even that, had it not been for a note addressed to her that I saw her open. I read the writing on the envelope as she did so. She was the type of hot-blooded little wriggler produced by the mingling population of any port or dockland. Young tarts of her kind emerge like timid mice in the mornings from the shabby terrace houses of the ports or the back-to-back streets that run from riverside to distance grange and grassy levels. They bustle to work in the shops and offices, then return at night to sit before the mirror of their cheaply-furnished bedrooms. There they paint their eyelids and their lips a second time, ready for the night to come.

Once, while she was busy at her work, dressing a wax mannequin, I heard two men talk as they passed the display window. One of them nodded towards Miss Jolly and said, "Little Miss Randy-Pants." The other man laughed. But that was perhaps the best description of all.

I had first seen her some time before, and on several occasions as I passed the store where she was arranging a display of fashions. I even made a note in my diary that there was a new girl, "a randy-looking girl," who worked there. I first studied Miss Jolly properly late on a Saturday afternoon in the autumn of '65—I see from my diary that it was 30 October—just when it was getting dark. She was then employed in setting out an autumn collection in the window of a shop that sold the latest modes. She displayed them to the passing world with the aid of another girl who was much fairer skinned and dark haired. I suppose the one who caught my attention was not more than about sixteen at the time. I knew her then—and still do—as Miss Jolly. I cannot tell if it was her name from birth. A young wriggler of her sort working close to such stylish and beautiful fashions soon fancies that she has an entitlement to a stage-title. But as Miss Jolly she always appeared.

I had not gone looking for her on the occasion when I inspected her closely for the first time. I noticed her entirely by accident. On that October Saturday, late in the afternoon, I was walking through the city streets with time to spare. It was getting dark and in another hour the shops would close. I paused to admire a display of the autumn modes behind the plate glass, not seeing at first that the girl and her companion were working there within a few feet of me. Then I looked up and noticed her.

If I am to describe her to you, you must begin by imagining a girl who is not more than average height with a neat trim figure that promises hot-blooded and knowing lasciviousness. Her satiny skin had the rich gold or tawny shade that one associates with Greece, or Egypt, or Provence, even a hint of the faintest duskiness of India or the Caribbean. If she combined a little of each in her blood, that is common in a little bitch who is born from the promiscuous copulations of a dockland city.

Her face consisted of a long sloping brow, a sharp young nose, a prim mouth and a demurely receding chin. She looked like a slave-maiden of the Nile or a sun-kissed Grecian girl. Her dark hair when I first saw her was in an elegant coiffure. It was back-combed in the '60s style and worn in a shape like a bee-hive on the top of her head, so that one was able to enjoy the delicate whorls of her ears with their little pearl ear-studs at the lobes of the slim elegance of Miss Jolly's golden-skinned neck. By the time my adventure with her took place several years later, the young tart had adopted the plainer and more proletairian style of a short crop of upward-brushed curls, hardly touching her collar at the back and just coming over her brow at the front.

Each time that I passed her in the street during those years, I paused and watched her inquiringly. I think she was self-conscious at being closely inspected for she would walk with a bustling little swagger, her chin tucked down primly and the tight-lidded ellipse of her almond eyes lowered to avoid the smiling gaze of a fancier who admired her in this manner. Miss Jolly's swagger was her habitual gait, caused I think by her legs being not quite as long as her figure warranted and by the erotic energy of her hips and backside.

She had the dark almond eyes of Eurasia, giving her the look of a cunning and eager little she-cat, in heat for the male. But this was misleading, for she would turn a cold and prim disdain on most of those who stopped to watch her at her work.

What interested me first was the way in which she dressed and painted to make the best of her charms. The eye-lashes were carefully darkened and the rather heavy lids painted with a little white cosmetic, for Miss Jolly made-up quite flagrantly even at seventeen or eighteen. She wore a thin woollen singlet fitting close on her slim straight back and her narrow waist, showing her breasts to be trim and firm as the rest of her. Best of all, for such a girl, she disdained long skirts, whose trailing hems would cause havoc among the carefully laid out display. Instead she had clad the lower part of her figure in snug-fitting blue jeans.

When I first saw her, I was more interested in the girl than in the display to which she was attending. It was past five o'clock on that October afternoon. She and her companion had finished their work and were engaged in brushing the felt carpet on which it stood. This was done by each girl in turn sitting on her heels and working the little handbrush hard in tight circles to raise the nap. From time to time, as they laboured with such energy, it was necessary to stretch forward and go on all fours.

How ordinary this will seem to anyone who has not watched Miss Jolly at her toils and not become totally infatuated with her! Let me explain.

I stood there and watched as she sat on her heels with her face bowed to her work, scouring the felt with hard little circling motions. I smiled at the way she jutted her haunches back and naturally I stood where I might get the best view. Presently, in order to reach further, she went on all fours and offered a sight that almost took my breath away.

Sometimes there is randiness in the very shape of a girl's body, however prim its owner may think herself, and so it was with her. As I stood behind her I saw that her slim thighs branched quite widely upwards from the knees. Her hips were lithe and neat enough but I must add that her bottom-cheeks are the most perfectly rounded I have ever seen. They are not large nor fat but deliciously and smoothly rounded. The sharper upward and outward branching of her legs also caused her buttocks to be deeply and suggestively parted in her present posture. Miss Jolly's bottom-crack is more widely and deeply revealed in this innocent posture than I have ever seen in a girl of her age. She seems to be opening herself at the rear for an admirer or a ravisher who will take her by that route.

The slope of her warm-skinned brow and sharp young nose was lowered in concentration and in the energy of her work. But the perfectly rounded globes of Miss Jolly's bottom in the tight and smooth denim of her pants would surely have held any man's gaze. I had no intention whatever of entering upon a great romance with the girl. A randy young piece of Miss Jolly's kind will do for an hour's amusement but she is not of the type to whom one vows a life-long attachment. Yet it was pleasant and amusing to see the way she tucked the small of her back downwards and provoked the onlooker by a fuller and more lewdly opened spread of her bum-cheeks.

My guess was that she had been born almost precisely at mid-century, had left school only a few months and that this was her first job. Perhaps she was too young to think of the sight she presented—or how mankind might react to it! I will only say that she glanced up and saw how I was standing over her, not six feet away beyond the glass, and that I was taking a survey of the rear view she presented. I believe she also saw the stirring of manhood under the tight pants of my suit. It was the bold movement of tightly-clad and stiffening penis that caught Miss Jolly's attention at once. Even if she had been innocent before, the effect of this on her was immediate.

If you would know her, you must understand that all her primness and evasion, her demure and enigmatic manner is a mere bluff. Back-street beauties of her kind are well-versed in the shape and functions of the penis by thirteen or fourteen. Turning to the dark-haired girl who was with her, Miss Jolly bared her teeth in some devilish private giggling, glancing back once or twice at the front of my pants. But the soft pale brunette was visibly apprehensive at the thought that she had stiffened a male tool by presenting herself in such a posture.

What of it? All this might have been nothing. What could possibly come of this encounter? But I watched them finish their work, kneeling and brushing in turn. Miss Jolly did so first and then her softer companion with pale skin and dark hair took over. At last they stood together, heads close in murmured conversation, glancing at me uncertainly from time to time. They seemed to agree upon a plan of some kind. With her back to me, Miss Jolly bent over with her hands on her knees, looking round to see if I would admire this view of her backside with as much enthusiasm. Indeed I did. At the same time, I made out the lips of the fair-skinned and dark-haired girl, who said quickly, "He's watching you again." Then they called an older woman to witness that they had an admirer.

Now this incident was in itself so trivial that I should not have dreamt of preserving it, had it not been for the sequel. I suppose Miss Jolly was sixteen or so when I first watched her brushing the display carpet behind the glass. Over the next year or two I saw her in passing, employed in a grander establishment. Occasionally I idled there and studied her, feeling a desire to possess her which had no very rational basis. As a rule I observed her when she was not looking and when the camera might record a picture or two. The lynx-eyed beauty of her face with its sharp young nose and dark gold tan might have been that of a prude. She was dismissive and even disdainful. Miss Jolly knew beyond question that I privately admired her. When I passed her in the street, however, as she went to buy a meat-pie at lunchtime or on some other errand, she would still deliberately lower her gaze and stare at the pavement until she had hurried by me. Sometimes I would see her walking with one of the other girls, Miss Jolly moving with a tight lascivious little bottom-swagger that is her natural gait.

I got to know the windows in which she appeared and discovered that the beginning or end of the week was the best time to observe her. I found myself in the city on occasions when I could not deny that I had travelled in merely to enjoy watching the little bitch. I would pass and pause. Then I could walk on, only to retrace my steps a few minutes later, caressing the lithe seductive grace of Miss Jolly's arse and hips with my eyes. Sometimes I would stand just outside her view, as if waiting for someone near the shop entrance. As she turned to stoop or brushed on all fours, I would take a long view of her. With her head bowed as she worked the stiff brush on the felt, her waist hollowed down and her succulently rounded bottom-cheeks suggestively and deeply separated, Miss Jolly was worth studying. Occasionally while I was making a purchase in the store, I caught an exchange between her and one of the other women. On the first occasion I heard her ask, "What's the time, then," in a fluting and lilting voice. The woman behind the nearest counter told her and added teasingly in the same lilting tone, "Do you want to go home, Car'?" To my other store of information about her, I was now able to add the sound of Miss Jolly's voice.

But how did I sense that beneath her apparent indifference to my gaze, Miss Jolly was a randy little wriggler? I think it was only her figure and the way she presented it. One had but to watch, as I did, the manner in which the girl went forward on all fours to brush. Under the tight seat of denim pants, the cheeks of Carol Jolly's bottom were trim and yet sensuously rounded. The manner in which they separated so deeply, like the way her thighs were always a little apart, gave the young working-class houri a look of lewd invitation—of which, I think, she was entirely innocent. But her body showed how easily her randiness might be roused.

Of many snapshots taken impromptu, some will be inartistic and some will succeed. I look at one as I write. The randy young piece is working on all fours behind the glass with her rear to the street. The patch-pocket jeans show the label "Ritzy" in silver thread on the rear of the waist. The jeans are drawn skin tight on the perfectly rounded young cheeks of her spread bottom in this posture and on her trimly seductive thighs. Beautifully rounded, her buttocks are also deeply separated in this pose and the stout central seam of the jeans-seat pulled hard between them. While she worked like this, setting out the perfumes and powders, I cannot imagine there was a man who passed and did not want to do many things to her as she presented her rear view to him on all fours.

Another lucky photograph shows me Miss Jolly waiting in the lamplight for the bus near Frederick Street, wearing a smart black winter coat that allowed one to glimpse her trimly rounded calves and ankles and carrying a neat white valise. At that time she was seventeen or eighteen and still wore her dark hair most elegantly on top of her head, back-combed into a bee-hive shape. It was just the style that a little tart of the '60s would copy to make herself look smarter and more expensive. Standing back from the lamplight, I could not resist discovering where she might live. It was a simple matter to wait until she had boarded and then follow discretely. We rumbled over the river bridge and into the meaner streets with their rows of little houses. I saw plaques on the left naming York Street and then Grosvenor Street as she got up to alight. She walked down opposite this, a long road past cramped houses and little shops. Then she turned into a doorway beside a betting office as I observed her from the shadows. But I soon rebuked myself, as I imagine you doing while you read. It was surely absurd, this surveillance of a girl whom I was never likely to meet and who belonged to a class of little tarts that one does not introduce to one's friends.

Was it curiosity or fascination that she inspired? I could not tell you. Because it was spread out over some time, my interest was less intense than it sounds. For the most part I observed and noted. How little I knew of her, it seemed. At first she might have been Miss Jolly or Miss Jones for all I knew. It was only seeing an envelope with her name on it that had enlightened me. I had not often heard her voice, the words a little accented and drawn out, so that she seemed to say "Y-a-as," for "Yes," and "No-o-o," for "No."

Precise dates elude me during those few years, though I spent a few pleasant moments at each opportunity of watching her kneeling or bending, admiring the tight-lidded and lynx-eyed enigma of her young face, as well her randy thighs and delectable bottom. At times she was unaware of this and at others she must have known that I was standing over her, separated only by the thin glass. A young tart like Miss Jolly was probably well-used to such rough admiration from passers-by and I suppose she had ceased to respond to it. In my case, I found it amusing for her to realize that she had presented herself for my sardonic inspection of her arse and thighs without even knowing it.

I recall trivial changes in her appearance during these few years. Somewhen she abandoned her elegant coiffure that she had at seventeen or eighteen. Now Miss Jolly assumed that shorter and rounded bell-shaped cut of sleek dark hair which was cut just above her collar. Later still she progressed to a shorter crop of lightly curled brown hair, brushed up in the utilitarian manner of a working-girl. I followed the progress of her looks and the development of her figure with great intensity. I could picture at will her face with its high and rather pointed cheekbones narrowing to a neat chin. In winter her warm skin-tone was apt to yellow a little, restored to seductive gold by her May holiday.

Very often, I would merely pause in passing to watch her briefly as she sat on her heels with her impudent little rump thrust back while she tricked out some display or other. Sometimes I met the tight-lidded slant of Miss Jolly's dark eyes, which caused her to turn away quickly. Was it disdain or did she want to hide her confusion at accidentally meeting the glance of a man whose interest in her she recognized? I cannot imagine that Miss Jolly ever doubted the kind of interest I felt in her! The manner of my looking at her when our eyes met left no room for misunderstanding on that point!

Sometimes I would spend a pleasant few minutes studying her before she was aware of it. On a winter afternoon with the lights bright behind the glass, the little tart was brushing on all fours, backing towards the opening of the display. The sharp young nose and weaker chin of her warm-skinned profile was bowed with the energy of her work. The jeans were tightened hard over the cheeks of Miss Jolly's bottom in this posture, showing how trimly rounded and deeply separated the two halves of her arse were. I naturally admired the strain and squirming of this view as she backed towards me.

I made no attempt to move, finding a certain amusement when Miss Jolly realised suddenly that I was standing over her just a few inches beyond the glass. I inclined my head so that she should see I was watching her young backside as she worked on hands and knees. She turned her head, her eyes were level with the front of my pants. I drew the cloth a little tighter to show Miss Jolly the penis shape full and hard as a result of admiring her. She sometimes tried to pretend that she had noticed nothing but I caught her quick and uncertain glances in my direction as she finished her work. She had no doubt of my interest in that part of her. On our very first encounter, you recall, she guessed as much and had bent over while the other girl observed me to see if I would step closer and admire Carol Jolly's bottom-cheeks presented to the window-glass in this way. I had done so to ensure that the little tart learnt early the way in which she appealed to a man. I believe something in my gaze must have alarmed her, for she never deliberately did this again!

Winter evenings, when it was dark by five and the lights were on, offered the best opportunity for observing her after work as she went home. Sometimes Miss Jolly would pause on her way to the bus, gazing with envy into a jeweller's window. She liked to wear rings and bracelets, though they were of the cheaper kind. Several times I went after her as she left her work. Once on the pavement of the shabby street that was her destination, she was greeted by another young woman from the house and a small fair-haired child that ran into the arms of the young odalisque. I had a misgiving that Miss Jolly might have dropped a cub on the sly, but I do not think this was so. The child looked much more as if it had popped out of the fairer girl who stood there.

It is often more difficult to possess oneself of a little scrubber like Miss Jolly than of a more elegant beauty of better class. Had it been possible to do so, I think I should not have hesitated. But the feelings she inspired were of passion rather than affection. I felt no vindictiveness towards her but I would not have saved her from any ordeal of the sexual kind, for she seemed a perfect object of such tyranny.

I thought a good deal about her after those occassions when I saw her, perhaps several times a week. Often I would put my feelings about her to the test and always with the same result. Suppose she had been abducted to some country where the trade of torment is inflicted in the vaults of the governor's palace. Picture Miss Jolly strapped naked and bottom-upwards over the trestle, the whips and implements of the torturer prepared. Had I been given the choice of rescuing her or being permitted a peephole to watch her night-long ordeal, I would have chosen the peephole without hesitation.

It was not a matter of heartlessness. My obsession with

her tight-lidded almond-eyed beauty and her golden-skinned figure had begun when she was fifteen or sixteen and was so great that it did not even shrink from contemplating a night for Miss Jolly in the torture-chamber. Obsession is more than affection. To be sure I wanted to see the trim young odalisque randy and energetic in passion, mewing and swooning with ecstasy. But I also wanted to hear Miss Jolly screaming, the tight-lidded almond eyes brimming over with tears, from the leather whip or the glowing implement. Of course, I did not wish that this should happen to her frequently but I knew my knowledge of her could not be complete until I had seen and heard her under such desperate circumstances. A man's obsession with such a girl is a matter of extremes. Have no fear, I did not see Miss Jolly tortured at that time. I mention the paradox only to explain what follows.

It was some time later when I was to sail on business to the southern hemisphere aboard the steamer *Alcazar*. At that time certain "backward" cultures still showed themselves robust in defending the institution of slavery. Girls whose ancestry was as much Italian or Spanish were still slaves by accidents of birth or abduction. A girl of Miss Jolly's appearance would be deemed a slave in those places if her master claimed her. What he did with her on a private estate or a grand house was a matter in which the authorities did not interfere.

I had not thought of all this before I set out on the voyage. My intention was to enjoy the amenities of a fine vessel, the luxury and elegance that accompanied her journeys. The oak-panelled saloon, the white linen and silver upon the tables, would have done credit to many a stately mansion of the Tidewater country or the Delta in the old days. I had taken one of the first-class cabins on the upper deck, for I was proposing to make an important purchase of a concession in the sugar trade.

The girl was far from my thoughts as, in the thicker light of evening, the liner weighed anchor and slipped out down the tidal channel from the city docks towards the open sea. It was that time of year when the blossom had fallen and the long summer had begun. I was cooling myself in the first draughts of the ocean when I noticed a man who was a stranger to me.

He was standing by the ship's rail with a golden-skinned girl of somewhat oriental beauty. I can only say that Mr Aziz, as he liked to be known, seemed the last man on earth to attract a young and fiery creature. He was middle-aged and rather gross, perspiring somewhat in his pale linen suit. The girl stood rather strangely beside him. She wore a coat loose upon her shoulders, her arms not in its sleeves. Presently she moved, her hands being clasped at her loins, and the coat slipped from her. It fell to the deck, from which her companion hastily picked it up and looked about him. Then, as she turned her face full towards me, I saw the flash of feline temper in her almond eyes. I knew at once the long slope of brow and sharp young nose, the weaker mouth and chin. She was Miss Jolly. Had I known the destiny awaiting her and the part I was to play, I should scarcely have contained my excitement.

If I had been less attracted by the girl, I might have been apprehensive. What was to stop Miss Jolly pointing me out and complaining of me as the man who used to "pester" or ogle her? Nothing at all. I do not say that much would have come from her complaint but it might, at the least, have been embarrassing. As it was I felt only eagerness and excitement at the thought that I was going to be in such proximity to Miss Jolly and that I should learn so much about her. For many hours of the voyage she would be in the next cabin to me. What might I not hear and even see, if I kept up a constant surveillance? You see the extent of my obsession with one who was no more than a shopgirl from the back streets!

I would deceive you if I pretended that I was outraged at the thought of her in captivity abroad. Miss Jolly was a randy young bitch and, though I might long to have her under my own sexual dominion, the next best thing was to know that there was a man who would take her to the Orient and sell her into sexual bondage there. All this was the stuff of dream and fantasy, of course. Yet, if you had seen Miss Jolly walking with the tight lascivious little swagger of her hips in close-fitting jeans, or sitting on her heels in the shop-window and jutting out her sexily-rounded arse at the passers-by, or staring with the knowing enigmatic look of her tight-lidded almond eyes, you would understand how easily she inspired such dreams. I remember the day when she was standing in the shop window. She drew her hand up over one cheek of her bottom, the painted nails red against the blue denim as if to advertise herself. She was just touching herself there and yet it was a most sexually suggestive movement. Respectable women of the bourgeoisie, seeing her as a rival for their own menfolk, might have wanted to give her a whipping for that self-display!

So please do not mistake me for Sir Galahad to the rescue. Mr Aziz was the owner of the girl. Miss Jolly the young window-dresser, shop-girl, counter-jumper, was his to dispose of as he wished. He had nothing to fear from me. Nor indeed would the master of the ship interfere in his affairs. The girl was being carried abroad with the consent of the vessel's owners. In the list of passengers, next to Mr Aziz's name, there appeared that of "Miss C. Jolly."

All the same, I could not help noticing that Mr Aziz was not at dinner that evening in the panelled saloon. He seldom appeared in the public rooms of the ship, nor did the stalwart duenna. As for Miss Jolly herself, she might as well not have existed for all that the other passengers saw of her. On every night but one, Mr Aziz chose to dine alone in his cabin, attended by "Miss C. Jolly," the lynx-eyed young odalisque.

The cabins on the upper deck, above the wash of the prow and forward of the smoke from the funnel, were arranged in a row. Outside was the deck-walk with the rail beyond it. It was only when I returned after dinner that I realised what Mr Aziz's domestic arrangements were. It was possible, you see, for a family to hire two or three cabins in a row. Private doors communicated between them. But there were bolts either side of these doors so that each cabin might be used in complete privacy when strangers travelled in them. Such a door could be opened only by the consent of the parties on both sides. If I listened hard, it was just possible to hear Miss Jolly in the washroom but our acquaintance was limited to that!

Mr Aziz had taken two cabins. That immediately next to mine was occupied by Miss Jolly herself and the redoubtable duenna who kept watch over such a randy young piece. Mr Aziz occupied the further stateroom. In my fantasy, he or his duenna possessed the key which would permit Miss Jolly a stroll on the deck. Such permission was rarely given and never when she might try to escape them or call out to anyone. I indulged myself in these fantasies about the girl, whom I rarely saw during the voyage. I could not know that I was on the verge of a far more dramatic reality. After so many years of watching and spying on her, I thought of nothing but Miss Jolly. Matters continued much like this until the sweltering morning of our arrival off Port Xantra.

I had no intention of remaining at Port Xantra, a hot and

fly-infested city. It had been built as a pastiche of Marseille or Algiers but with more of the tropics than of France about it. The *Alcazar* docked in the inner harbour where the cobbled quays stank of hot oil and fish-meal. Our stay was three days, after which we were to sail again for Reinamare. As usual, several quarantine and customs officials came on board, the sweat drenching their light grey uniforms even before the sun was at its height. They were polite and even deferential to me. But Mr Aziz was soon in trouble and, to this day, I cannot tell you precisely what became of him. The door between our two cabins was left open, for it is the custom that passengers go ashore here to the Hôtel Terminus in the Grand Boulevard du Sud while the ship is thoroughly cleaned and disinfected.

Having seen my luggage on to the tender, I went back to the empty cabin and found the communicating doors open. Of Mr Aziz and his duenna there was no sign in the adjoining suite. Miss Jolly, in her white singlet and jeans faced two swarthy gendarmes of the Port Xantra civil guard. One had three bars on his blue epaulette and the other only two. The girl was standing with her back to the porthole, watching the two men blankly from the tight-lidded slant of her almond eyes.

"Your companions are detained for being in possession of contraband," the senior officer said in his accented English. "You also know something of this, I think?"

I cannot tell you whether it was true that Aziz and his woman had attempted to smuggle contraband into Port Xantra or whether these officers had so arranged matters as to have Miss Jolly as their suspect. She shook her head. The one who had asked the question nodded to his assistant. This younger man squeezed past him in the hot cabin, seized Miss Jolly's arm and twisted it up behind her back. This forced her to bend over with her back to them, the thin and faded denim of the "Ritzy" jeans stretched tight on her buttocks and legs. The younger man worked his way round and clamped her head between his knees to keep her bending.

"Is this your first time at Port Xantra?"

"Ya-a-a-s!" wailed Miss Jolly, indistinctly and with her head still trapped. I stood there, astonished and intrigued by the sight through the doorway. Neither officer of the civil guard seemed to notice my presence.

"I do not believe you," said the captain to the bending girl. "The passport of your friend Mr Aziz is false. You know that?"

"No-o-o-o!"

"Do you have prohibited goods concealed? Hashish, perhaps? Diamonds?"

"No-o-o!"

"We shall see." The captain who stood behind her undid the press-studs at the waist of her jeans. He drew them down, laying bare the paler coppery smoothness of Miss Jolly's bottom and thighs. Then he made her stand astride with a light kick at her feet.

"I do not believe you. Feet apart. Spread yourself for me. I must search and then we shall see what is to be found."

His fingers were rough between her legs. I am sure now of what I suspected then. His accusations were deliberately fabricated in order to search her in this way. He rummaged the girl's loins and backside in a rough and prolonged manner to goad her into retaliation. If he could make her resist him, he had a pretext and witnesses for doing as he pleased with her.

So he stroked and fiddled, caressed and pinched, fondled her intimately and contemptuously until even Miss Jolly could bear it no more. She knew that he was not searching her at all but enjoying himself at her expense. Whether it was that he hurt her sharply or whether the tears that scalded her were anger and humiliation, I cannot tell you. But as he was doing it, Miss Jolly kicked back at him wildly. She did him little damage but the man—Captain Shavez, as his companion now called him—smiled to himself and wiped his fingers on a sheet of tissue.

"If you smuggle a little hashish, we make an agreement with you. An afternoon on the mattress in the cell and then we let you go. But you attack an officer of the civil guard. For that you will go to prison. Pull up your jeans and dress yourself. You will come with us."

I still stood beyond the open door, an accidental witness of this little drama. Captain Shavez turned and saw me there.

"You," he said, in the tone of a man who exercises power over people of all ranks, "you are a witness of the attack. You will also come with us."

I might have sworn that I saw nothing. But looking at Captain Shavez, I thought my best hope of being on the *Alcazar* when she sailed next day was to do as he said. I felt unease at what might happen to me but a growing excitement to see what would be done to Miss Jolly. Captain Shavez reassured me.

"It is only for a written statement of evidence. You will be back here before the ship sails. For the girl it is different. She will be in a cell of the civil guard until the investigation and report are completed."

I had little choice. We went down the gangway and across the waterfront railroad tracks of the port. Beyond the tall dock gates there were bars with tin signs advertising whisky and driftwood stalls selling strips of lottery tickets. There were thin dogs and naked children. A seagull hovered in the hot sky with the patience of a vulture. The

Boulevard du Sud with its palms and cafés was cracked and unpainted, stretching inland to the scrub-dotted hillside where the city ended among isolated shacks painted pink and white. In half an hour my routine voyage had become a drama of menace and uncertainty—but the prospect of Miss Jolly's punishment also caused me a little excitement. The randy almond-eyed young teaser was now at the mercy of a barbaric law. That law in Port Xantra was Captain Shavez, as in Charleston it had once been Colonel Ashbee or Colonel Randolph.

Off the decayed avenue that the French engineers had built lay a street of bars and stores, the bare concrete strip of a gasoline station. Here, in a green shuttered house and with the shield of the civil guard over its door stood the headquarters of law and justice in Port Xantra. The two officers led the girl up the sour reeking stairs of pitted marble to the landing at the top. All the doors were double and grandly carved. Once it had been the residence of a French or Spanish merchant, or perhaps a German consul. Since the revolution, such people had left Port Xantra. The city lived nowadays for politics and police interrogations. We entered a suite at the first level. With its barrel-vaulted ceiling and window pillars, Captain Shavez's office was like an opera-house foyer. A room opened off it, a stifling little cell with a prison bed and a chair, a barred window overlooking the yard.

I waited in the office while the two men marched Miss Jolly into this sweat-box with its steel door.

"Lie down," said the captain sharply. "On the mattress. Give me your hands."

There was the click of a thin steel cuff round one of Miss Jolly's slim wrists and then a metallic bump as the other cuff was locked round the steel frame of the bunk.

"You must wait here for a few hours," Shavez said to

her. "A few hours while the papers for your detention are signed. After that the charges will be brought against you. And you will not forget that I have a personal score to settle with you. When I come back, I shall bring a whip with me. I shall use it to avenge myself and also to begin your interrogation. In the case of a girl of your sort, it is best to begin with a whipping before the questions are asked. You will answer more readily. And after the cheeks of your bottom have been skinned, you will learn to do as you are told. So we shall begin with that at seven o'clock. Have you ever wondered what it would be like to be tortured? At seven this evening, you will know what it is like."

Miss Jolly seemed so stunned or terrified by their promises that she could do no more than gasp and squirm. Presently Captain Shavez came out into the spacious office with its balcony windows and venetian blinds.

"You must stay here also," he said. "I regret that—but it is necessary. When I return there will be a statement for you to sign. After that, I will have you driven to the Hotel Terminus."

"And the girl?"

He shrugged.

"Her case will be investigated. She will be with us a few months while that is done. Perhaps many months. After that, it is a matter for her judges. But she has also attacked an officer of the Civil Guard. Tonight she will be whipped for that. In your country you would not do such things. Here it is different. It is also a method we use to discourage her resistance to the charges that will be brought."

The other man came out of the cell, pulling the door to after him.

"You can make yourself comfortable," Shavez said to me. "But we must lock you in until we return."

They went out together and I heard the key in the double-lock. It was out of the question for me to leave in any case. I should be looked for everywhere in Port Xantra, without a hope of boarding the *Alcazar* undetected.

The heat of noon seemed to have stunned the fetid littoral city into silence. The footsteps of a single passer-by sounded in the street below. I looked from the window across the tin roofs of the shacks and the long avenue of cracked stucco that had tried to ape the elegance of metropolitan France. Heat shimmered from the tarmac and the polished rails on which the rusty wagons stood idle by the Gare Maritime. Beyond the city limits there was nothing but a reddish coastal plain with dark scrub and the sharp limestone escarpments of the inland mountains seen through a smoke-blue haze.

Because I write as a stranger to those who read these pages, I need hide nothing of my thoughts or acts in the next few hours. I imagined the girl lying handcuffed to the bunk on the sweat-stained mattress in the steel and concrete oven of the little cell. The thought that Miss Jolly was going to be whipped by Captain Shavez before the investigation began excited me. He believed that the randy little piece was less likely to lie or prevaricate if she had tasted the lash first. I did not suppose that I should ever have any more to do with her. But my heart beat a little faster with excitement at the hope that he might whip her while I was still there to watch her getting it. That excitement will tell you all that you need to know about my romantic feelings for Miss Jolly.

I went across to the steel door, thinking that there must be some chink or peephole which enabled the prisoner to be observed. I put a hand on the cooler surface of mat steel and, to my surprise, felt it move. Captain Shavez's assistant had pulled it to, but not hard enough for the lock to engage fully. I could, of course, have pushed it shut. But I did not. It even crossed my mind that it had been left like this deliberately, so that I could divert myself with Miss Jolly in the hours while she waited to be whipped. I cannot describe the intensity of the thrill I felt at this thought.

Very slowly, I pushed the door open and stood there.

To avoid lying on the stained mattress, she had wriggled far enough to kneel on the cement floor. Her wrist was still cuffed to the far side of the metal frame. The best she could do was to kneel over the bunk with hips raised.

I could not help smiling at the irony of it. With the jeans skin-tight on her slim branching thighs and deliciously round young bottom-cheeks, Miss Jolly appeared just as I had admired her when she was brushing or arranging the display of goods. As she turned the deep gold of her face and looked back at me now over her shoulder, the tight-lidded almond eyes, the sharp young nose and tall brow, showed her recognition of me as the man who had so often watched and admired her.

I stood over her, speaking to her familiarly as Annie, Lizzie, Viv, and the other girls used to do.

"Are you feeling scared, Car'? I'm sure you must be. They mean to torture you with the whip. You may just as well have a good time for the next few hours, rather than squirm and fret. Shall we try to take your mind off what's going to happen to you, Car'?"

She made no objection, though she could hardly bring herself to accept eagerly the passion of a voyeur! As she knelt over the bunk, I undid her at the waist and worked her jeans down to her knees with Miss Jolly's underpants inside them.

I helped her back on to the mattress, one of her wrists still being cuffed to the metal frame of the bunk. I had no key to unlock it and in any case it suited my purpose to have her fastened like this. Miss Jolly was lying on the bed, naked but for her short white singlet and a coquettish little pair of black shoes with high heels. She lay on her belly and the slim coppery tan of her thighs was parted a little as if to admit the rousing and caressing of my fingers. I pulled the hem of her singlet higher yet, so that her trimly rounded golden-tanned hips were properly bare. She was curved forward from the waist and the smoothly swelling rounds of Carol Jolly's bottom had a paler coppery tan compared with the darker brown of her trim-waisted back.

Standing over her, slipping my fingers through the rear of her thighs, I began to manualise her gently. I stroked and tickled, squeezed a little and teased out the folds of sensitive flesh until I felt her shiver with grateful excitement. The young tart was looking back over her shoulder again as I roused her, her firm golden-tanned thighs squeezing and squirming on my fingers.

I lay over her and roused her like this for half an hour or more, while she lay with her head turned aside on the mattress, her mouth open breathlessly and the tight-lidded slant of her almond eyes almost sightless with desire. Soon she was moist enough to assure me that I had taken her mind off the torment awaiting her. I made her turn on her back and kissed the sandy gold of her firm flat belly. Then I guided her knees wide apart and took my place.

Miss Jolly's legs clung to me, her heels on the small of my back, as I rode her loins in this manner. She was like a drowning Venus who clutches the swimmer that rescues her. In the fierce heat of the little cell we were both sweltering as we toiled to the climax and release of passion. At the same time she fastened her little teeth in my flesh with the extravagance of her lust and tried to score me with the nails of her free hand. I possessed the narrow passage of her loins, while she thrust her hips and belly up to receive it deeper, all the strength of her trim young figure pressing against me. I continued, restraining my own compromising tribute. She gave a short cry and then another, as if seizing upon a relief that almost escaped her. Her thighs tensed in a spasmodic rhythm and she relaxed gratefully.

Then I coaxed her to turn over on her belly. She knew quite well that I was going to make use of her delectable copper-tan backside as a safe receptacle into which to direct my sperm, as well as enjoying the tightness of Carol Jolly's arsehole. She was tense and rather unwilling as I turned her over but offered no true resistance. Miss Jolly's natural randiness made her a little curious to try the experiment of having her arsehole stretched by a man. She ceased pushing against me and allowed me to turn her properly on to her belly.

I made her twist her short crop of dark upward-brushed curls on the pillow so that I should be able to enjoy watching the long slope of her profile and the randiness of her tight-lidded almond eyes while I was busy behind her. I think she liked to be made to keep her face to her master in this way. Miss Jolly is one of those girls who are more excited the more extreme the demands made upon them by their lovers.

The beautifully-rounded cheeks of this shopgirl's bottom were satiny to the touch and a light coppery tan by contrast with the brown of her waist. It was delicious to fondle them while that warm rear cleavage was stretched open so lasciviously. Parting the pale gold satin of her rear cheeks, I gazed at Miss Jolly's forbidden little vortex. I think she may have been a virgin in that part but she showed no fear nor shrinking. There was a scrap of hard white soap in the little basin. I spat upon it, worked it to a slippery perfumed pulp and used it to ease her tight postern gate. There was uncertainty in her slant eyes but neither resistance nor refusal. Once again, the natural randiness of Miss Jolly is hard to exaggerate, though she was more reluctant to try this experiment than I. So the intruder touched the tight rear button and there was a moment's ordeal for her. At last I felt her give and was at once held in an exquisite tightness. She caught her breath a little with alarm. I smiled teasingly at her, knowing that she felt the swelling of the hot masculine gristle very large in the tight fit of her behind.

To feel the tightness of her was a delirious thrill. She took it quickly and responded with her natural lewdness. She thrust to impale herself more vigorously and deeply without the least apparent fear of what the consequences might be. I have known girls of all kinds whose eagerness is an object-lesson in self-indulgence. But I have never known one to equal Miss Jolly as she was in her attempts to put the fear of the whip from her mind. I tailed this almond-eyed little wriggler thoroughly, and determined to express my passion as deeply as possible.

I employed her in this way until just before Captain Shavez had promised to return. In the final minutes, Miss Jolly's fright at being whipped presently gained the upper hand. She began to shift a little with uncontrollable panic and her breathlessness betrayed fretful little sounds. I enjoyed her then more than ever. Through the barred window, which gave us a view of the yard as we lay there, Captain Shavez appeared at the far gate, a whip in his hand. I rode the randy young shopgirl's backside harder, excited at what was going to happen to her now. I whispered in her ear, drawing her attention to the return of Shavez with the whip. By this time my hand underneath her could feel the flutter of panic in her warm-skinned young belly and the cheeks of Miss Jolly's bottom must have been itching with a fearful anticipation. There was no purpose in pretence. A man's release brings the truth with it. I confessed softly in her ear all my thoughts as I had watched her at her work in the last year or two. I called her a randy young piece and a hot little wriggler. I promised that far from trying to save her, I should greatly enjoy watching Shavez whip her. And I assured her that I hoped her place of detention would be one with soundproof vaults where strapping down and muffling was the prelude to whips and more severe discipline.

Then I let out my quick constricted squirts of sperm in the depths of Carol Jolly's backside, which caused a cry of dismay as she felt it and a tensing of her coppery-smooth, sweat-lathered bottom-cheeks that came too late. I went in at a full length, so that the soapiness of the knob would stir up some very unladylike needs while she was being whipped. But I also knew that she would feel the squirting of my passion more sensitively in such an intimate place. The liquid pulsing dwindled and ceased. I did not withdraw from her at once, knowing that it would take Shavez at least five or six minutes to reach the office. The truth was that I was stiffening again, partly from natural excitement at possessing Miss Jolly in this way and partly from the tightness of her rear hole on my shaft.

"I want you again, Car', before they come to whip you. In your backside again. Quickly now! Go to it, fast as you can! Move your arse, you randy little tart! You have only yourself to blame for provoking your admirers by the way you used to display yourself!"

I went at her hard, my loins slapping against the pale copper smoothness of Miss Jolly's seductively rounded bottom-cheeks. She gave several frightened little cries as she felt the knob very deep, where the workings of her bottom made a man's presence very improper. The hours I had spent watching her at her work, the lascivious posture on all fours while she used the brush vigorously in its tight circles on the velvet nap had prepared me to enjoy the young shopgirl's bottom in this way.

I warned her that she had only herself to blame if I inconvenienced her, since she had not made a movement to assist me. I caught a backward glance of the tight-lidded slant of her dark eyes and then she pushed up with her hips, hard and rapid.

"You like it now, don't you, Car'?" I teased her breathlessly.

It took several minutes to pump up the second tribute of passion. In the end there was nothing for it but to push her down by the scruff of the neck and ride like fury, smacking her flanks and letting loose a second squirting of warm gruel in the hot young tightness of Carol Jolly's bottom.

Hastily I withdrew from her. I worked her jeans up again, zipped them up, and fastened them at the waist. Then I smiled at her knowingly as I went out, pulling the door closed after me. I heard the lock engage and knew that I had an alibi if it were required. Captain Shavez found me sitting quietly, the cell door locked beyond any power of mine to open it.

He said little before he and his assistant went into the cell, leaving the door open an inch. There was muttered conversation and orders given to the girl. Miss Jolly's voice was raised in lilting protest. I could tell that she was kneeling on the floor again and that Shavez sat on the bunk.

"Like that," Shavez said. "Is it the first time you have knelt before a man? I cannot believe it is the first time you have seen such a thing as this! Your lips, if you please. You will show your gratefulness for the lesson I am about to teach you. Make good use of your tongue. You shall have practise like this several times a day with the guards so long as you remain in detention here."

For ten minutes there was a silence, except for an occasional creaking of the bunk and a gasp from Captain Shavez. Several times, from Miss Jolly, there was a sharp involuntary sound in her throat. After one of these there was a pause.

"Begin again now," Shavez said presently. "Your tongue a little more."

It was about ten minutes later when a harsh gasp escaped him and his breath came unevenly.

"Show it me on your tongue," he said breathlessly. "Ah, a big spoonful of medicine for a naughty little girl, I see. In this place you are not permitted to reject a man's passion. The taste is one you will get used to. Swallow it down like a good little girl. It will not be the last time you have to do so. At once! Show your tongue again. Good."

Then he spoke to his assistant.

"She knows what to do. Someone must have taught her when she was still a child in the back streets! But I think that is the first time she has been made to swallow."

He came out into the office, his face a little flushed. From within the cell, the sequence of sounds was repeated. Once again, Miss Jolly had to show her tongue and then swallow her medicine like an unwilling little girl.

The drama of the whipping might have been witnessed in a hundred such cells of the world's police-states. Miss Jolly was held kneeling over the bunk, her backside on display in the skin-tight jeans. Captain Shavez, the short lash of the whip dangling from his hand, stood over her. A number of people had come into his outer office. Soon the door of the cell and the area immediately inside it was crowded by onlookers from elsewhere in the building.

The typewriters in the other rooms had stopped. The

civil guard lieutenants, and pretty dark-skinned office girls had pressed eagerly to the open doorway to watch what was happening. Captain Shavez undid the waist of the Ritzy jeans again and tugged them down, the bare coppery tan of Miss Jolly's bottom-cheeks swelling a little fuller as the restriction of the pants was eased down. The guards and the office girls edged forward a little more for a better look. Shavez worked the jeans right down to the ankles of the kneeling shopgirl, her underpants inverted inside them. Then he strapped the slim golden-skinned thighs together just above Miss Jolly's knees.

The perfectly-rounded pale gold cheeks of her young bottom shifted and tensed. She uttered a soft questioning little cry of dismay. The bunk creaked under the nude pressure of her strapped but restive hips. There was a dry squeak of leather as she strained against her straps. Her head twisted round with its rather short crop of slight upward-brushed curls, the slim bare neck and the pearl studs in her neat ears. The profile of the long sloping brow and sharp young nose was admirably shown. The watching civil guards licked their lips eagerly and there was excitement in the eyes of the pretty native girls.

Captain Shavez drew the snakeskin lash lightly across Miss Jolly's copper-toned backside. One heard a smoothing of the young window-dresser's bare belly on the mattress as she tried to squirm in fright. He raised the whip high behind his shoulder, then waited while the clock in the office ticked away ten long seconds. At last the sleek ripple of black leather caught the light as the curling whip lashed down. It landed across the bare Arabian gold cheeks of Carol Jolly's bottom with a vicious smack that made the stone walls sing. Her gasp rose to a wild cry as the pain swelled to its climax. He timed the next stroke to catch her across her backside just as the agony of the first reached its crescendo. Before she could contain the second, he whipped her hard a third time. And then Miss Jolly screamed. There was a shiver of excitement among the men and the girls in the doorway. But at Miss Jolly's scream, there was a peremptory pause in the punishment-lesson, while one of the guards found the girl's briefs, dampened them, wadded them, and used them to muffle her shrillness.

For half an hour, the satin-smooth orient-gold cheeks of Miss Jolly's bottom jumped and quivered under the sharp impacts of the whip that curled and clung to her nude rear curves. Desperately she tried to tense her bare rear cheeks, to jam her knees into the bunk as if that pressure helped her to contain the agony. The tawny cheeks of her backside flesh creased and surged in the moment of torment that followed each kiss of the skinning whip. Urgently, she twisted this way and that. But the effect was merely to receive an agonising taste of the whip across the bare flanks of her hips or across the backs of her slim gold thighs. She was far removed now from the quizzical and giggling odalisque working in the window of a fashion display. The prim young mouth was open in a wild cry and the tight-lidded almond eyes were brimming over. As the hot twilight gathered across the dusty streets and shacks of Port Xantra, the copper-toned cheeks of Carol Jolly's bottom danced to the tempo of the whip, while she heard her own screams muffled to a trapped mewing and she tasted her own tears on her lips. The young bitch's backside seemed to be performing a lascivious tango with the lash as her partner.

Captain Shavez was unsmiling, though his assistant grinned at the girl each time she looked frantically in his direction. As she turned her upward brushed curls, the tight-lidded almond eyes brimmed over and the mouth was strained to a howling oval. Some chastisers might have been moved to leniency by her whip-marked bottom. But to have the young tart in this predicament was an irresistible temptation to the captain. He paused to use a sheet of tissue to wipe sweat from between the cheeks of her young arse, for the energy of writhing had made her lather herself there a little in the sweltering cell. Twenty or thirty thin raised weals curled across the pale copper tan of Carol Jolly's bottom-cheeks. She would be superbly responsive to a further whipping. The captain prolonged the torture of the young shopgirl's bottom and thighs with his lash, making it impersonal and pitiless as a prison whipping. Here and there on the swollen plum-coloured weals a darker droplet rose and trickled down. Then, stroke after stroke, the delectable cheeks of Miss Jolly's arse were thrashed—and thrashed—and thrashed.

Seeing Miss Jolly at her work for several years had conditioned my thoughts about her, for which her own natural randiness was to blame. But now I would not have saved her from the whip, even had it been in my power. When she had been really well thrashed by Captain Shavez with his short snakeskin lash, I felt only a slight disappointment that her ordeal could not be prolonged.

Once it was over, he left her to writhe and weep on the sweat-stained mattress. The onlookers went back to their offices and the door was closed. Captain Shavez sat across the desk from me and asked a series of formal questions. Then he produced a document. Upon it were the accusations against the girl and her accomplices. I must sign those to which I was a witness. Had I witnessed an assault upon Shavez by Miss Jolly? I signed it in the affirmative. Then followed a series of others, asking me whether I could confirm that I had overheard her talk of contraband and false passports with Aziz. To agree that I had would be to hand Miss Jolly over to Shavez for a month or two of investigation, followed by judgment and sentence.

I paused as I read them through, knowing that I lacked any such evidence, apart from the assault. But I was haunted by that image of her on that first October evening, brushing up the nap of the carpet with such suggestive thrustings of her bottom at sixteen or seventeen years old. I thought of the snapshot as she worked on all fours among perfumes and silks, skin-tight jeans offering the spread cheeks of Miss Jolly's arse to the world. With a slight stiffening of manhood, I took the pen and confirmed every accusation against her. Captain Shavez smiled in anticipation of the months of interrogation that lay ahead with Miss Jolly as his prisoner. Then he arranged for me to be driven to the Hôtel Terminus, where I should be just in time for dinner.

I was delayed in Port Xantra for the best part of a week, thanks to the blowing of a boiler-pipe as the ship was getting up steam. But this enabled me to attend one of the most diverting entertainments I could have wished for. Before the *Alcazar* sailed again, her captors had found for Miss Jolly a lesbian companion, Alexis. She was quite the opposite of the little wriggler with the slim straight back and almond eyes who had given me such pleasure as I rode her and such amusement as I watched her bare tawny bottom-cheeks whipped. Alexis was a lazy-eyed fair-skinned trollop with a plain crop of light hair and a certain weight about her figure. She was the bigger of the two girls. It was several days later, just before my departure, when Shavez invited me to visit him in his quarters one evening. I accepted without demur.

I can only guess the punishment with which Miss Jolly had been threatened if she refused to take part in this display. The two girls were to perform on the spacious dinner-table round which we sat and which had been cleared of all but coffee cups and brandy glasses. They both knew what was required of them and that the only reward for virtuous resistance would be several months longer in detention before their cases were judged. One could not deny that they showed an amusing contrast. Alexis with her lank fair hair and rather stolid face had a lazy heavy-lidded glance. Her jeans tightened over a pair of sturdy hips and thighs. She undressed in a matter-of-fact way, just as if she had been alone in a bathroom or going to bed. When she was naked one saw that her body had that slight pale heaviness of a girl who is a little dull but sensual at the same time. She clambered first on to the table and stretched out on her side, while we admired the rosy tips of her breasts, the brown fleece that clustered in the shelter of her loins, and the sensual fullness of Alexis's bottom-cheeks. Examining her from the rear, it was possible to see the fading traces of a thin bruise or weal on one cheek that had been inflicted by Shavez with a whip or cane some weeks earlier.

In a moment more, our almond-eyed little odalisque was naked, too, pulling herself up and lying to face the larger fair-skinned girl. They wound their arms about each other, pulled close together, squirming naked and nuzzling long breathless kisses on one another's lips. It was not quite what Chaptain Shavez wanted but he allowed this performance to continue for several minutes with a tolerant smile.

In a charmingly awkward way, they drew close and kissed each other's lips. The bigger fair-skinned girl hugged the randy almond-eyed little wriggler but only with the awkward affection that girl-children show each other. Miss Jolly, however, kissed Alexis round her sensitive bare neck and ears so that the paler big-hipped girl shuddered with sudden excitement and anticipation, spiced by a perverse thrill at doing such things with another young woman.

Alexis did what she must. She drew back and kissed Miss Jolly repeatedly on the lips, as if she did not know what else to do. Miss Jolly ran one hand down the bigger girl's back, slid her fingers between the pallid and fatter cheeks of Alexis's bottom and came to the sensitive feminine flesh by a rear approach. But at this touch, as if stung by an electric shock, Alexis bucked her hips back to escape the caress of the randy young odalisque.

Miss Jolly drew her hand away and stroked the plain crop of Alexis's straight fair hair, kissing the tight-lids of the bigger girl's closed eyes. Alexis would permit kisses and cuddles but could not bring herself to share more than that.

I had no doubt that Miss Jolly would seduce her unwilling partner with a little encouragement. Captain Shavez interrupted them and ordered the two young sluts to change their position on the table. They must not lie as before but head-to-tail. Each girl lay on her side and presented herself to the face of the other in what I would call an upward squat. Miss Jolly guided Alexis to draw her knees up a little more. Alexis's broadened thighs and hips, as well as her bottom, were offered to Miss Jolly's kisses and caresses in a more fully spread and revealing posture. At the same time, the lascivious darker-skinned girl posed so that her femininity peeped between the rear of her slim legs while the coppery tan cheeks of Carol Jolly's bottom almost sat naked on Alexis's face. The two girlfriends made a charming study for a camera portrait.

We leant forward round the table for an hour or more and watched at close range the seduction of pale-skinned lethargy by hot-blooded randiness. The two girls had never before had amorous feelings for one another, not even of the most secret kind.

Miss Jolly's nimble fingers took Alexis's sensitive femininity, teasing and rousing it. She worked slowly but coaxingly, no doubt judging that what she had sometimes done in private to herself would cause arousal when she did it in the same way to another girl. In this she was proved right, as Alexis's hips began to stir. Miss Jolly also kissed the bare fattened pallor of the cheeks of Alexis's bottom. Alexis gasped for breath and her big pale thighs squirmed like a girl riding the most exciting love-saddle in the world.

Meanwhile, the tightly-swelling copper-tone cheeks of Miss Jolly's bottom and her spreading thighs were presented patiently and expectantly to Alexis's gaze. The fair-haired girl's lazy face with its hooded blue eyes was a charming study in hesitation. Her own enjoyment troubled her. As one watched, it was clear without any question that Alexis was receiving pleasure. At last her fingers tentatively stroked the peep of Miss Jolly's feminine flesh between the rear of the girl's thighs. Miss Jolly lifted her upper leg a little, crooking it back from the knee, to make herself more fully accessible.

Alexis closed her eyes as if to create some vision of her own while Miss Jolly caressed her. Her fingers began to fondle Miss Jolly's intimacy, although she did it rather inexpertly.

"Keep your eyes open, Alexis," said Captain Shavez sharply. "Don't try to hide your feelings from us while this randy little piece makes love to you."

The blue eyes opened again, startled at the command and a little dismayed. But Alexis looked closely at what her fingers were doing, as if fascinated by Miss Jolly's secret anatomy. Despite herself, Alexis was intrigued by the other girl's body and the effect that her caresses were having upon it. The eyes of the big fair-skinned girl grew gentle and loving as she continued to gaze at the moistening and roused feminine flesh of her warm skinned partner.

"Use your other hand as well, Alexis," said Shavez coaxingly. "Your girlfriend's bare bottom is beautifully presented to you. You needn't be shy about doing anything to her. See how sensitive she is there as well, especially just round her rude little arse-dimple."

There was no protest from the bigger girl. Alexis looked lovingly and tenderly at the deeply and suggestively parted cheeks of Miss Jolly's backside. While her other hand remained busy with more important matters, she also stroked the young almond-eyed bitch's copper-bare rear cheeks. Then, as if imagining what she would like Miss Jolly to do to her, Alexis's fingers slid gently between the tan-skin cheeks of Miss Jolly's rounded arse, feeling and stroking.

Alexis's eyes were wider now and she was drawing breath through lightly parted lips. There was excitement in her bold young face where before there had only been bashfulness. Soon there would be no more difficulty in persuading Alexis to play the part of a boy with another girl. She began to kiss the backs of Miss Jolly's pale gold thighs, starting behind the knees and working up. Miss Jolly, excited at this, touched her lips to the fair-haired girl's roused and moistened sexual flesh, kissing it lightly and then beginning to flicker her tongue upon it. Alexis shuddered and moaned but never ceased to kiss her girlfriend's thighs. Without more ado, they settled down to kiss and nuzzle and tongue-tease one another in the most intimate and sensitive places.

Both would have reached fulfillment in a few minutes more, but Shavez and his friends drew the girls' heads back and held their hands away. There were two bereft little sobs as the pleasure was interrupted. But it was interrupted only in order that it might be prolonged. By having their hands held away from one another for a moment, they lay fretful and restive, making self-pitying little sounds of frustration. When Miss Jolly and Alexis were permitted to resume, they did so in the most savage and passionate manner. Each was as eager to feast upon the other as to be feasted upon herself.

It was delightful to see Alexis, after so much reluctance, quite unable to hold back. Her fingertips played lightly and tantalisingly on the young odalisque's secret places. At the same time, Alexis kissed the cheeks of Miss Jolly's bottom which the darker-skinned girl now thrust out more fully. Alexis hesitated and then, flinging caution aside, kissed between them.

"Better than that, Alexis," murmured Shavez encouragingly. "No need to be shy. I want to see you being a rude girl with her there. Use your tongue between the randy little bitch's bottom-cheeks, Alexis. Make her scream with excitement."

Miss Jolly was manualising Alexis all this time with great skill and had brought her close to a crisis. An excruciating pang of pleasure seemed to paralyse the pallid-thighed young Amazon, as if she had been impaled upon the cruel pike of a conqueror. Then in its spasm, Alexis's tongue was stuck out, firm and urgent, its tip disappearing where Miss Jolly's bottom is better imagined than described. Alexis was shuddering with the first release of her tension. Shavez and one of the police matrons held her firmly while she was having it. When it was over, there was a danger that Alexis would burst into sobs of relief and remorse. She might lie there in dismay, cold and ashamed at what she had done. They held her so that there should be none of that. The caressing must continue so that the last spasm of her release would merge with the first tickle of her next arousal.

"Lie still, Alexis," whispered one of the uniformed women. "You'll come several more times on the table tonight."

As she did this, the middle-aged prison-matron also began to rouse Miss Jolly with quick expert fingers, bringing the tart to a gasping and shuddering conclusion. Then the policewoman smilingly ordered them to begin all over again, at once.

And so they did while we watched them. This time there was no holding back, They hurried to regain the tension of excitement from which they had just relaxed. There was no doubt of the exertion which the labour involved during the warm night. A gloss of sweat shone on the swelling pallor of Alexis's bottom and hips, the wetness slippery between her legs and rear cheeks.

This time, Miss Jolly reached her reward first. Her back arched and she flexed her legs, her mouth opened in a long soft cry and her almond eyes rolled back as if she might swoon. But she never ceased to caress her fair-haired girlfriend. When Alexis had finished as well, they lay together, touching lightly and apparently exhausted by their labours. I think they could have slept then and there, upon the table.

It was the uniformed woman whose cunning prevented that. Gently with her own hands she began to rouse the moist and sensitive flesh of each girl again, one hand attending to Alexis and the other to Miss Jolly. Despite their langour, it was not long before they stirred, squirming and sighing. The second bout of love-making had been hurried and eager, this one was slow and luxurious. The girls studied each other's loins and thighs and bottoms, fingers examining and testing rather than caressing. The slipperiness of their sweat made them look like two beautiful girl-wrestlers sleepily united after combat.

There was nothing to keep me in Port Xantra after this. What I had seen determined me that I should not interfere with the destiny proposed for Miss Jolly, nor for that matter Alexis. I returned to the ship. On my way, I paused to visit a bookshop in the heat of the main avenue. Here I bought a little reading for the rest of my voyage. I could scarcely hope that I should have a real-life diversion of the kind Miss Jolly's presence on the ship had provided. I must make do with the next best thing. I left the shop with a small parcel containing such memoirs of men and women as *Noreen: A Strapping Young Trollop*, *Elaine Cox*, and *The Captives of Cheluna*. They would provide me with instruction after dinner, as the bows of the ship cut the waters of the southern ocean. Combined with what I had witnessed in the little port, they would afford ample material for a learned monograph before I reached my destination.

I cannot say whether these events laid to rest my obsession with my randy little odalisque, or whether they merely satisfied it for a while. Time must tell. I walked down the cracked and palm-lined paving of that colonial boulevard towards the dock. One of the last shops was a saddler's. Passing it, I saw in the window a fine whip of black leather, a three-foot switch that tapered to a fine quivering point. As a mad freak, I bought it. In my cabin before the ship sailed, I wrote a farewell note of thanks to Captain Shavez. In it, I also confessed that Miss Jolly had begged me to assist some plan of hers for escaping his justice, when I saw her for the last time. I had, of course, refused her. Wrapping the note with the handsome switch, I sent it to him with my compliments.

I thought that was the end of the matter. We put to sea and were several hours out of port, cruising international waters. There was a knock at my cabin door just before dinner. It was the steward with a message received by the ship's telegraph service. Captain Shavez thanked me sincerely for my present and my advice. He hoped that I should find confirmation waiting for me at Reinamare, the

Alcazar's next port of call. So I did. His package contained a remarkable pair of photographs. One showed me the face of my randy young odalisque in a moment of shrieking frenzy. The other showed the coppery rounded cheeks of Carol Jolly's bottom in such a state that she must surely have learnt obedience and submission at last. I preserved these mementoes but was careful not to say a word to anyone that might interfere with what Captain Shavez planned for her.

Perhaps it is only in such places that the truth about mankind is revealed, where there is no need for pretence or any veil of conformity. On the voyage south to Reinamare, I read of such things. The extremes of amorousness or sadism are common in southern cultures. I read of Tania Nicoll, the nineteen-year-old shopgirl *garçonne* with her curls and high-boned slyness, who was required to lie naked across the top of her master's bed every night so that her backside provided him with a pillow. He fondled intimately and fiddled with her there at every stirring so that the girl was in a state of restless sexual arousal the whole night long. From midnight until dawn, the warm air of the room stirred with the liquid caress of feminine arousal between her pallid thighs and the whispering touch of a hundred kiss-prints on the rather ungainly swell of Tania Nicoll's bottom-cheeks and the teenage weight of her thighs. Only as the rest of the world woke did she fall into a profound sleep, her passion released and her desires calmed.

Though Tania resented her state of bondage in which these things happened, how many girls would envy her! How many brides on their honeymoon nights would have longed for a master as passionate and as insistent in loving as the one who possessed Miss Nicoll! Extreme in its demands and its goading to pleasure, the southern Tropic of Venus shocks the sensibility of cool northern blood.

One is accustomed to regard the white-slave trade as a commerce in innocent girls, kidnapped and carried south to destinations like Port Xantra or Cheluna. Yet a sensible man who reads of Cheluna is bound to conclude that the girls who were cherished or chastised there deserved something of their fate. Girls like Brigid Price had certainly behaved vindictively against a man in such a way as to remove all sympathy for them. The bold-faced insolence of Mandy Worth or Louise Neville made it hard to regret their fates.

I had reason to ponder this as the *Alcazar* left a broad wake across the fierce tropic glitter of the ocean between Port Xantra and Reinamare. Just as the Tropic of Venus produces men who have no scruple about bending a girl to their will, are there not girls who invite such attention? I do not mean soft and pliant creatures but those who act with sullen resentment towards mankind or play fast and loose.

I thought of this as I sat on deck and read a very private edition of the dark romance of Elaine Cox and her sadistic admirer. The sinister erotic melodrama was such that I thought all adolescent girls should have it put into their hands! At fifteen years old this ill-mannered youngster attracted the attention of a man who was more than a match for her, a trader in captive beauty far to the south. But surely the youngster's boldness and insolence were as much to blame for her abduction and subsequent fate as the man's susceptibility to schoolgirl tomboys. Everything about her slum-child insolence challenged and excited him.

He first saw her striding up the hill on her way home from school, shouting to the boys, defiantly tossing the lank fair hair which lay loose on her shoulders from its central parting. The broad pale oval of her face with its thin mouth and narrowed eyes was a study in snub-nosed impudence. The striped tie and white blouse of her school uniform were accompanied by a little grey pleated skirt, worn scandalously and deliberately short, leaving her sturdy adolescent thighs bare. A puff of wind on the hill wafting up the skirt at the rear, showed the full cheek-swell of Elaine Cox's fifteen-year-old bottom tightly clad in the white stretch-briefs of her school knickers. He was determined to possess this ruffianly fifth-form girl.

I looked up from my streamer-chair, as I read this, across the white-painted rail to the glittering sea. A good many teachers and disciplinarians, who were moralists rather than villains, would want to deal severely with the conduct of a youngster like Elaine. Is she not the loud insolent schoolgirl of whom there are far too many in this day and age? You see how the argument goes? Most men and quite a few women would like to see this problem pupil bent over the classroom desk and the teacher's strap used vigorously on the full tomboy pallor of Elaine Cox's fifteen-year-old bottom. Some would admit this, the rest would secretly approve.

As a well-behaved and courteous girl, would she have inspired the obsession that her follower felt for her? I think he would have paid her no attention at all. Had she been demure and obedient, as she should have been, I think he would have felt no challenge. Of course he could only respond to that challenge because he was able to arrange her abduction and to hold her as securely as any slave-girl was held on the plantations of the Mississippi or in the harems of Arabia. He followed, photographed, and spied on her. What contempt there was in her young face for this middle-aged admirer!

He also observed her when she went out in the evenings or returned from casual work in the holidays with her big sister. The photographs accompanying the tale showed her on these casual occasions in a white short-sleeved singlet and trousers of a smooth grey-blue material pulled drumskin tight over her hips and backside by a shiny black waist-belt. Elaine's fair hair had been washed and brushed for an evening out with a boyfriend of her own age, even lightly waved as it lay loose across the top of her shoulders. I have a photograph taken of her, a rear view of her walking up the hill after work dressed like this, turning her head to say something to her big sister. The smooth tightness of the blue-grey trousers emphasises the sturdy rather heavy-cheeked swell of Elaine Cox's fifteen-year-old bottom.

The Tropic of Venus is more than a geographical location. It is a system where such girls, dusky beauties like Monnelia or rebellious youngsters like Elaine, can be held against their will as the property of a master. It would be absurd to blame them for the fate they suffer. Yet why is it that some girls are ensnared and others are not? Elaine's conduct and manner was such as to draw the attention of a man who contrived her downfall. In that, at least, she is warning to all girls of her age and type.

The account of her fate attempted no sanctimonious evasion but told the stark truth. The man whose passion Elaine had roused was one of the greatest villains among the abductors of girls into white slavery. He would not rest until she was his property. Her destination was "a remote house beyond the Danube where he was free to inflict the final severities." It was, in truth, far beyond the Danube and closer to the Atlas mountains of the north African littoral. He had a secret room, to which he would escort a girl and from which he returned alone, calm and satisfied, the room empty. The girl was not seen nor spoken of again. The guilty evidence had been tumbled through a trap-door in the floor of that private room to rocks below where predators snuffled for food. The ogre of a fairy-tale was an amateur by comparison.

Elaine walked ahead of him one night to that room, unaware of the sombre fate in store for her as his assistants escorted her. The heavy stool bolted down at the centre of the floor was equipped with the usual restraints and convenient for holding her on all fours. The scandalously brief pleated skirt and the tight white briefs of Elaine Cox's knickers were cast aside. The straps were sturdy and her school uniform blouse with its striped tie was no inconvenience to her master. The servants left him alone with her and he locked the door, turning to tuck the white blouse well up above the youngster's waist so that the full tomboy pallor of Elaine Cox's bottom-cheeks as well as her hips and thighs should be properly bare.

It is easy to imagine how a man of normal lechery might have employed her. But he gave rein to his passions in a decadent retreat of the tropics and had no scruple whatever in his dealings with women. He did things to this insolent fifth-form girl that night which would have cost him his liberty if he had been brought to account under any law of the civilised world. Night long, he took her beyond endurance in every way. It was impossible that she should ever be permitted to tell tales or bring accusations of the pleasures he took with her. Indeed, he behaved as he did because he had planned the finale from the start. Long after midnight, he slipped a noose of strong black silk about Elaine Cox's throat, as the straps held her kneeling bare-bottomed over the trestle. His face calm and movements leisurely, his strong hands drew the black silk fatally tight. A few minutes sufficed from the first sinister adjustment of the looped silk to the completion of the dark deed. After that he draped Elaine over a bar lodged across the open trap, her head and feet dangling, bare bottom facing up. A band of black lace with an elegant bow, tight round one tomboy thigh, suggested the final hour of sombre excitements.

The youngster's fate was a warning to womankind—to girls of her kind, at least—that they cannot indulge themselves in ill-manners and impudence without the risk of a sinister penalty. They may talk arrogantly of the privileges due to them and the obligations owed them by mankind but their reward may be to challenge the passionate sadism of such a man as this.

But whether in the sensuality of Tania Nicoll's master or the sadism of Elaine's, there is a dark romanticism in places that lie on what I call the Tropic of Venus. Whether his passion for a girl be amorous or vindictive, the master of Cheluna or the gaoler of Port Xantra will be extreme with her. They are not citizens of the dull provincial towns of America or England. Such men live close to scenes of violence and dereliction, however rich they may be and however surrounded by immediate comfort. Cheluna and Port Xantra have seen revolution and insurrection, a landowner with throat slit dangling by his heels from a house window, his daughter taken by revolutionary justice and spread-eagled on the butcher's table for a queue of peasant soldiery to ease their desire between her thighs. The people of such turbulent places do not shudder like pale Anglo-Saxons nor demand prosecution when a temperamental young woman complains of being ravished when she did not mean to be or of having had a smack or two on her bottom.

The ways of Xantra and Cheluna scandalise the sensible north but the south is used to dramas like that of Elaine Cox. They are part of nature. Even the civilised north is ambivalent. It is outraged at the girl's fate. Yet the town where she lived had endured her shouting striding insolence and contempt for her elders and betters. Privately its folk confessed themselves "well rid of an impudent little scrubber like Elaine Cox." Others thought her appealing only as an insolent schoolgirl. But she was already accommodating the penis of a lad of her own age. By eighteen or nineteen she would have been a fattened drab with several squalling brats for the nation to feed. Captain Shavez added that each woman has a different time of greatest sexual appeal. Elaine's appeal was that of a rebellious schoolgirl. When her adolescent charms faded in a year or two, no man of taste or sense would pretend to desire her. It was sensible and logical to make her yield pleasure early, as much for Elaine's sake as for that of the men wanting to use her for their own.

I may add something which I did not know at the time but can now assure you was true. The sinister room in "the house beyond the Danube" had been used for the same sombre purpose before its sadistic master dealt with Elaine Cox. It was not spoken of in the household but it was known. The servant entering to tidy the room next day, knew that the final severities (as he quaintly called them) had been carried out there the night before on Elaine. I have heard him admit it, when returning to Port Xantra and dining with Captain Shavez a year later. By then there had been a mutiny in the remote mountain province and the man who had strangled Elaine Cox as the conclusion of his night's pleasure with her had died defending his property against the depredations of the rebels. Secrecy was no longer important to him. Indeed, he seemed to want posthumous fame for his exploits with such girls.

The servant described how he had entered the room the morning after the drama and picked up Elaine Cox's underpants and skirt, where they still lay discarded by the kneeling-stool with its judiciously fixed straps. He put the bamboo cane back in the cupboard and hung the pony-lash on its hook. The fine erect rubber penis was the very largest in the tool-box and he saw that after the direct approach it had taken Elaine's "bottom way." He rounded his lips and drew a breath of amazement. He conceded that a man who chose a rubber tool of such stoutness for the tight fit of Elaine's behind had a passion for the girl that was bound to prove her downfall. He took the pencil-shaped metal probe from the brazier coals that had almost lost their glow and returned the vaseline jar to the shelf. He saw that the bottle of smelling-salts was almost empty and replaced it with a new one. Last of all, he picked up the discarded noose of black twisted silk and smiled to himself significantly as he returned it to its drawer.

When I pressed him, he said that he did not approve of such frolics but it was none of his business. I did not believe him. He confessed that as he tidied that room, he noticed several photographs of the youngster discarded in a basket. They were copies of those taken as she walked from school in short skirt and uniform blouse, showing the impudence in her young face, her contempt for the admiration of the middle-aged man with his camera. And there was one of her in those smooth-strained tightly-belted trousers, walking up the hill with her sister, the tomboy cheeks of Elaine Cox's bottom showing a full robust shape. The servant slipped the twenty or thirty discarded photographs under his coat. He also picked up the white cotton web of Elaine's stretch-briefs and tucked them in his pocket. The master had nothing to fear from this loyal fellow, who wanted only to brood over the photographs and the discarded pair of Elaine Cox's schoolgirl knickers as his mind reconstructed the events of that previous night. Before he did so, he reached up to the top of the cupboard and took down a little recorder, casually concealed behind the wooden pediment. He had hidden it there to chronicle the hours of the night's drama.

Such cavalier voyeurism is a sardonic amusement in

places like Port Xantra. The servant smiled and withdrew to his room for the hours of the siesta, locking the door to avoid interruption. He laid out the twenty or thirty photographs of Elaine Cox where he could see them. He unfolded the little wad of white cotton web in his hand and laid Elaine Cox's knickers on his pillow where he could also study them, as he stretched out on his bed and listened to the tape. The tape played. Its sounds were those of perverse passions that took the bottom way eagerly with a schoolgirl tomboy. There was the drama of a punishment-room in a strict reformatory. The singing sharpness of a whip suggested an unbroken filly under correction in a training-yard. The harsh pant of bellows was followed by the stirring of coals and the rattle of metal against brazier bars. Defiance, insolence, amazement, and wild shrillness mingled in Elaine's response. The servant lay back and sighed as he listened, studying the photographs of her and the suggestive schoolgirl underpants. Presently he unbuttoned and relieved his stiffness a little.

I tell you only what I know. For those who are easily dismayed, the casual manner of the servant will inspire more horror and outrage than the most randy of perverse sexual acts.

There is a hardiness about the attitude of some men to some girls that is only seen or accepted in those southern climes. Yet it is not all girls who inspire it, perhaps only a few. Elaine Cox was one and Miss Jolly was another, the fifth-form schoolgirl and the randy young odalisque who had little in common otherwise. Brigid and Tania in the dramas of Cheluna were strangers in taste and character. Had it not been for the accident of Port Xantra, I should probably never have got closer to my hot little wriggler than the adoration at a distance I had already shown her. The match-making Captain Shavez offered would have been unthinkable elsewhere. Such is the state of mind that makes certain enclaves of the southern world the Tropic of Venus. Perhaps such places cannot be judged without putting oneself in the situation of their men of influence and seeing the opportunities and temptations confronting them.

In our own society, men of strong and self-confident tastes find the robust attitudes of Xantra or Cheluna appealing. Only one in a hundred will risk the wrath of his own self-centred and indulged womenfolk by saying so. Put yourself for a moment in the place of Captain Shavez or Manrique or Colonel Ashbee. You sit in your chair after dinner, attended by a selection of captives. Monnelia approaches with your glass, clad only in her little white panties and bra, elegant dusky thighs moving demurely, eyes lowered, the upward-brushed warrior-maiden hair ribboned at the nape of her neck. She places the glass on your table and turns. Bending for the cigars, the graceful African-tan cheeks of Monnelia's bottom swell with a sheen like chocolate-dark satin.

To one side, Tania leans over a table, chin in hand, reading a paper. But unlike her posture in the shop, she is naked from waist to heels. The short crop of light curls clustering on her forehead a little softens the pert young face with its high-boned cheeks and rather sly deep-set blue eyes. As she leans over like this, bare tomboy thighs a little out of line and hips slightly twisted, tapping time with one foot, there is a careless and rather sluttish look to the pallid cheeks of Tania Nicoll's bottom.

Brigid is curled naked in a chair, the tumbling red tresses partly obscuring her firm pretty face as she reads. One hand is pressed between her lithe well-exercised thighs, as if for comfort, though the fingers move suspiciously from time to time.

On your valet's instruction, the mature beauty of the harem is naked but for a short white singlet, ending in a tight belt round her waist, and lying on her belly over a chair-arm. You will not mistake the turning of the high-crowned boy-crop of her short fair hair, the sulkiness of the mouth and chin, the aloof disdain in the blue eyes under the parted fringe. You may have your way with Lesley but she is defying you to try it. The means for that may be suggested by the firm fair-skinned length of her bare thighs, the full-moon pallor of Lesley's bottom-cheeks, and the bamboo lying on the table.

The valet's note reminds you respectfully that you must do your duty in bed with at least one of the four female slaves. You may command love-making between two of the others. He notes that Lesley has earned your chastisement for her wilful defiance during the day and that you may care to discipline any others whom you judge to merit it. He has left the cane and a tailed strap on the sofa-table.

What would your decision and judgment be? Master of your fate, you may back away in horror from the scene and take flight that same evening for cooler and more rational northern climes. There you may hang your head and humble yourself by making public confession of male iniquity to the female sex. Or you may consider the four possibilities before you. You may go as far as you like with any of them and in whichever direction your preference lies.

Monnelia. Is your taste inclined to the controlled but savage beauty of a tribal princess? She walks so gracefully and demurely towards you, eyes lowered and bare dusky thighs brushing invitingly. She turns and bends for the cigar-box, the elegant negress-skinned ovals of Monnelia's bottom-cheeks suggestively offered. Will you order her to kneel before you, open-mouthed and agile tongued, or command her to lie across your bed. Will you test the punishment-cane across the swarthy African gloss of Monnelia's backside?

What of nineteen-year-old Tania, prim and sly? With her cropped clustering curls and the slight teenage weight of her hips and buttocks, her appeal is that of rogueish and tomboyish prettiness. Will she be the one to part her thighs on your bed tonight? Will the slight pallid fatness of Tania's bottom-cheeks show the prints of bamboo or strap tomorrow? Or will it be Brigid? Perhaps she is the prettiest of them and scarcely able to stop furtive self-arousal, even in your presence and that of the other girls. At least one of them is to be your bed-companion and at least one, according to your duty, is to be spanked. Brigid would make an appealing subject in either case and perhaps for both.

The final candidate shakes her long parted fringe into place and looks back at you with cool indifference in her clear features and blue eyes, verging on contempt, while she lies on her belly over the chair-arm, as commanded by the valet. From the rear of the waist-strap securing her singlet-hem, the bare full-moon pallor of Lesley's bottom-cheeks swells in the firm self-assured maturity of an experienced young woman in her late twenties. There is a peep of light-haired sex in the rear parting of her long well-kept thighs. She is well-experienced between her legs but Lesley's rear entrance will be virgin-tight, if your inclination lies that way. Indeed, if you make her submit in this way, she is perhaps better able to adapt to it than Tania at nineteen. In any case, you will not win your way without a little conquest, though the means are at your disposal. Moreover, the valet requests you to train her a little with the bamboo or the strap. Knowing that she is to get this afterwards, perhaps she will behave more seductively in bed to try and soften you.

To be sure there are many more possibilities offered by your four companions. As you study them, your eyes move from Monnelia's dusky loins and calm beauty to Brigid's silky red tresses and graceful young thighs, from Tania's rather tomboyish hips and thighs to the firm pearly-skinned maturity of Lesley's bottom. You have the means to allot pleasure or punishment to each in the hours that follow, even to command pleasure and punishment for the same girl. Brigid may be irresistible but you can hardly ignore Tania. Lesley must not escape your attention but the dusky-bottomed Monnelia bending for the cigar-box is not to be overlooked.

A sensible man might surrender to prudence and make his escape from such a place—so at least he would assure those good ladies who preach the evils of women's submission to male dominion. But when a room is secret as this and there is not the least risk of tales being told, few men would wish to be sensible. Perhaps you will perform a judgment of Paris, making the four female captives stand in a line before you, or turn their backs to you and bend over in a row. It may take half an hour to make your choice. Command your four beauties to parade up and down before you, if that will assist you. Let them lie over the sofa together for your consideration. Line them up and consider Monnelia's tribal-princess beauty, Lesley's boy-cropped emancipation, Tania's curls and slyness, Brigid's red-tressed prettiness. Turn the row and bend them. Lesley's bottom firm-cheeked but fullest from regular sex and the child-bearing that follows. Monnelia's swarthy but graceful backside tensing uneasily. Tania's behind with the pallid weight of a nineteen-year-old tomboy. Brigid's rear cheeks finely-rounded and lithe as a dancer's.

Pose them, consider them, command them. Perhaps it will assist your choice to turn back the pages and consider each in the toils of pleasure or the ordeals of punishment. The choice remains yours. Shall it be Brigid's silky red hair spilling over your thighs as she kneels? Monnelia's knees drawn up and thighs parted as she lies on her back across your bed? Tania bending over most reluctantly for a bare-bottomed strap-spanking long overdue? Brigid and Monnelia making love while Tania writhes and mews under the strap? Lesley lying bottom-upwards over your bed, peevishly protesting on behalf of her backside's feminine dignity as you unbutton? Lesley unable to take her eyes off the bamboo cane that must print a smarting willow-pattern on her rear cheeks after your own weapon has discharged deeply between them? Make the choice at leisure. There are means to employ all four female captives until dawn. The natural ambition of men who dream of the Tropic of Venus is to enjoy the power and privilege of such a choice—and the delightful consequences that come from it.

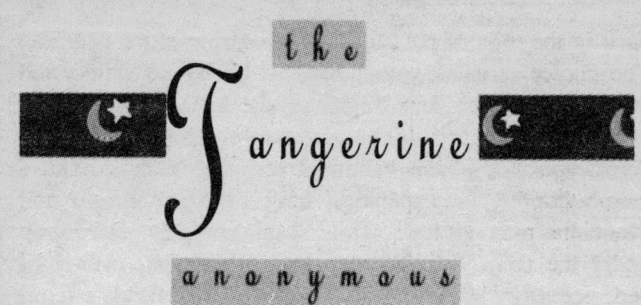

the Tangerine

anonymous

A dreamlike tale of erotic pursuits by lovely young English ladies at the turn of the century. Whether aboard the yacht, The Tangerine or in their own abodes, all traits lead them to pleasure and amusement.

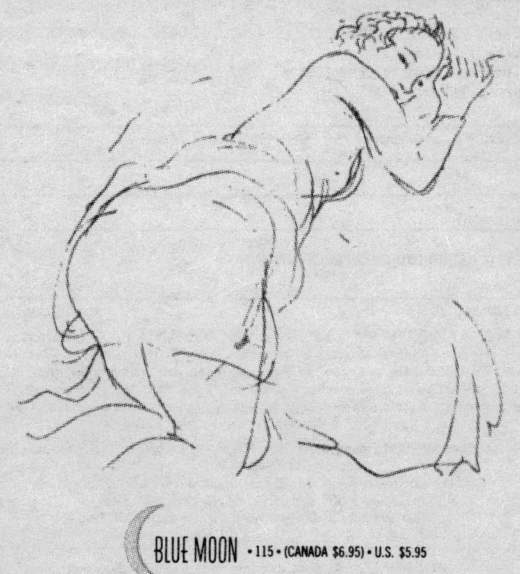

BLUE MOON • 115 • (CANADA $6.95) • U.S. $5.95

SELECTED BLUE MOON BOOKS

_____	Afternoons of A Woman of Leisure (#126)	$5.95
_____	Algier's Tomorrow (#127)	$5.95
_____	Amanda (#131)	$5.95
_____	An English Education (#025)	$5.95
_____	Beating the Wild Tatoo (#132)	$5.95
_____	Blue Velvet (#082)	$5.95
_____	The Captive (#043)	$5.95
_____	The Captive II (#098)	$5.95
_____	The Captive III (#123)	$5.95
_____	The Calamities of Jane (#024)	$5.95
_____	The Encounter (#078)	$4.95
_____	Frank and I (#002)	$5.95
_____	The Hidden Gallery (#121)	$5.95
_____	Ironwood (#022)	$4.95
_____	Images of Ironwood (#063)	$4.95
_____	The Hour of the Wolf (#054)	$4.50
_____	Man With a Maid II (#088)	$4.95
_____	Man With a Maid III (#104)	$5.95
_____	The Merry Order of St. Bridget (#122)	$5.95
_____	Miss High Heels (#020)	$4.95
_____	My Secret Life (#027)	$9.95
_____	Professor Spender and the Sadistic Impulse (#045)	$4.50
_____	Romance of Lust (#116)	$9.95
_____	The Rites of Sodom (#026)	$4.95
_____	Sundancer (#125)	$5.95
_____	The Tudor's Bride (#030)	$4.95
_____	The Vicar's Girl (#122)	$5.95
_____	What Love (#117)	$5.95
_____	The New Story of O (#102)	$5.95
_____	Secret Talents (#005)	$5.95

Signature (I certify by my signature that I am over 21 years of age)

Name

Address

City   State   Zip code

CREDIT CARD USERS CHECK APPROPRIATE BOX
☐ MasterCard   ☐ VISA

Credit Card Number   / Expiration Date

WE ARE NOW ACCEPTING PHONE AND FAX ORDERS!

Call us at 1-800-535-0007 to order by phone or 212-673-1039 to order by fax 7 days a week. We will require your card number, expiration date, name and current mailing address. Include your phone number if possible. If you have any questions about your order please call us. We request a <u>four book minimum</u> credit card order. Forthcoming titles will be shipped as they become available.

Please make all checks payable to Blue Moon Books Inc. in U.S. currency only
THANK YOU!
Postage Information: $1.50 first book. $.75 each additional
Canada: $2.00 first book. $1.25 each additional
Other foreign: $4.00 first book. $2.00 each additional
<u>NO C.O.D. ORDERS</u>

Blue Moon Books Published by: Blue Moon Books, Inc.
P.O. Box 1040, Cooper Station, New York, NY 10276
Phone: 212/505-6880 or 1-800/535-0007 Fax: 212/673-1039